Tyne O'Connell divides her time between LA and the Isle of Wight where she lives with her two husbands. Her previous books include *Sex, Lies and Litigation* and *Latest Accessory*. She is currently working on a sitcom adaptation of *What's A Girl To Do?* for American television.

Praise for Tyne O'Connell:

'Evelyn delivers some superbly sassy one-liners in this hilarious romp. Definitely a book for the modern girl' *Chat*

'Well might this be called a girlie novel for the nineties' *Oxford Mail*

'Ex-pat Australian author O'Connell's début is an extremely sure-footed romp, spiced with spot-on bad-taste humour, à la Kathy Lette and the *Ab Fab* team, and some excellent characterisation. Bravo!' *Who Weekly*

Check out the Tyne O'Connell website:
www.tyne-oconnell.demon.co.uk

What's A Girl To Do?

Tyne O'Connell

review

First published in 1998
by REVIEW

An imprint of Headline Book Publishing

First published in paperback in 1999

10 9 8 7 6 5 4 3 2 1

ISBN 0 7472 6028 1

Typeset by Palimpsest Book Production Limited,
Polmont, Stirlingshire
Printed and bound in Great Britain by
Clays Ltd, St Ives plc.

Headline Book Publishing
A division of Hodder Headline PLC
338 Euston Road
London NW1 3BH

Dedicated to my parents, Veronica and Bernard O'Connell, for providing me with the strenuous humour workouts that made me the girl I am today.

Acknowledgements

must go to Hollywood film industry for providing all those sassy role-models for girls everywhere. Special thanks must go to Tricia Davey and Maryann Kelly in LA for all their upbeat transatlantic phone calls that reminded me what life in a hot climate is all about. Thanks also to my agent at Curtis Brown UK, Vivienne Schuster, and Lisa Bankoff at ICM New York, for proving that sassy girls outrank their less sassy male counterparts in everything, every time.

I must also tip my sunglasses to the staff of Château Marmont for providing their service with such formidable style and for changing my suite so that I could get better acquainted with the Marlboro Man on Sunset Strip.

Thanks also to the usual suspects – Martin Gibson and Rupert Wilkes for their encouragement, and Jason Fisher, aka the Star Maker, for his glam shots. These guys prove that what men lose by way of testosterone they can make up for in charm and talent.

As always though, the lion's share of my gratitude must go to my children, Zad, Kajj and Cordelia, and the men in my life, SP and Eric, for keeping the humour and the espressos coming.

'The men like me because I don't wear a brassière. And the women like me because I don't look like a girl who would steal a husband. At least not for long.'

Jean Harlow (1911–37)

CHAPTER 1

'Maybe love is like luck – you have to go all the way to find it.'

Out of the Past, 1947, b/w, Kirk Douglas and
Rhonda Fleming

'TRAP A MAN'

Three words guaranteed to make a girl like me who has just got her single shit together squirm with repulsion. Thing was, back in seat 4A, en route to LAX (business class at last!) was sitting a man going by the name of Mr Right (in his dreams) who had accused me of just that – his idea of humour.

I'd laughed myself sick obviously.

The thought was out there though. As much as I modernised the concept, and played with the inherent irony and post-modern playfulness of those three little words, the brutal realism was quite clear. Trapped or not, I had a boyfriend for whom I was thinking of tossing aside my career as a barrister, friends, family and membership to Soho House, and emigrating to the States to be with.

You didn't need to be a French deconstructionist to see the problem. I was (choke on the words) one half of a couple.

So what kind of freak zodiac line-up led to this state of affairs – that I, queen of the successfully single of London, could without warning be transmogrified into the other half of an Irish-American guy who insisted on calling me *doll*? I kept telling myself that this was just a trial run. Just checking out that all the orgasms I'd been enjoying these last months weren't faked.

But what was going to happen to my cherished Mary Tyler Moore single girl's life? That's what I wanted to know. Would I cope in my new role, transformed from a 'meet you after work for drinks' sort of girl into a 'will you be home before six tonight, darling?' person?

Would my wardrobe work?

Would my heels be too high?

My lipstick too bright?

My skirts too short?

Would my voice be too loud?

Would I need altering?

These were the questions plaguing me. Because this was reality, not a bad hangover or a case of, 'Oh my God! Who is that in the bed beside me?' No, I was in love – or at least in serious long-term lust.

I had just pinched myself black and blue in the

plane's toilet cubicle in case this was all a bad nightmare, a case of too much cheese before bedtime. But I was still there – dehydrating, my feet exploding from my Manolo Blahniks with retained fluid. Love or lust, the effects of altitude and flight cabin air pressure were turning my late-twenties' complexion into crepe paper.

All this for the sake of a man? Basically there was no getting away from it. I was about to become one of those creatures who had for some time floated on the periphery of my life. 'The Couples', as we affectionately dubbed them.

I mean, before you call the PC-police on me, I'm not a couplist or anything mad like that. Honest! Some of my best friends are couples. I've even talked about the viability of Coupleland with my girlfriends at times but we'd all agreed that it probably couldn't sustain life as we know it.

Stuff like:

Deciding you need to dye your hair at 3 a.m.

Drinking daiquiris on Sunday mornings.

Really believing in fashion as a form of spiritual awareness.

Telling your girlfriends absolutely EVERYTHING!

Declaring that size really *does* count.

Asking cute blokes for a light even though you don't smoke just so you can flirt.

Calling the emergency services because you left your keys and your mobile phone locked in your flat.

Hanging knickers out to dry in the bathroom.

Shaving legs/armpits in the bath.

*Joining health clubs on a whim.

Paying extortionate health club joining fees with money you have no intention of earning.

Never attending said health club and later forgetting you even joined. Joining another health club on a whim. (see*)

Deciding you simply adore the new minimalism. Throwing out everything you ever owned (including all health club memberships).

Swiftly growing sick of minimalism and taking on a new overdraft to buy a normal off-the-floor bed and other essentials.

All this and more would have to stop!

Once you start living with men they don't find any of the above cute, sexy, admirable or proof of a healthy menstrual cycle. With men comes change. Not for them but for us.

Face it, we find somewhere less satisfactory to dry our knickers while they go right on taking off their socks with their toes and leaving the seat up on the toilet.

For all their good points, boys don't play by the rules. Take Eve for example: she tried the apple, politely asked Adam if he wanted a bite and bingo, he ran off to Yahweh to tittle tat. It's not a good look boys. Not good at all.

Whatever fine points boys might have, one thing is for sure, they don't get 'it'. They don't understand GR. Girlfriend Rules. They don't understand why you have to tell your girlfriends absolutely everything and your boyfriends only edited, heavily censored bits.

It all started when one of them wandered down a mountain side one day with a stone tablet of rules for the boys carved into it and they declared the game theirs from then on in. Nice try guys.

Sorry boys!

Your innings are up. Have been for years actually, we just didn't want to have to upset you. We know what your pride thing is like. Remember the time we brought up the *size* matters issue in the seventies? Ouch!

There has been full and frank disclosure of our gender positions these last few decades. It's nothing to do with penis envy or womb envy or anything anatomical like that. It's a simple case of game, set and match.

Lad culture, *Men Behaving Badly* and the antifeminist backlash were all a nice try at holding on to the power but we've all got a pay packet now and it's not going to wash. We put it to the vote and the girls have it. It's time to put the seat down, guys, and to start taking your socks off with your hands. The boys-only club culture is over.

Putting it simply we are now living in the age of The Girls Are Going Out Tonight And They Don't Know When They'll Be Home. PS. Don't wait up.

I'm not anti-men. Hell no! I love them. They can be

really handy with an espresso machine in the morning and sweet as buttons when they're sleeping, only less so when they start oozing out of the side of their mouths.

Men are one of my favourite sources of affordable fun on Thursday nights, although normally the first sign of the post-coitus condom is enough to make me run back to the quasi-comfort of my own futon (the remains of the latest minimalism-gone-mad binge).

Love them as I do, men are like champagne, a little goes a long way. 'Men are best treated as a celebratory beverage', according to my gran. Don't think you can live on a diet of men alone. Coupledom rots your liver and makes drying your knickers in the bathroom next to impossible.

When we are drawing up lists for parties, my friends of both sexes and I always ask each other: 'Should we invite *The Couples* this time?' Very magnanimous of us, we think, considering how boring couples usually are at parties, doing things like:

Getting stroppy when you accidentally snog their partner when it's late and dark and everyone's snogging everyone.

Going to pieces when they find their 'partner' holding opinions outside the jurisdiction of their relationship,

Or worse, when they find their 'partner' talking to people they'd both agreed were no-go areas.

Couples see no flaw in having a domestic in your bathroom when everyone else is queuing up to use it because we overlaced the fruit punch, as one does after a difficult week in court.

Invariably couples are the type to accept all Saturday night invitations, proof of how sad they are, wanting to hang out with a bunch of reprobate singles when they should be beyond that and far too busy flicking through the IKEA catalogue and mapping out ovulation projectories.

Not that I have crossed Coupleland off my list of places I might eventually want to visit. It's just that like Canada, it was way down on that list. I have even checked out the brochures with a bloke going by the name of Giles, but that's ancient history: we never shared a toothbrush and I never gave up going out with my girlfriends, or gave him full disclosure of my shoe collection or anything really intimate like that, so he doesn't really count. Besides, he's dating my therapist now – but that's another story.

I must also admit that I have even observed The Couples at our parties, clustered together in cosy *tête-à-têtes* holding forth on the latest videos they've hired and how tasty the food was at the Conran restaurant where they went to celebrate their anniversary, and how they're giving up smoking together, and I concede that I have sometimes wondered what it would be like having an *other half*.

I offered my 'couples are dull' theory to my therapist Maddy, to see what sense she could make of it, but she was even more in the dark than me. She told me it was an 'image thing' which kind of suggests that I could get over it by changing designer labels or getting a new hairstyle instead of paying her ninety quid an hour.

Then again my therapist isn't the person I go to for advice so much as someone to yap away to about myself for an hour. I mean, I can't afford to pause for breath or she'll invariably start making prescient, incisive remarks like, 'Perhaps you are running from your fear of commitment, Evelyn.'

Like wow! Slap me round the face with a diaphragm Mads. Like I never thought of that! 'Puhlease! You needed a degree and a licence to practise psychology to come up with *that*?' I replied. 'I've had better advice from desk calendars. I mean, even the wandering insane are afraid of commitment Maddy.'

Should I commit myself or run? I asked my girlfriends when Giles proposed to me a while back. 'Run you fool, run like a mugger up Bond Street,' they urged. 'Blow your rape whistle, kick off your heels and don't stop until you are back in the convent.'

'Commitment is scary Mads,' I told her, and cancelled my next appointment so she could ponder the concept for a bit. You have to keep your analysts in check or they walk all over you.

Self-empowerment aside for a minute though, just occasionally, on miserable Monday nights when I've eaten too much Häagen Dazs and realised what a slug I have become, I sometimes try to visualise what it would be like to live in Coupleland.

Sharing bills (now that's a thought), browsing

through holiday brochures together, taking a romantic weekend break in Paris. We'd travel Eurostar and toast our love with Perrier, having given up alcohol for the sake of our health. Couples do stuff like that. They are altogether more health-conscious and careful than us singletons.

Wandering along the banks of the Seine, I envision us swearing off birth control and talking excitedly of natural birthing methods. In the evening, we'd enjoy memory-making moments sipping alcohol-free cocktails in the Hotel George V, whilst chatting animatedly about prospective prep schools for our offspring. It's at this point, you see, that the fantasy ceases to appeal. Even sleeping in a cardboard box on the Strand has got to be better than commitment.

It is the actual word *commitment* that scares the G-string off me, according to my hairdresser. While at Bar school we used to say: 'Tried as a couple, sentenced as a couple and committed to Coupledom for the term of your natural life.' Boyfriends come and go, but up to now I've never met a man up to the job of facing my knickers hanging in the bathroom long term.

OK, so what started me off on this rant was Rory – Mr Right as he calls himself – being possessed of an overdeveloped irony gland. It's a long story, but one minute I was successfully single, living in my mortgaged-to-the-hilt loft in trendy Clerkenwell, reeling from my latest attack of minimalism, contemplating my hugely brilliant career prospects in one of London's most successful chambers – and the next minute I'm in love with an American private eye.

Big deal you might say – so you fell in love, why does that require a trial period? At this point I have to direct your attention to Mr Right's serious physical credibility – call it the body I had dreamed about all my life and occasionally even searched for down at the gym (on the several occasions I had a pre-membership tour). At the risk of sounding shallow, Rory's was not a body to be walked away from lightly.

Apart from his looks, his charm and questionable blue-collar upbringing, Rory also had that important exotic aspect to his personality guaranteed to make me question my single girl vows.

ISOH – Irish sense of humour.

Now, I am pretty much putty at the first glimpse of Irish humour. When it comes laced with an American drawl, let's just say that I am the proverbial gum on the shoe of the bloke in question.

As a private detective to the rich and fabulous, Rory lives in the States and *ipso facto* I had agreed to spend a month in LA in the lap of luxury with him. A girl's got to do . . . etc.

I let it pass that he was very cagey about his latest assignment, muttering things about catching husbands *in flagrante* and counter-surveillance tactics. Like I said, it was only a trial period – just to make sure that I wasn't faking my orgasms.

Anyway, no sooner had the plane ascended than Mr Right dropped his 'trap a man' bombshell.

'Why is it that once you girls trap your man, you all start demanding the window seat?'

He had asked this question with wide-eyed incomprehension, fluttering those pornographically long eyelashes at me. He had then added insult to injury by ruffling my hair the way he knows my hairdresser hates. You see, Rory has me down as a kind of Giget figure, despite the fact that I am a barrister of some five years called, and, at least I like to think, sassy – in that Jean Harlow kind of way.

Normally a girl renowned for being quick off the mark with the genital wit-kick, I was slow to respond to Rory's sexist slight on this occasion because he had referred to me and my sex as *girls*, which was like a huge leap for an Irish-American diehard sexist like him. Previously we'd all been 'dolls'. More of his overdeveloped irony gland later.

Obviously I didn't want to discourage him if he was about to get sensitive on me or anything, so I decided against my usual strategy of employing my lightning-fast wit to castrate him. Instead I just smiled and said: 'Why, Spencer Tracy, you must be thinking of someone else. Trapped? By little old moi? I don't think so.' At this point I raised my left eyebrow the way I know raises his libido and smiled my most come-in-your-pants-boyfriend smile.

His response was to kiss me rotten which is how I came to be in the toilet cubicle, reapplying my lippy and thinking about 'couple stuff'. Asking myself complex questions which there was no handy twelve-step programme to deal with. Questions like:

Would I have to expose my debt figures?

Would I have to pretend to love a baseball team and wear ball-hats and colours injurious to my looks?

Was I now about to enter the twilight zone of shared tastes, favourite songs, favourite restaurants and favourite designers?

Would I start getting teary-eyed whenever I heard *our* song?

Shit, would I have to start scanning the *Cole Porter Song Book* for a song to call *ours*? Make a note.

And would my brown bob have to go in order to make way for matching hairstyles à la Pitt and Paltrow? Scratch that. That was never going to happen!

Horror of horrors – would I have to start accessing all those gyms I'd joined and learn how to spell cellulite?

Oh the Vivien Leigh pathos of it all!

I rifled through all the dispensers and cupboards for a Valium drip or something poisonous that I could swallow and never wake up from. Nothing. These airlines run a suicide-proof operation. It's a wonder they don't take your laces off you before boarding.

Deep breaths, I told myself. In out, in out, in out, just like the natural birthing method. 'Saints in heaven preserve me!' I cried, raising my eyes heavenward for divine intervention. I tried to kneel but there wasn't the room. And this was business class? Hello? How do all those poor people in coach manage to have sex in their cubicles?

I settled for babbling out decades of the rosary but someone started banging on the door. No doubt they were imagining I was notching up points in the mile-high club. I banged back and turned on the taps, splashing my face with water which a sign by the tap warned against drinking. Suspicious about its safety as facial splash, I turned it off. You can never be too sure where your pores are concerned.

I calmed down a bit and told God not to bother with interceding, basically because he would probably really approve of a nice lapsed Catholic boy like Rory. Particularly given the sorry bunch of Proddy Dogs I'd served up since I'd been living in England.

'Puh-lease!' my mother would cry down the long distance phone line from Sydney as if I'd just declared that I'd had an abortion. 'I send you to predominantly Catholic Europe and you start fraternising with the enemy!'

Yeah right! I mean, no one has bothered to tell my mum that the Huguenots' rebellion was successfully squashed. She still thinks that she's been charged to take over where Catherine de Medici left off. Another cross I have to bear.

Back in my seat, I resisted Rory's attempts to canoodle. 'All right, have the window,' he relented.

'I'm not bothered about the window any more,' I

told him sulkily, by now finding the whole seating arrangement issue a bit shallow after the incredibly lofty stuff I'd been dealing with in the loo.

He stretched out exposing his six-pack stomach which he knows always makes my womb miaow.

OK, so maybe Coupleland wasn't going to be the absolute end of me, I conceded, too dehydrated to be bothered. Besides, it wasn't as if we were getting married or anything. I still had my single-girl parachute attached. I could jump at the first sign of an IKEA catalogue, right?

A trial period. That's what I had promised my girl-friends who had looked none too pleased on hearing that they were about to lose the best shopaholic friend they had ever had to LA – the natural habitat of shopaholics.

'You're mad!' they warned me.

'You don't know the first thing about this guy!'

'What about your career, your loft apartment, your friends?'

'What about Sam and Charles' party on Friday night?'

'What about the summer sales?'

'You'll be back in a heartbeat,' they promised me.

'Yeah, like the first day you realise they don't accept your Harvey Nichols' storecard at the Beverly Hills shopping mall.'

I'll admit this last threat did leave me a bit uneasy but on balance I decided that I was prepared to take the rough with the smooth. I was prepared for sacrifices. Course I was. So what, I'd be in a Harvey Nicks free zone with no friends to have fun with, no job prospects, no family to run to in an emergency and limited funds of my own.

I would in short be partially dependent on a man who, bar this one exception, referred to me as *doll*! A man I could never tell my parents about without risking them turning up on my doorstep with a straitjacket and prepared speeches about the dangers of mixed-income marriages.

What the hell was I doing? I was at the mercy of Rory, a man I hardly even knew and had no hope of ever understanding. I looked at him with a critical eye. As the first inedible tray of space food arrived and I watched him tucking into it with gusto, I admit I was beginning to feel nervous about the journey I was embarking on. 'It's a trial period,' I repeated in my brain like a mantra.

Trial period!

Trial period!

Trial period!

CHAPTER 2

'Hollywood is where they write the alibis before they write the story.'

Carole Lombard (1908–42)

Events seem to change their emphasis as time goes on. I have learnt to my peril that trusting one's gut instinct is about as reliable as the vaginal orgasm. Even my clitoris generally has a better idea about where I'm heading than my stomach. Left to its own devices, mine is a gut that will head for the mini-bar everytime.

'Always judge a book by its cover,' my gran advised. But there again her advice fails me. I've never spent a lot of time studying the covers of life. I'm more a storm past the window display and get the latest Gucci pin-stripe suit before somebody else does, sort of girl. Anyway, as a barrister it all comes down to dreary details and tedious content. When I see excitement, I charge at it with everything I've got.

I spend my work hours poring over deeply boring briefs and writing madly detailed advices for solicitors with whom I later go on to exchange tediums *ad nauseam*.

Law is coma-inducingly dull; *ipso facto* lawyers are too. Lawyers are so boring in fact that they should be forced to wear tell-tale costumes and be kept in enclosed areas of the city – whoops, we are. At least in London.

Criminal lawyers may be an exception to the bore rule but not what I would call an attractive exception. It's a nose thing see. Hang around criminals for long enough and you get 'the nose'. I've seen a lot of hold-onto-your-libido, gorgeous noses ruined by a life of crime at the Bar. I don't know whether it's an acid they put in the pages of *Archbold* or the acrid air of the Old Bailey cells or the pettifogging with police that does it.

I almost turned to crime myself as a pupil, but apart from the woeful Legal Aid budgets, I didn't want to risk my nose getting all bulbous and pitted with big pores like the QCs you see lurking around the Bailey. PS. Check out El Vino's in Fleet Street if you don't believe me.

'You should study law,' I occasionally remark to party bores who get me in an ear vice. 'The Bar needs people of your calibre,' I assure them. This advice usually makes them glow with pride and prickle with pleasure, as if I've told them they deserve a knighthood.

Occasionally my ruse backfires though when they start pleading with me to tell them about my cases. I blame *This Life* and *LA Law*. People think 'law' and their thoughts immediately turn to riveting sex scandals and the debauched carry-ons that the townspeople of Sodom and Gomorrah were warned about. But that's politicians actually, lawyers are altogether more conservative and dare I say it – dull.

The truth is, behind the extraordinary Gothic edifices of the Royal Courts of Justice and the Old Bailey, lawyers spend their time labouring points of jurisprudence and watching tufts of hair growing out of judges' ears. It is soul-destroying stuff for a girl like me.

Get yourself an invite to a lawyers' party sometime and see what I mean. They are relatively easy to get hold of, hardly red-letter chic occasions. More often than not you get the Coldstream Guards sweating up in the minstrel's gallery while the rest of us observe Princess Margaret putting a few judges through their paces at High Table – and that's if you're lucky. Put it this way, *Tatler* and *Vogue* never cover Inns of Court bashes.

Watch lawyers at play; talking in funny voices and laughing immoderately at trifles, lurking around the wine waiter with intent to cause tedium, getting legless and pretending to recite laws of precedent in Latin or impressing one another with the latest EU directives they have discovered in their beard. Not a whip or a leather cowl or a cross-dresser to be seen amongst them most of the time. More's the pity.

The first American bore, sorry lawyer, I met in LA was at the Hertz desk of LAX airport and as much as I am loath to admit it, he was anything but dull. More of that in a bit.

As it was, I wasn't really up for the challenge of anything more exciting than a coma after US customs and immigration had finished with me. Next time I'm doing as the Mexicans do and crossing at night by flashlight with my possessions in a plastic bag. So what if Texans take pot shots at me – it couldn't be worse than the cruelty those soulless blokes in charge of the official stamps had just inflicted on me, I decided.

'You go hire the car *doll* while I make a few calls,' were Rory's instructions to me as he vanished into the crowds. If he thought I was going to play a Katharine Hepburn to his Spencer Tracy, he had another think coming.

Fuming, but too jet-lagged to react, I did as my liege bid, and it was while fumbling around for Rory's licence and my own synapses that my first American bore focused on me.

'So, your car didn't turn up either?' he enquired.

I turned and faced the stranger. He smiled at me warmly, like my parish priest used to do after confession when I was a kid. A smile that said: 'I know all your secrets, little girl.' (Such as they were, sadly.)

I will concede that this bore was attractive, i.e. no tell-tale hair growing out of the ears, no unsightly pockmarks or bulging of the nose. No beard, which always helps. Late thirties, tall, good body, all the bits and bobs that make a guy worth checking out twice at a cab rank, actually. All right, so he was a Richard Gere clone and my eggs started jumping round in my womb.

'Hello?' I said, in the questioning tone the kids use on *Friends*. I was getting into my American dialect stride – 'blend and conquer' my gran said, like the Trojans did.

He smiled at me; his eyes seemed to be laughing.

I didn't smile back. I have to say that it was very hard *not* smiling back when faced with such cuteness but I stood firm. Good-looking or not, living in England for seven years prepared me for this moment. I was knackered and not in the mood for idle chit-chat.

No offence but I'm not into strangers at the most hydrated of times, no matter how ravishing. With all my doubts about the human race, I need a whole series of formal introductions and insurance policies, disclaimers, recommendations and CVs before I'll even consider speaking to a stranger. Unless I'm at a party and hitting the Martinis particularly hard, that is.

'I asked if your car had stood you up?'

I looked at this man, his kudos dribbling away with every attempt at light banter. My look was unfeeling, blank, uninterested and laced with a suggestion of loathing. Actually it was a look I'd just recently picked up from my immigration official. I proceeded to fill in my form and imagined that he would get the message and shut up.

Fat chance.

'Lawyer?' he pressed.

'Excuse me?' I snapped, not looking up from my form.

'I can smell it on you.'

All right, this was too much. I looked around for a policeman. How dare someone accuse *me* of being a lawyer. It was outrageous. I mean, so what if I am? I prefer to think of myself as a bit of a fierce individual, a trailblazer of irreverent, iconoclastic magnificence – that sort of thing.

In a nutshell, I'd prefer to be mistaken for a lap-dancer than recognised as a lawyer.

'We exude a kind of animal danger don't we?' my Richard Gere clone grinned, as if his groin wasn't in the slightest bit of danger from attack. 'I can smell that unmistakable stench of ego and love of the hunt a mile away. And you've got it bad. My name's Daniel anyway. Daniel Silverberg. Mackay and Berk – Media, although I do a bit of litigation, if pushed.'

He offered his hand for me to shake. It was a large, well-manicured hand. The sort of hand I probably would have been happy to shake if my internal organs hadn't been gasping for moisture.

Instead I gave it a withering sneer. 'I'll thank you to keep animal smells and my good self out of the same sentence,' I told him tartly, turning back to my form.

'What's your line?' he continued, seemingly not at all perturbed. 'Let me guess. Not Family, too hopeful for that. Not crime, far too arrogant. Civil Litigation? Maybe. Don't tell me you're in Media too? Is that why you're here, wrapping up a deal?'

I turned and gave him another dismissive look. It was the 'arrogant' bit that rankled. Calling an Australian who's lived most of her adult life in London arrogant, is like calling a kid from Queens a snob. It doesn't happen, my friend.

'I'm right aren't I? Huh?'

I motioned to the Hertz guy to call the security guards but he was imploring another customer to be satisfied with a Merc SLK as opposed to the Merc SL he'd requested. I turned to Daniel and said in my haughtiest tone. 'I'm at the Bar in London. Now if you don't mind!'

I know my dialogue stank but give me a break, I wasn't in full charge of my faculties. Basically a whole hemisphere of my brain was still struggling to cross the Atlantic. It was proof of my incredibly good breeding that I was even stringing words together.

My Richard Gere clone collapsed into paroxysms of mirth. I mean serious, hearty laughter. He was falling about and slapping his thighs and his ass so hard that he suddenly had to grip his knees to keep himself from toppling over.

I aim to amuse.

'Sorry about that,' he said, after he'd totally annihilated any chance I had of keeping a low profile that evening. The whole airport was watching now, trying to work out what I'd done that was so funny. 'It was just the way you said you were at "the Bar in London",' he explained, miming inverted commas to make his point.

'Don't spare it a thought,' I told him. 'Now if you'll excuse me, my boyfriend will be back in a minute.'

'Take my card,' he urged. 'I can see you're worn out from the flight but even so, you've got style coming out your ass. Give me a ring while you're here and I'll show you some genuine LA legal drama. Called the phone over here,' he joked and held his thumb and pinkie to mime a phone set. 'I just love that – "the Bar"!'

He gave one final chuckle and shook his head in a knowing way which suggested he was planning to entertain his buddies back at the office tomorrow with my hilarious turn of phrase.

As he passed me the card, I caught a whiff of his scent, something spicy, distinctive and indefinable. Something dangerously sexy. Our fingers touched and he smiled. I can't lie, no matter how much I tried to loathe this guy, the fact was he was sweating charm.

A voice inside me said, 'Warning, warning you

are no longer single, you are no longer permitted to find strange men attractive and remember, he's a lawyer. You have sworn an eternal vow never to find lawyers attractive. All sensations of sexual desire for people other than your current lover must disembark. Disembark now!'

'Oh? Glad to oblige,' I said as I raised my lip at one corner in a 'shrivel up and die' sneer. And make no mistake, my shrivelling sneers have been perfected on QCs whose careers have never recovered. My clerk is forever congratulating me on them and promising me that one day in the not-too-distant future my 'looks' will lead to Silk.

At this point the Richard Gere clone's car arrived. 'Nice talking to you anyway,' he said, grabbing my hand and pumping it heartily before leaving.

'Who was that?' Rory asked, suddenly by my side in true private detective style.

'Some lawyer. Gave me his card,' I told him nonchalantly.

Rory took the card, glanced at it. 'Partner at Mackay and Berk? Big law firm here, represent a lot of star players in the industry.'

'Industry?'

'Hollywood, doll. Hollywood. This is America and the stars are our Royals. We take our cues from them. When you represent star players you represent money, lots of it. That guy is rolling in it in a way a pig rolls in shit. What'd he say?'

'Said he'd show me some LA courtroom drama.' I

refrained from mentioning that he also thought I had style coming out my ass.

'That's LA speak for getting laid, doll.'

He passed the card back to me and I ostentatiously shoved it inside the cavern of my Prada holdall – my pride and joy – boy did I have to queue for this little baby! In the end I had to impersonate Lady Weinstock to get it. The guilt was such that I sent her a little Chanel key ring by way of compensation. So sue me.

I guess I kept Daniel's card to wind Rory up. Even though he had never done anything to suggest jealousy, I knew he was turning green inside. Rory was madly jealous. It's one of his best features actually, not just that he's jealous but that he never lets on. Not letting on is what makes Rory so irresistible to anyone who spent their childhood in love with Roger Moore – the Pupil-Master of not-letting-onness.

Rory kissed me hard on the lips and I felt that familiar wobble in my Blahniks – like my heels were about to collapse. I pulled away first because I'd only just done with cleaning up my lips from the last kiss. That's the worst part about being in love – the cost of lipstick and the hours spent reapplying it after kissing.

Once back in London when we were just newly lovers, Rory had let me go off to court looking like the gothic guy out of The Cure. Candida, the QC leading me in the case, could have said something or passed me a tissue, as could my clerk Lee, but obviously they saw fit not to mention it. Judge Threep-Smith, I'm pleased to report, was more forthcoming but only after he'd practically burst his prostate giggling.

I handed over the form and pen to Rory and told him to deal with the car-hire himself. 'They said I can't hire a car because I can't drive,' I explained.

He went a bit white at that and smiled at me oddly like my accountant does when I turn up loaded down with shoe boxes full of receipts – most of which *are* for shoes actually. A 'why are you doing this to me?' smile.

'What do you mean by *can't* exactly?' he said, getting all pedantic.

'What, you think I can drive in these heels?' I joked, pointing to my Manolos.

He didn't even grace my feet with a cursory glance. 'Yeah sure doll. But let me get this straight, you *can* drive. You just *don't* drive. Right?'

'No. I can't drive and don't drive, as in never tried, never will. Call it a decision made in the interests of public safety,' I told him.

'No, doll, listen to me,' he insisted, getting more agitated. Then he did something that men in the sixties agreed they would never do to women again. He took my shoulders in his hands.

I decided then and there that if he tried to shake me or called me 'doll' again the spell would be broken for ever. I would cease to be in lust. I would be free to return home to Harvey Nichols and the new gym on St John Street.

'You can't be serious,' he insisted. 'You don't come to this town if you can't drive. Driving is what this town is all about. Right?' He asked this last question of the Hertz staff and the airport at large.

'I'll take cabs,' I breezed, breaking free of the shoulder hold.

'Did you hear this girl?' Rory called out to the Hertz guy who was by now dealing with another customer. 'Says she'll take cabs.'

The Hertz guy shook his head in sorrowful disbelief.

Rory probably didn't notice but my *joie de vivre* levels were plummeting rapidly, and after my transatlantic flight they hadn't been all that high to begin with.

'You see doll, you don't hail taxis on the corner in Beverly Hills. It just doesn't happen.'

'So I'll walk,' I snapped, ready to show him then and there how it was done.

'You get arrested for walking in this town. Walking ain't natural,' he explained, looking at me meaningfully. He had me by the shoulders again. 'Just tell me you can drive,' he pleaded.

His obdurate incredulity was beginning to seriously grate. My faith in the future well and truly evaporated, like expensive scent left out in the sun. I thought of how much I missed my analyst.

You never really appreciate what you've got till it's gone.

'You have to evaluate the dynamics of your relationships or you'll find that the dynamics start controlling you, Evelyn.' This was the last thing Maddy had told me after hearing that I was taking off to the States to check out the validity of all my orgasms. 'After years of faking it, a girl can't be too sure,' I'd explained.

'Evaluate the dynamics, Evelyn. Separate the dynamics from the feelings. Otherwise, the dynamics will become destructive.'

I was evaluating the dynamics now, that was for sure, and I could feel that any minute I was about to separate my dynamics from the floor and lodge them in Rory's groin.

I told Rory that if he didn't cut out the 'you can drive' shit, he was going to drive me straight back onto the next flight to Heathrow.

Rory wasn't listening.

He was well and truly bonding with the Hertz staff, leaning over their counter like a latterday Socrates getting into his oratorical stride. 'I drive – therefore I am,' he declared expansively at one point. I started to rummage through my bag for a toga.

A few unwise customers at the desk chuckled heartily.

'Isn't that right?' he asked the Hertz girl, who was flaring her nostrils with the excitement of being spoken to by this genetically advantaged Y-chromosome.

'I'm pissed off. Therefore your balls are in danger,' I told him.

'Isn't she a doll?' he asked the Hertz guy.

The Hertz guy looked at me and muffled a chuckle, realising he was in a minefield and that the person in charge of the detonator might very easily be me.

I gave him an approving 'you got that much right buddy' nod.

'Don't air your dirty linen in public' was the domestic standard that governed my parents' generation. Forget it. 'Let's get it all out in the open!' is the catch-cry of the nineties. And that evening was the wash day of our relationship.

Another good motto is never run from a fight when you're wearing heels! And so I stood my ground. Between Rory, the Hertz staff and me, we upped the entertainment on offer at LAX airport that evening until a voice behind us asked, 'You doing OK there?'

We all turned and faced our interlocutor. Daniel Silverberg. Sex on legs himself. Smiling, distinguished and waving a pair of keys to his newly rented Merc SLK.

Casting aside all the Stranger Danger warnings of my childhood, I told Rory that he could deal with his 'I drive therefore I am' theories the way his mother had dealt with his foreskin, and I asked Daniel for a lift.

Rory was gutted. He begged. He pleaded. He got down on his knees and wept and told me he loved me.

Yeah right. In my dreams.

Actually, he was still chatting up the Hertz girl when I left.

Minutes later, I was tearing along the freeway with Daniel. We discussed his client base, which read like a Who's Who of *Entertainment Tonight*. OK, so I suppose I should have thought twice about charging off into a strange city with a total stranger in a fast car, but I had made a conscious decision to piss Rory off after his 'I drive therefore I am' thesis, and I was prepared to take risks to achieve my aims.

An inner voice suggested that those risks could involve sexual assault, GBH or even the risk of being bludgeoned to death and dumped in a plastic garbage bag at the bottom of LA harbour. But given that it was the same inner voice that always warned me that a second bowl of Häagen Dazs could ruin my thighs, I ignored it.

Anyway, by now my biorhythms were shot and I was running on pure adrenalin. I mean this was one of the greatest exits of my life – ever. Whoa, was I exhilarated. The roof was down, the wind was in my hair and 'Champagne Supernova' was playing on the radio. I was on cliché overdrive.

Daniel asked where I was going and seemed impressed when I answered, 'Château Marmont.'

'The dump where John Belushi died?' he asked.

'Well yeah, I guess.'

'Cool,' he said, risking both our lives on a dangerous overtake.

'People fuck like they drive in this town,' he

announced later, just as I was beginning to switch off my reality principle and make a dive for the door handle. If this was how he fucked, he should be classified as a dangerous warhead and never sold to unstable governments.

'So where does that leave me Daniel?' I asked tentatively, realising that as I couldn't drive at all, I was for all intents and purposes a eunuch.

'Go figure!' he shrugged, staring at the long road ahead with cold menace. 'Impotent maybe?'

As far as I could make out, watching the Lotuses, Corvettes, Mercs and BMWs whizzing past, by Daniel's definition, sex in this town was fast, flash and everyone wanted to be on top. I relayed this to him.

'You got it,' he agreed, putting his foot down hard on the accelerator to overtake a red Corvette. 'Drive or die,' he said, 'that's how LA works. Without a licence, you're a nobody in this town.'

'Oh,' I said, starting to think that maybe Rory wasn't being such a bastard after all, maybe he was right with all his 'I drive therefore I am!' rhetoric.

Shit.

CHAPTER 3

'I saw you and I said, "Boy, this is going to be one terrific day, so you had better live it up 'cause tomorrow you'll be nothing," see, and I almost was.'

Rebel Without a Cause, 1955, colour, Natalie Wood and James Dean

For the duration of the journey, we did what Mads refers to as 'bonding exercises'. Daniel told me all his 'stuff' and I hedged around the edited highlights of my own personal history.

Like all the Americans I have ever met, Daniel was unafraid of the declarative sentence – even if he did have the aura of a man who might in a pinch lean more on drama than content in his court appearances.

All my life I have walked through the NOTHING TO DECLARE channel of emotion. Especially where my therapist is concerned. That's the best way to survive the London underground actually: wrapped up in the steel plating of all your hang-ups and angst.

Americans are the opposite, they are big on individual expression where we are big on mass repression. Socialism never had a chance in America. They are a nation of individuals, ready and willing to declare it all. No self-exposure too daring, no confession too compromising. They learnt this honesty shit during Watergate I guess.

Americans wear their feelings like their weapons. Having feelings is no crime but carrying concealed is a serious offence. Listening to Daniel speaking frankly about his life was refreshing stuff for a girl who'd spent years at Oxford perfecting the stiff line of her flabby Australian upper lip.

Actually over the course of our journey I learnt more about Daniel than I knew about myself. At one point he even gave me his analyst's card. In brief, Daniel had run the gamut of DIY life-enhancement from Buddhism to Scientology, he had meditated and chanted with the best of them.

He had been in two committed relationships and almost married once but shied away around the pre-nup stage. Daniel explained that he was now successfully using a personalised form of self affirmation that involved a macrobiotic diet and Zen meditation techniques to raise his *chi*. He was also a strenuous Feng Shui enthusiast and if pushed too far, pro-gun lobby.

In a nutshell he was everything that my girlfriends had warned me about Californians, and then some.

Previously, on meeting blokes into inner-self exposure I had been inclined to make an unflattering remark about size being all and run, but there was something incredibly disarming about Daniel. Something about the way he laughed, especially when he saw me wincing over some particularly intimate revelation he'd made.

It was a laugh that suggested he didn't want me to take a word of what he was saying seriously. I gathered he was aiming to amuse, or as we say in the UK, winding me up.

He was certainly a mould-breaker as far as lawyers went. He had a wry sense of humour and a way of looking at me out the of corner of his eyes which I always find sexy. Plus he got all my jokes which is tantamount to finding my G-spot.

We talked about love and dreams and why I'd come to the States, about Rory and my fear of being a couple and my cynical buttoned-up nature and the way I always ran from commitment. It was like talking to my hairdresser really, only Daniel was most definitely not gay. Daniel was a guy to run with the pack, preferably up at the front.

Daniel said that as a lawyer we knew better than most what commitment could cost. I told him that I was never a girl to run shy of a price tag.

'Don't sweat it,' he advised when I told him how nerve-racked I was over this commitment thing.

'Life's too short. Love can't be predicted or controlled. If it's right, it will work out regardless of what you fear.'

'Sounds very wise coming from a lawyer,' I told him.

'Probably something I picked up in a film,' he teased. 'This is California after all. Chill out and enjoy the pace. The only thing you have to stress about here is the Richter scale and casual violence.'

'Sounds like Nirvana,' I said.

We were getting on very well. I told myself it was because we shared a similar career. Whatever. I made a big decision that night as we pelted at breakneck speed along boulevards of bright lights, palm trees and billboards towards Hollywood.

If I was ever going to enjoy this country, if I was ever going to make a good couple, I was going to have to turn off my cringe meter. I was going to have to stop being so dubious about things that involved letting oneself go. I was going to have to open up to the new.

Irony would, by necessity, become a thing of the past. I have seen enough films in the romantic genre to know that love and irony are hardly on a nodding acquaintance.

When you think about it, love is like Hollywood. Full of bright lights and aspirations and everyone wanting to be a star in their loved one's eyes. You don't think about the gutters of disappointment while you're studying your map to the stars.

When you are in love, anything is justified. Cornyness goes down particularly well, cutesy talk and schmaltzy sentimentality rate highly too.

Thinking about it, Hollywood is like a giant metaphor for love. It doesn't matter how many casualties you see limping down the boulevard, you really do think that your love will be different, your star will shine brighter than all others. Your love will justify all the schmaltz. Your love will make all the gaudy sentiment worthwhile.

Glitz, after all, conquers all. The major studios will back me up here.

I put my theory to Daniel.

'Absolutely,' he agreed. 'Love is like the box office. The ends justifies the means.'

At various times my girlfriends had warned me about both LA and love. They had warned me that I was going to have to stop saying 'erk!' every time someone spontaneously started singing *I Say A Little Prayer For You* in a lobster claw restaurant, or started dancing along the pavement out of a sheer celebration of life, or expressing their affection for their countrymen in an open self-growth kind of way, i.e. embracing strangers on daytime chat shows.

It was time to let it all go.

Goodbye to subtle inference.

Goodbye to clever quips.

Goodbye to irreverent, politically incorrect humour (well not straight away, perhaps, but ultimately I would have to let it go).

Goodbye to my fear of self-expression and intimacy.

Goodbye to my arch scepticism.

Goodbye to doubt in all things good and positive and fluffy.

It would be a bittersweet parting and there would be regrets. But I was certain that it all had to go if I was to cross the border control of my limitations and enter the world of the declarative sentence. Concepts such as 'I am in love and content with COUPLEDOM', would only be realised if I renounced my cynical nature. Before I could announce that I was prepared to make sacrifices for love, certain adjustments were required. But I was a girl prepared for change. More than that, I was prepared to go blonde.

I was prepared to run into the future, arms outstretched, armed with nothing but a love of the first amendment and a flashlight, just like all those Mexicans and Cubans I'd seen on the news. Into the vistas of free-market possibility offered by this land of the licensed handgun.

When Daniel asked, 'Where to?' I told him: 'To my inner depths!'

He nodded solemnly like I'd said something really serious and then turned to me and burst out laughing. That was when I realised that we were flirting. Maybe it was just the loss of the left hemisphere of my brain over the Atlantic but I doubt it. Even lying on a gurney I reckon I could flirt – it's in my genes.

More likely I was just out for affirmative action. Innocent stuff, like kisses and diamonds and shared songs. I was feeling so Holly Golightly-ish that even my waistline felt waspish.

Thousands of miles from the constraints that characterised my life, I could feel the convent-educated, cold, ironic, buttoned-up, stiff upper-lipped, dubious lawyer within me melt under the bright brash lights of Sunset Boulevard.

'Tomorrow,' I confided, 'I'll buy a can of mace and in time, perhaps I'll progress to an automatic weapon.' I told him that I was going to take my therapist's advice and wrest control of my life from the guilt inflicted on me by my conservative religious upbringing.

It was a dangerous and risky undertaking but now that I could arm myself appropriately, I was willing to give it a try. I was prepared to tackle all those hang-ups my therapist had pointed out to me. I would cease to run from dilemma and engage in direct and volatile confrontation with my insecurities. Obvious stuff really.

On top of that I would learn to drive – kiss off my interest in public safety.

I would declare myself armed and dangerous – if still a little afraid of commitment and prone to use chocolate as a substitute for affection.

On Daniel's advice, I agreed to buy a fringed jacket and wear it with attitude – possibly even matching boots.

I would learn to drive and deal with my interpersonal dynamics behind the wheel of an automatic fast car. Just like in J.G. Ballard's *Crash*.

Daniel pointed out the Château on the hill, a Gothic edifice left over from the Addams Family set. 'Wow,' I said.

'Not exactly the Holiday Inn, is it?' he laughed.

'Not exactly,' I agreed.

'But they say if you're going to get into trouble, do it at the Marmont.'

'Sounds tailor-made for my needs,' I said.

As we negotiated the oncoming traffic and turned into the oasis of palm trees surrounding the hotel, I picked up a conversation we'd been having earlier about blondes in Hollywood and asked him if he thought I'd be better equipped to tackle commitment as a blonde.

'You've got beautiful hair,' he told me, suddenly serious, swerving to avoid a limousine. 'Don't you dare change a strand of it.'

I didn't really take his words in. I was closing my eyes and making a headlong rush for the future. It was as if I had been looking down the wrong end of a telescope all my life. Now the aperture of my dreams was opening up. Right or wrong, being in the States gave me a sense that anything was possible. Even love. Even 'innocent' flirting.

Oh dear.

CHAPTER 4

'Yes, there was something special about me, and I knew what it was. I was the kind of girl they found dead in a hall bedroom with an empty bottle of pills in her hand.'

Marilyn Monroe (1926–62)

Day one in LA was long and dull. Sort of like a marathon screening of daytime television soaps, only without the ads. Even Château Marmont with all its reprobate grandeur and history wasn't enough to amuse me. Billy Wilder once declared that he would rather sleep in a lobby toilet at the Marmont than take a suite at another hotel – and did exactly that when the hotel was full one Christmas.

The place had wall-to-wall kudos, and then some. It's hard to argue with the credentials of a place where the guest-list reads like a Hollywood walk of fame. I kept looking for handprints of the stars in the brown carpet and chenille bedspreads.

Here amongst the antiques, the icky brown carpet (an anti-cool statement) and the kitsch, I was reminded that LA was a place for stars and their deal-makers and that as a nobody, I was doomed to be part of the audience.

I was one of those people who vie to be part of the crowd scene in films. I was a bit-part player without a speaking part. I was a no one in a place full of someones.

Rory was sulking about the way I had run off into the Sunset (that's the boulevard not the solar horizon) with another man. He'd pretended to be asleep when I'd finally rolled in. I knew it was all a pretence because private eyes are not heavy sleepers by any stretch of the imagination and I'd made plenty of noise. Plenty.

Rory's way of expressing that he didn't care about something was, like most other men I have known, a long painful sulk. Mads calls it 'passive aggressive'.

'Why is it that men use sulking as a non-confrontational form of aggression? Tell me that!' I'd asked her when I was stuck for something traumatic to tell her about my childhood one session. God knows why I ever imagined that a woman like Maddy could throw any light on the subject of men though.

Let's do a reality check on my shrink for a minute.

Love her as I do, Maddy's romantic history makes even lighter reading than my own. In a nutshell,

Maddy once suffered from a handicap known in the cosmetic industry as being 'nasally challenged'.

In lay women's terms her nose was a schnoz and whether or not it was unsightly was beside the point, it coloured her view of life. She was obsessed with the thing to the point where she had *me* playing therapist.

'Do you think this jumper makes my nose look big?' she'd ask, just as I was about to explore a locked door in my psyche.

I got to thinking about how I might help her. God knows, Barbara Streisand used her nose as a self-empowering tool and made it the hallmark of her own individual beauty, but Maddy was never going to carry it off *à la* Babs.

Not only is she *not* Jewish, but as you've probably gathered she's not exactly plucky either. Not a hallmark-making woman in the least, far from it. Given the choice, Mads would put her hand up for Susan Sarandon qualities but you'd have trouble getting most people to see her as anyone other than Mia Farrow in *Hannah and Her Sisters*. Put upon is what Mads is. Mostly by me, she claims.

Let's just agree that like most therapists, Mads is a lie back and watch the world go by sort of a girl. A listener, not one of life's doers, a member of the jury.

'Do you think if I get my hair cut it would make my nose stand out more?' she asked one time when I was trying to wrestle with the issue of men and their passive-aggressive paybacks.

I decided to wrestle with the issue of Maddy's self-image instead.

'Why are you afraid of having cosmetic surgery?' I asked. 'Scalpels can change your life,' I had told her – look at Michael Jackson. Maybe that wasn't the best example though, I thought later.

The results she was waiting for came two weeks after the surgical swelling went down. Mads was a new woman, bursting with hormones and hope. Almost straight away she started dating my ex, Giles – or as he is known in my circle 'the superbastard'.

Anyway back to me. After whisking me off in his Merc, Daniel had taken me for a drink at the Skybar at the Mondrian *en route* to the Château Marmont. The Skybar is like *the* coolest place in the world – and when I say coolest I mean in the seminal sense of the word. All those other places you thought were cool become distinctly uncool once you hit the Skybar. If you're not a media babe or a player, forget it.

By the time Daniel handed his keys to the parking valet, I was way beyond jet lag, let alone babeness of any description. Two hours later I was moving through another time zone entirely. A sort of extra-terrestrial time zone still to be discovered by NASA.

Either that or I was just plain drunk.

Daniel had proved himself pretty damn adept at *cosmopolitan* ordering, though now I come to think of it, slightly less proficient at drinking the things himself.

Pretty soon I was making expansive declarations about my personal dynamics and my postmodern right to withhold sex as a valid form of self-empowerment. Daniel was laughing at virtually everything I said, and wise sayings I'd read on my desk calendar about not drinking when jet-lagged only came back to me the next morning.

The Skybar is one of those ultra-trendy bars where self-conscious coolness is obligatory. The patrons are all walking pieces of art with chic, understated sensibilities, who don't like to seem too interested in life – or even breathing for that matter. I had an urge to pinch them to see if they were real.

They kept looking really bored – even when I slid off my stool. And they hardly spoke except to say stuff like 'whatever', although they were no doubt packing the word with innuendoes which I was too uncool to comprehend.

I was flagging fast but it wasn't until around two in the morning that it occurred to me that Rory was probably waiting for me at the hotel, thinking of calling the police or something. There is nothing like a sense of guilt for sobering me up. I asked Daniel to take me to my hotel and he seemed pretty relieved to do so.

Once at the Château, Daniel arranged my check-in and had my bags carried to my room. A guy with a stud in his tongue appeared from nowhere and offered to carry my shoes, which I'd removed back at the bar just before my feet exploded.

Daniel shook my hand formally and insisted that I allow him to take me to lunch while I was in LA. He said he'd leave a letter for me at reception but I didn't believe him for a moment. It was obvious that the poor guy couldn't wait to be shot of me. I think he was going to think twice in future before offering strange women lifts from the airport.

Rory was snoring soundly on one of the enormous beds by the time I fell, giggling with the joy of *cosmopolitan* excess, into our fourth-floor suite.

I should have spotted then that Rory was in for the long sulk by the way he ignored my drunken entreaties to wake up. Normally any sudden moves make him reach for his gun.

'What's this with the separate beds?' I'd yelled in his ear after basic prodding and poking had failed to pay off.

Not so much as a flicker of an eyelash.

I started blowing on his face.

For those of you who know the type, Rory's got one of those orifice-panting mouths that make a girl forget she's lost her virginity. All my life I've been saving myself up for a bloke with a mouth like Rory's – although being of an enthusiastic disposition, I may have made that declaration about a few men with slightly less desirable mouths.

His Caravaggio curls were falling enticingly on his brow and I forgot all previous plans I'd had for petulant withholding of sex, as expounded to the chic men and women at the Skybar earlier. Instead, I tried my best to wake him up to start testing out my orgasm capacity. Still no go.

I became bored after a while and went off to rummage through the well-stocked mini-bar, which was more of a maxi-bar actually – a huge period fridge with cargo enough to destroy a thousand women's thighs. Heaven.

Following a massive binge-out, I ran a bath and tried to think of a song that I knew all the words to. A song which would express all the excitement of being in LA with Rory, and failing that I loudly tried a few bars of almost every song I knew. Floating in a lather of bath gels, aligning all the lovely little petite shampoos and conditioners with my toes, I felt all sultry, sexy and sirenish.

Maybe I wouldn't go blonde after all.

After my bath I made a few more goes of enticing Rory to make love to me. I must have stretched out on the sofa for a bit because I awoke the next morning in a Château Marmont-issue robe with an alarming pain in my right arm which was lolling about on the floor, all sort of blue and mottled.

There was a note in said hand, which read.
Back around 5. R!

Rory is the sort of guy who doesn't like to give too much away. Goes with the territory of being a PI I guess.

I wasn't overly troubled by his absence initially. The suite was altogether divine and the light altogether blinding. I had entered a place where Ray Bans were compulsory. Though I must admit that I felt quite perfect after three strong espressos gave me back single vision.

Hand on heart, I have never stayed in a suite before, although this was probably not your normal suite, taking as it did a more ironic view on taste than your average top-class establishment.

The substantial dining-table and chairs looked out over Sunset Strip, and down the stretch of Sunset Boulevard which was home to famous places like the Viper Room, Whisky A-Go-Go, the Comedy Store, House of Blues and the Mondrian. The Marmont was one of those places with a history that had managed to stay contemporary. A maverick amongst luxury hotels.

The suite had a CD player with a library of some four hundred disks, two televisions, a video, and most importantly a view over both Sunset Boulevard's Marlboro Man and the palm-fronded pool. Top of its virtues was the kitchen – bringing a new scale to the term mini-bar. A full-sized period kitchen packed with tasty goodies and calorie baddies, this was a lifestyle rather than an accessory.

I was like a kid in a candy store.

Part of being an embracer of fashion is that come August when the Inns of Court have disgorged their drones, I realise I haven't the money to go away. If I have any room left on my overdraft limit at all, it certainly doesn't stretch further than a charter flight and a tiny room at the back of the hotel over the disco with a leaking cistern and a balcony with an alarming sign reading *unsafe*.

This suite was everything I had always dreamed of and more and as I sorted out my jet lag with a few miracle cures I'd bought in Paris on my Eurostar phase, I realised that I'd fallen on my feet. I could easily become accustomed to this.

Feeling approximately at one with my DNA, I breakfasted on low-calorie muffins and more full-caffeinated coffee. I had a swim or rather lolled slug-like in a rubber ring in the pool while no one was looking (still wearing full bathrobe) and later I did, like, three seconds on the free weights in the attic gym before exhaustion drove me back to the suite.

I then reread the *Harpers & Queen* I'd brought with me from London and pencilled in the Gucci steel heel slingbacks that looked so nice on Kate Moss for next month's Visa bill. I was already paying off the outrageous boots from the same range.

By one o'clock, I was rigid with boredom. Panicking that my limbs were going to mottle again, I exercised my fingers with the remote control, flicking through every cable channel, first on one television and then on the other until I started to get a migraine.

I ordered up a few CDs from the hotel library and blasted my headache into another part of my body. It was around this phase that I started to become seriously pissed off with Rory for leaving me on my first day in LA and rang my hairdresser back in London. Stefan is usually far more useful than my therapist as far as advice goes.

'Cut a few crotches out of his trousers,' he advised when I woke him up for a bit of off-the-scissor advice. 'See if he still feels sulky then. Crotch cutting brings men round every time in my experience,' he promised. I had no doubt that he was right.

I should add that my hairdresser is also the sort of guy who believes firmly in always leaving a prawn in the mouthpiece of ex-lovers' telephones. More about my hairdresser's philosophy for self-empowerment later though.

Searching for fresh air and amusement, I ended up hanging around the lobby and generally wandering about the hotel with intent to divert myself. Later on, plumped up on a comfy velvet sofa sipping Perrier amongst the splendour of the lobby's Gothic retro-chic, I was eyeing up a few crotches with the boys still inside. PS, a detail like that wouldn't bother a guy with scissors as sharp as Stefan's.

For a while it really was quite relaxing, soaking up the Hollywood atmosphere, the sounds of nature coming from the palm-fronded garden and the sophisticated buzz of residents' conversations as they sipped espressos and smoked Marlboro Lights. But only for a while.

Absorbing faded opulence only goes so far even in this Hollywood lobby of lobbies, where Led Zeppelin had ridden around on their Harleys while fellow guests, who'd seen it all, blew smoke rings and pretended not to notice. Even here, boredom was only a heartbeat away.

Besides there were no signs of Led Zeppelin today amongst the celebrities, their just as famous agents, hotshot producers and deal-makers. And no matter how hard I tried to stay hopeful and pretend I belonged, no matter how disinterestedly I watched the parades of people going in and out, armed with scripts and ideas, I couldn't help but feel my lack of purpose.

I was a fake. These people belonged. They had people to see (and who wanted to see them!), appointments to keep. They had lives. No matter how groovy this place was, sipping espresso in the decadence of LA's only French château did not qualify as a life. Not quite.

Stuck for a driver's licence, I guess I was hoping to live vicariously, waiting for something to happen in the hotel which would take my mind off how bloated, pointless and unwanted I was feeling. Elizabeth Taylor, Dennis Hopper, Sting and all the other stars rumoured to have hung out here were significantly absent though.

I thought I saw Michelle Pfeiffer at one point but it could have been Goldie Hawn or Sharon Stone or a million other babes because she had her back to me as she flitted past.

F. Scott Fitzgerald once said of this hotel that the girls often seemed to be French and the boys English but I didn't think that was the case today. Everyone except me was smoking though. That's how cool this place was – the Marlboro Man dream was still a real possibility here.

I started to focus on my usual first-day-of-holiday bloat. Is it just me or do all women dread getting their period in the first week of their vacation? I mean, I seriously stress about this issue, even if I'm not due. And why, if all women fear getting their period on holidays, do hotels provide no pre-menstruating women's entertainment? Apart from food that is.

I mean, I know they say that we live in relaxed times and that our bodies are just our corporeal shells but hey, the sense of pre-menstrual bloat can ruin a brilliant holiday. Instead of painting the town red I was more likely to end up painting my toenails green in my room watching CNN. Or moping around the poolside, hugging my hotel-issue robe around me like those guys in tight black bathers who don't want to get their medallions wet and risk the gold plating flaking off.

Besides, this hotel was the sort of place where Sting might pass you a towel or tell you there was someone on the phone for you, so I was definitely not going to risk having my motley white thighs exposed. God forbid, what if some paparazzi lurking in the fronds thought I actually was someone and took a shot of me – or worse a shot of my thighs and they appeared on the front page of *Hardcopy* under a jokey heading, 'The Thighs of the Rich and Famous'.

Oh my God!

My therapist blames the nuns for most of my hang-ups, and fear of exposing my thighs is right up there on the long list of crimes she has accredited to them. Which, if you want to be ironic, is really amazing because if the confession of Sister Conchilio that I eavesdropped in on in fifth grade is anything to go by, those nuns think they've got a pretty clean slate.

Think about it.

While the rest of us Catholic women are slinking through life with a heavy burden packed to bursting with a multitude of sins designer-made for our sex – lustful inducement, vanity, pride and general coveting, etc. – nuns on the other hand sit back smugly, resisting all the temptation that the rest of us girls grab at like it was the last chocolate biscuit on the plate. This sense of safety from evil is one of the main perks of the job for the brides of Christ.

Nuns have never incited anyone to lust (apart from the cute albeit sicko Italian guy in *The Flying Nun*) and are sadly without vanity. They don't grab at sin or covet their neighbour's husband or wife (not without a quick trip to the confessional and a thorough absolution anyway). Nuns feel pretty confident of their virtue, only not too virtuous because that would be prideful.

Nuns think of themselves as good eggs. Apart from the odd scuffle over whose turn it was to say the Hail Marys during washing-up duty at the convent, the nuns who taught me had every reason to think that they were living relatively sin-free lives.

Now, as we catapult into the next millennium, armed to the teeth with gestalt, Freud and a hell-ish host of reclaimed memories, these same nuns are finding to their horror that their sin slates are suddenly full. Laden down with king-size portions of the blame for the way Evelyn Hornton turned out basically.

'Be fair now,' I pleaded with my therapist the last time she had urged me to stick pins in an effigy of one of the nuns she has down as oppressing my sense of self. 'She was only following rules from on high. Pull yourself together Mads,' I told her. 'My fear of thigh exposure has nothing whatsoever to do with the nuns who taught me algebra, so just drop it OK?'

'What is it about your body that depresses you so much?' Maddy asked by way of a put down. Whenever she sees herself losing an argument she always gets me to discuss my body. It's one of her favourite ploys to trap me and keep me where she wants me – in the pathetic and needy seat.

Like most women with a pronounced fear of retain-ing fluid, I am naturally more than happy to oblige.

'Um, let's start with my head and work down,' I suggested gamely.

Talk about a depressing session. The whole hour discussing my body and we didn't even get as far as my thighs. Like most women, I can go on all week about my thighs but Maddy had another patient so

I went home and rang up my girlfriend Charles and bitched about my therapist instead. Far more edifying anyway.

I think I might leave therapy when I go back to London. After all, I only took Mads on as a fashion accessory really and since she started dating my ex, I get a feeling that her questions are laced with a smug secret knowledge that new girlfriends get about old girlfriends.

Men are so disloyal.

Maddy is thirty with a figure like a greyhound and not the merest hint of cellulite in her aura. Miss perfect A-cup to my difficult D-cup basically. The Maddies of this world don't know what it means to be a woman with breasts in a world of designers who have never let a thing like a woman's anatomy get in the way of a good frock.

We live in a world where line is all. It's tough out there in the dressing rooms of Gucci and Calvin Klein for a girl genetically designed for breastfeeding. Anyway I don't think it's ideal having a therapist who is dating your ex, it's probably against the Hippocratic oath or something.

Although as it turned out, Maddy was perfectly suited to my ex, Giles Billington-Frith. They both wear the same brand of in-steps and they both look at me like I might have an alien inhabiting my body.

Anyway, back to crotches.

Watching their groins go by I decided there must have been a stud convention going on at the Marmont that day. Either that or they were casting for beach bum of the year.

Rebel Without A Cause had been cast in this hotel, in one of the bungalows out the back. That was when Dennis Hopper first met Natalie Wood, although romance didn't bloom till much later. She was only fifteen at the time.

These stud-of-the-month guys with their flowing locks and massive pecs could have held James Dean, Natalie Wood and Dennis Hopper in the palms of their hands. Everyone of them had a suntanned Adonis body and a head of bleached hair that made Fabio look like he was thinning. Actually they looked like a bunch of Fabio clones.

How do American men get to look like that? I mean is it the breakfast cereal or the sun's rays or the simple lack of socialist history? I have a theory that socialism makes the men thin, bearded and weedy. Maybe Romanians would all have been strapping great manifestations of health: big-chested tanned people with tumbling bleached locks and big crotches if it weren't for Ceausescu? I flirted briefly with the idea of going into politics once but I couldn't think up a manifesto that would hold mass appeal.

In a corner, nursing a *Variety* magazine like a press pass, I caught one of the Fabio's leering at me, although maybe he was just wondering why I wasn't smoking. I was feeling madly uncomfortable. Sometimes, and to be honest this was one of those times, I feel like a giant set of thighs, swelling and swelling and swelling.

During these periods of imagined thigh swelling, if a man stares at me for more than a nanosecond, I can become totally convinced my thighs are going to explode cellulite and splatter innocent victims.

Not wishing to go down for manslaughter during my first week in LA, I struggled out of my comfy sofa, put on my sunglasses and took my thighs off down the road to straddle a stool at Bar Marmont.

A *cosmopolitan* or two later, I realised that this LA bonding exercise with Rory was not turning out as well as it might. Proof of this was in the fact that I had started to think fondly of my loft apartment back in Clerkenwell – an albatross-type manifestation of minimalist misery and debt consumption.

I had even begun to wonder how things were back in the clerk's room at Chambers – hitherto a black spot of spite and bitterness at 17 Pump Court. Was my clerk Lee missing me, I wondered. Was he standing in my rooms now perhaps wondering who to hand a fraud brief to?

I even began to wonder whether the soulless solicitors of Clifford Chance were missing me, envying me, or even sparing me a thought as they filled out their time and motion reports on the intranet.

My excuse of abandoning everyone for the sake of an orgasm check-up now seemed a tad pathetic, given the fact that I hadn't had so much as a clitoral flutter since we'd arrived. Not even a vaginal test drive actually.

My visions of him making hot love to me all night and languorous love to me by day (apart from when he was pumping up his chest doing free-weights in the attic gym) were fast disintegrating under the heavy grind of boredom. I mean if he didn't hurry up and get his libido together my period would arrive. Sometimes I feel that I spend my life racing against the tyranny of my menstrual cycle.

What was most troubling to a paranoid depressive like myself was that Rory hadn't said anything about rushing out on our first day – quite the opposite in fact. He had tantalised me with images of lying on beaches, rollerblading down Santa Monica and eating marvellously healthy food – and most enticing image of all – shopping on Rodeo Drive.

Either I had been lured to LA under false pretences, or I was being punished for accepting a lift from a stranger, or for not being able to drive. Both of which seemed equally grave and heinous crimes to Rory.

What was driving me crazy was the thought that there was an unexplored city out there. More importantly, there were unexplored shops. I could hear the heart of consumerism pumping the blood of purchases around shopping malls and designer stores. Tills ringing up charge cards in the Beverly Hills Mall, designer frocks crying for attention in Donna Karan, cocktails with parasols in them under cabanas, imploring me to rush out and gulp them down greedily.

It was infuriating. I just knew that there were Azzedine Alaia dresses that could change my life, hanging listlessly on racks in Barneys unnoticed, calling out my name: 'Evelyn! Evelyn! Evelyn!'

Oh, it was heartbreaking.

Bloody hell this was my first chance ever to wear a size six and here I was tempted by the idea of sticking my fingers down my throat as a valid form of passing the time.

I began to castigate myself for not learning to drive. So what, my heels might have got caught under the accelerator pedal, I might have mown down old women on pedestrian crossings but by God I would have mitigated my way out of it like a million other reckless drivers before me.

Rory would come to my defence in one of his smart suits and recite his 'I drive therefore I am!' speech, and the judge would nod solemnly and agree that after all it was a car's world and that hapless pedestrians like the sweet old dears I'd just mown down were a small price to pay for the triumph of motoring.

By two o'clock I began to hope against hope that my watch was wrong and that it was really five o'clock and that any minute now, Rory was going to saunter through the palm trees in the courtyard. Whereupon I would melt into his arms in a puddle of unemancipated subservience and allow him to carry me back to our suite and do manly oppressive things to me like kiss me all over my body. Every inch.

Eventually a weird Australian guy in the lobby took pity on me and told me that a small-time soap-opera star was staying in one of the bungalows of the hotel, and that for a substantial tip he could probably get me photos of him in the shower.

Gasp!

I had obviously fallen much further than I'd initially thought. What had happened to Evelyn Hornton, super career girl with bags of sass and style? Mistaken for paparazzi. Reduced to shelling out for blue snaps of wannabe soap stars in the shower? If you're not someone in this town you must be a sado who wants to take photographs of people who are someone.

I got a grip pretty smartish after that and marched myself off back to our suite where I couldn't shame myself further.

By four o'clock I was more or less prepared to throw myself on Rory's mercy. 'Forgive me, oh testosterone host,' I was going to sob.

'You were so right, oh masterful one!'

'How pathetic of me not to have a licence!'

'I deserve your total opprobrium but in the meantime can you shag me out of my boredom and arrange for me to have a limo with driver on your expense account?'

Within my subconscious though, all was not suppliant harmony. There were doubts as well. My inner-therapist voice was warning me to doubt my choices and being of a paranoid nature and, let's face it, deeply bored, I began to listen.

The inner-therapy voice – which sounded more like my hairdresser than Maddy – was talking sense. There was something unreal about my whole relationship with Rory. Surreal even. I mean his name for starters?

His real name was Gary but that's probably best left for late-relationship humiliation – just before we divide up the CDs and own up to all the stuff we could never stand about one another.

Rory had been introduced to me by my builder which is about as unsuitable an introduction as you can get really, discounting those women who fall in love with men on death row after reading about them in the *National Enquirer*.

OK, so being introduced to your boyfriend by your Irish builder isn't that bad in the classless 1990s but I am almost certain that a psychic once warned me about dating a tall dark gentleman, linked to a man I should be suing for destruction of property.

My first impression of Rory was that he was the most odious man alive and once again the evidence was stacking up. What kind of low-life bastard leaves a girl in a hotel famous for the way its guests die? What kind of man leaves a girl without a licence in a luxury suite where smoking is practically obligatory and the mini-bar is a lethal weapon capable of discharging enough artificial colorants and flavours to kill her in an afternoon of compulsive bingeing? The West should be made to decommission men like Rory – before more sex-starved women get hurt!

First impressions are almost always right. Then again my first impression of my mother is apparently that she was a selfish evil bitch who gave me milk formula rather than ruin her figure with breastfeeding – I have this on Maddy's authority.

Rory was thrust on me by Paddy as a possible solution to a slight stalker problem I had at the time but he ended up bringing far more chaos to my life than the stalker ever dreamed of.

Adding up the clues, i.e. his background, his education, his Neanderthal attitude towards women, his profession, his address (a few thousand miles away), it's hard to imagine why I fell for Rory but fall I did.

PS. He was hold your breath gorgeous. He looks like Cary Grant and he knows it.

The thump in the stomach that goes with love first began when he disappeared back to New York, which as far as seduction technique goes was a pretty good way of guaranteeing my interest. More men should try it.

We then spent an unsatisfactory few months conducting a transatlantic relationship that ended up with a phone bill of which a phone-sex fiend could be proud. I ask you, is any man worth spending £198 just to speak to for the evening?

No doubt it was to my peril that I hadn't focused

on these doubts before deciding to accompany Rory to LA.

Five o'clock came and went.

I ate more high-calorie mini-bar snacks, mainlined full caffeinated coffee and searched through the carpet for residual heroin and speed rollerballs that might have been left behind by other guests. No luck.

At six, while waiting for the mini-bar to be refreshed, I went back to the gym and tried the walking machine.

While trying to look cool in my sweaty, sludge-green leotard – a near impossibility for any woman – I politely declined a lesbian affair with a Sharon Stone lookalike and watched a man burping. I tell no lie, he was shamelessly burping by the free weights, over and over again. Not so much as a hint of a 'pardon me'.

When I sought assistance from the gym supervisor guy, I was reassured that burping repeatedly was a valid way of invigorating the digestive tract during fasting. 'Speeds up the detoxification process,' he assured me.

I still had a lot to learn.

Around seven, I familiarised myself with the major studio executives' career climbs in the *Variety* left behind in the lobby by the leering stud. I then read the society pages of *Harpers & Queen* for the first time in my life. Who are these people? I have always wondered, flicking past their asinine grins and going straight for the back page in the hope of finding a last perfume sample.

Maybe it is jealousy on my part that makes me despise them and their jovial society romps. Secretly I hope that the people grinning out of the pages of *Jennifer's Diary* are actually stunt people. Hired for the day to be photographed looking privileged and happy, showing off their stately homes and idle lifestyles. Hired to drink vast quantities of Veuve Clicquot, to dance tirelessly, to frolic agelessly and to misbehave in kilts. Oh, for a job like that!

I tossed the magazine aside listlessly and started to pace my suite.

My parents would not have been proud of me that night – both televisions blaring, the stereo going hell-for-leather, the mini-bar taunting me, empty now but for a Diet Coke (rumoured to cause shortening of the bowel or cancer or something – or was that petrol? I didn't want to risk it anyway) and a mini bourbon.

I was like a caged puma prowling round an unfoliaged cell in Regent's Park Zoo. Greta Garbo used to hide out in this hotel when she was in Hollywood – and I wondered what she did to alleviate the boredom of all that aloneness she always professed to 'vant'. Perhaps I just wasn't cut out for mystery and fame?

Outside my window the Marlboro Man sneered, as if goading me to jump on my horse and get the hell out of this town.

My plan to throw myself in abject remorse at Rory's feet had totally deflated by eight o'clock. His absence was obviously part of his sadistic plan to break me. He no doubt figured that if he left me like this for long enough, I would admit to being able to drive.

I could have arranged for the hotel to provide me with a car and driver and charged it to Rory but I was still clinging to the independent woman thing. Come on, women have thrown themselves under horses and been force-fed like geese so that I could enjoy the privilege of my right to say 'no' to Rory and his expense account.

Instead I took two Temazepams and fell asleep, draping myself dramatically across the bed. Naked.

Oh, the utter Vivien Leigh-ness of it all!

CHAPTER 5

'She's got those eyes that run up and down a man like a searchlight.'

The Women, 1939, colour & b/w, Joan
Crawford
and Rosalind Russell

Rory finally rolled up at the hotel at about 8.30 p.m. Just as the Temazepams were beginning to seep into my medulla.

'Come on, doll, we've got company,' he declared, slapping my bare rump heartily.

Who did he think he was – I thought, gathering a few functional brain cells together, Clark Gable in *Gone With The Wind*? Actually there are rumours that Clark Gable conducted an affair with Jean Harlow in suite 29 in this very hotel.

Jean is one of my ultimate girl idols. It was she who uttered that famous pre-coital line, 'Excuse me while I slip into something more comfortable.' I mean, how's that for an aphrodisiac? Suggesting not only sex but the promise of a new outfit! My two most favourite pastimes.

Just at this minute though, I wasn't up for slipping into anything other than unconsciousness, but articulating this was a bit of a struggle.

'Company?' I repeated woozily, my eyes glued together, my jaw collapsing with the mammoth effort of speech. I was in one of my Shirley MacLaine-as-hungover-French-prostitute moods but Rory wasn't cutting me any slack.

As I tried to sit up, one of the society pages of *Harpers & Queen* got stuck to my cheek. Let's be frank – Temazepam has never been the drug to present me at my best.

Rory peeled the page off my face and began to study it while I slumped back to the bed and groaned.

'Rise and shine doll, we have a visitor,' he told me.

'Fuck off Rory,' I murmured into the pillow. 'I hate you. I have always hated you. Go away. I want to be alone.'

I may not have been quite *compos mentis* but I was recognising my disadvantages for what they were and they sure as hell didn't need an audience. I tried to look aloof and remote and smoky-eyed as I uttered my Greta Garbo line but I could see my enigmatic expressions weren't cutting any ice with Rory.

'Your eyes are rolling around in your head doll,' he said. 'What have you taken?'

That was when I realised that I needed a pair of dark glasses and a head scarf, I wasn't dressed adequately for my role as siren. I wasn't dressed, period.

Rory was sitting on the edge of the bed in a dark Armani suit I'd never seen him in before. To be honest I'd never seen him in any outfit that didn't offer at least a glimpse of his six-pack stomach. It made him look kind of dignified. Dignity – now there was a thought.

I was bereft of dignity, clothes and basic mental function. I was nodding off. I think I may have started to dribble actually. Whatever, I wasn't looking my coolest.

In true Clark Gable style, Rory took control of the situation and before you could say the word 'bimbo', I was showered, brushed, dressed (stuck in a pair of dark glasses) and sitting at dinner with a woman introduced to me by Rory as 'Alexia Dean, a *great* friend. She's so great, you'll just love her.'

Confronted by this 'great' friend I longed to be back in my coma. She grinned a grin so wide, the luminosity of her well-flossed teeth burnt through my iris and gave me a migraine. 'Isn't this just *great*?' she squealed.

This word 'great' was to mark the beginning of a very bad phase in my romantic relationship with Rory and the cause of sisterhood generally. In the fullness of time I would come to see the word 'great' as the most grating thing about that evening. I slumped down in my chair and tried to hide behind my menu for a quiet snooze.

The evening wore on and on and on. It was on its uppers before our first course arrived in fact. Introducing me to Alexia was Rory's biggest mistake ever, and Rory was well versed in the big mistake stakes. Let's just say that she was not my kind of girl.

Alexia was a blonde, toned, tanned 'babe' in her late twenties with a tense enthusiasm for life. A sort of surgically enhanced Sharon Stone. Her nose bore the classic hallmark of a good surgeon, her lips pouted with collagen and her breasts were the shape of a moulded silicone desk-toy. I doubt her thighs had ever threatened to explode on her or anyone else for that matter. On reading the menu she pronounced it fatty!

She was no doubt the faithful member of a fitness club and, I hazarded, noting the tendons in her neck, she regularly took to a free-weight machine with unbridled gusto. She was pretty, confident, organised and probably really popular in a prom queen sort of way. In short, she was a girl I would never have got to know by choice.

Initially I had mistakenly thought that she must be Rory's latest job lot. The hotshot Hollywood agent who was paying him to catch her husband with his pants around his ankles, but I was wrong. Only I didn't know just how wrong. Actually I was worse than wrong. But the worst of it didn't become clear until much, much later.

In Hollywood terms I was still rehearsing my *Age of Innocence* lines. I was playing Michelle Pfeiffer under the influence of sleeping pills, not to mention the wrong hair colour. You see my problem.

I have watched the Alexias of this world all my life and make no mistake, I know the type. I have met them at taxi ranks, in bars and on the shoe floor of Gucci on Old Bond Street. Sloane Slappers I call them, and Alexia was their American counterpart.

These are the girls who just when you are about to be served, cry out from the back of the store, 'Excuse me, but I have been waiting for ever!'

Yeah right!

These girls have had the world handed to them on a silver salver all their life. Alexias wait for no man. These are the girls who have measured out their lives in Gold Cards and trust funds and yet try to pass themselves off as having been waiting patiently in the wings like the rest of us. Pah-lease!

When you are as genetically gifted as the Alexias of this world, it is always your turn and it is the lot of the rest of us genetic unfortunates to wait.

My PC conscience rumbled me immediately. I was jealous.

Only hours before I had thought that the worst thing that could befall my relationship with Rory was a faked orgasm.

Sad.

'Well, isn't *this* just *GREAT*?' Alexia said for the

millionth time, just as I was about to happily nod off again into my Pacific Rim cuisine.

Amongst her many irritating qualities, Alexia was a woman skilled in the art of speaking in CAPITALS, *italics* and inverted commas. If this woman was in a cyber chat room she would be flamed from the Internet pathways. Chased into cyber Coventry.

But the only thing being chased at our table that night was the food around her plate. Just looking at the way she didn't eat made me feel mentally and physically huge.

'Could I have an espresso?' I asked a passing waiter who happened to catch my eye.

'Need! Say NEED!' Alexia insisted, grabbing my wrist in her pincer grasp.

I looked at the starched white knuckles and blinked. 'Excuse me?'

I couldn't help staring at the muscles in her neck which were throbbing like something out of the X-Files. I decided then that Rory's client or not, I hated this woman as no other. She was like a greyhound on amphetamines, psyching herself up for a race.

PS. No prizes for guessing who the bunny was.

'Tell him that you NEED an espresso, don't ask him IF you can have one,' she advised. 'Act like a *schmuck* in this town and assholes like him will TREAT you like one.'

The words 'chill out' came to mind but I didn't utter them.

'You know something Evie?' (She dared to call me Evie!) 'I used to drink coffee all the time before my surgeon showed me what it did to the skin.' She looked at Rory, wrinkling her nose job prettily.

He nodded understandingly.

Fully alerted to her implied insult on my skin tone, I began to act like a spoilt girlfriend. I wanted to hurt this woman in true Meg Ryan, *Addicted to Love* revenge-fest style.

Now!

'Coming from Australia you really ought to take better care of your skin,' she advised me, giving my wrist a sisterly squeeze.

When thirty is on your horizon the last thing you need are complexion jibes. It was official, in six months' time I would pass the cut-off point for being a 'babe' and become a 'flirtysomething'. In my early twenties babe-prime, my skin had been referred to as dewy. I may have grown up on the north shore of Sydney but I had never left the great indoors without factor-fifteen sunblock slapped over every part of my body.

OK, so I was pushing out the membrane of my babedom but give me a break, I was getting over the shock that I wasn't one of the immortals anymore. I still harboured the illusion that I was bulletproof. It seemed like just yesterday that I could stay up all weekend, imbibe all manner of complexion-deteriorating substances and still get asked for identification to get into a club.

'Lucky you have such long legs,' she sighed wistfully. 'Men love a woman with long legs no matter how wrinkled up her face might get. Rory's always been a leg man, haven't you hon?' she simpered.

Hon?

I shot Rory a don't-you-dare-say-a-word look and then smiled my most acid smile. Legs were a bit of an issue between us, mine being longer, stronger and faster than Rory's – or any man's I've ever met actually.

Quite a few men have been put off by my legs. Oh I know they go on about legs in a voomba-voomba kind of way, but confront them with legs as deadly as an Exocet missile coming at you close range and watch their libidos shrivel.

Anyway, so Alexia was really getting to me. Although if I am honest it wasn't so much the barbed remarks or the blonde brittleness or the speaking in CAPITALS that bugged me as much as the fluttering eyelashes aimed in Rory's direction and the way the two of them kept sharing in-jokes and speaking in a shorthand which excluded me almost as much as it irritated me.

As one of life's great flirts I was probably a hypocrite but Daniel aside, I believe that flirting should only begin by mutual consent, and preferably it should be begun by me – with my boyfriend of the moment looking on green with possessive desire. What's more I had given Rory full disclosure on this fact.

Information he had obviously decided to disregard at his peril.

He was behaving very out of character in other ways, too. All my cleverly subtle, hilariously bitchy remarks – stuff that would normally have him laughing himself sick – were instead being met with swift kicks under the table. My shins were beginning to resemble a hockey pitch and my ego wasn't faring brilliantly either.

Talk about giving my self-image a beating – what was Rory trying to achieve here? What had happened to his hitherto cherished belief in my sense of humour as one of the most significant talents of the modern world? Not to mention his previously sworn hatred of all hair colourants derived artificially and his heartfelt loathing for all the plastic fantastic breasts of LA?

'So Alexia, what does a Hollywood agent do all day?' I asked in an attempt to get her attention away from Rory. I mean, the two of them were gripped in an eye-lock of positively steamy ferocity.

Alexia dragged her eyes from Rory significantly and smiled at me like I've seen mothers smile at hysterical children in department stores. A smile that warns the child that danger awaits them when no one else is looking. 'Ideas, Evie. I get IDEAS,' she explained, tapping the side of her head and turning her attention back to Rory.

Rory gave her one of his 'you said it kid!' winks.

'I sincerely doubt that,' I muttered under my breath, earning another kick to the shin. But I guess I deserved that one, because despite my feelings for Alexia she seemed quite taken with me in a superior, condescending, supercilious kind of way.

'Isn't she just GREAT, Rory?' she declared during the main course when I dropped a bean in my cleavage. She said it with such genuine warmth too, with real glee. Now glee is something you just don't usually see exhibited much in the adult population of the UK. Particularly in London.

Glee gets short shrift in the UK where a sort of generalised cynicism in all things positive prevails. Positive is not a good look to master in Britain. It suggests an almost infantile trust in the future, that two wars and ten years of torture by unions, followed by ten cruel years of Thatcher-inflicted misery, basically kicked out of the population.

I made a face to show Alexia that her glee was a little saccharine for my world-weary taste.

On the other hand, Rory seemed totally comfortable with this glee thing of hers. So comfortable in fact that he gave me one of his cold, hard stares. One of those looks I had previously thought were reserved for people who had drowned puppies or offered small children poisoned sweets. I could feel my belief in this American-dream orgasm thing with Rory draining away.

'You didn't tell me she was so "great",' Alexia said, now looking not only gleeful but worryingly like she might be about to burst into spontaneous song and embrace me.

'You've been talking about me?' I asked, looking from one to the other like a kicked dog.

Rory shrugged, avoiding my hurt expression by summoning a waiter.

Meanwhile Alexia was gazing into my eyes like a hypnotist, her whole expression spilling forth a saintly human kindness. I couldn't stop wondering what would happen if I injected her with a dangerous hallucinogenic drug.

'I couldn't WAIT to meet you, could I Rory? As soon as I heard about you Evie, I said, YOU HAVE GOT TO BRING HER OUT HERE RIGHT AWAY! Didn't I hon?'

I cringed.

'Yeah, you did,' Rory mumbled into his beer.

The waiter arrived and was promptly dispatched by Rory for a double shot of Irish whiskey.

'"Rory," I told him, "I have simply GOT to meet her. She just sounds so GREAT, so, so, so, WACKY!" Didn't I say that, Rory?'

'Wacky?' I enquired. If anything, 'wacky' is one of those adjectives I shy away from using at all, let alone in reference to myself. I pride myself, if not on unerring sobriety, at least on an emotional depth and intellectual complexity devoid of all wackiness.

Wacky is an adjective I use to describe guests on *The Dave Letterman Show* – the ones that appear on New York street corners demonstrating their dance moves to strangers or who jump out of the audience in crazy hats or waving local craft produce from Vancouver.

'I mean WACKY as in GREAT, don't I Rory?'

'She thinks you're great,' Rory conceded, looking into my eyes all of a sudden. God, his eyes were gorgeous. And the lips! Just that one glimpse was enough to make me want to take off my shoes and walk across hot coals to sleep with him.

All my internal organs wailed out with desire.

'Bear his children!' my womb cried.

'Do anything to be with him,' my hormones urged.

'Subjugate yourself and wash his socks!' my ovaries screamed.

'Have him now! just tear off his clothes and lick every inch of his skin!' my clitoris moaned.

I crossed my legs and said my seventeen times table.

'Just GREAT,' Alexia repeated. 'Hey, I LOVE wacky.'

I was fairly sure she was being genuine here. Feeling guilty for my earlier dreams of injecting her with dangerous hallucinogens, I smiled and nodded politely. The nuns were very big on manners, even where Satan's emissaries were concerned. Courtesy was a cardinal rule. Don't stoop to their level, Sister Conchilio had warned.

I tried to make eye-contact with Rory again but he was looking extremely edgy now – slunk down in his chair, gazing uncomfortably into his beer.

He was wearing what my analyst calls the Mask of Masculinity – that is he was pretending to be a casual observer, a neutral passerby, rather than an integral player in the dynamics of the drama unravelling before us.

Alexia squeezed my wrist. 'And I'll tell you something else,' she whispered. 'I am in the "market" for a wacky project right now.'

Looking around the room for an assassin for hire, I noticed the Australian who had offered me the nude snap of the daytime TV star. He was in a dark corner table with his arm around an older man who seemed to be sobbing. My heart went out to him. I hoped that he wasn't still upset because I'd turned down his offer.

Alexia nudged me. 'A little bird told me all about you. Not mentioning any names of course but you know who I mean,' she added cryptically.

I had a vision of Alexia in a white robe, calling down doves from the sky.

'You talk to birds?' I asked, mortified. This was serious.

Little or otherwise I am not big on people who talk to our feathered or even our furry friends actually. Let's face it, for the most part we are shooting them out of the sky, sticking them in cages, chopping down their native habitat or spreading oil slicks on their food source. My attitude is to keep a low profile with them as far as possible. Head down in shamefaced repentance is the attitude I take around the ducks and swans in Hyde Park. Anything else is just patronising.

Alexia winked at me and grinned triumphantly at Rory. 'Isn't she CUTE?'

I stuck my fingers down my throat and gagged.

Rory slunk lower in his chair and stared out into space like he'd taken one Prozac too many.

Alexia was unperturbed by my gagging. Still as gay as a young debutante out to buy a new frock, she fluttered her eyelashes coquettishly and purred, 'Tell me Evie, have you seen *My Best Friend's Wedding*?'

'The one with Julia Roberts?'

'Right. *That's* what I mean by 'WACKY'! Don't you think she's SO Julia Roberts, Rory? I mean the body, the smile, the hair. LOOK AT HER.'

'Right, that's it. I am going blonde this minute. Ask the waiter to bring me a bowl of peroxide,' I demanded.

'See,' she gurgled.

Rory gave me a cursory onceover before returning his eyes to his beer. At this point I should add that Alexia had actually grabbed a hunk of my hair and yanked, not hard enough to bring tears to my eyes but hard enough to warrant a kick under the table.

Rory was still captivated by his beer, watching the little bubbles deflating like all my hopes for our future. My internal organs weren't crying out in lust now. The only voice inside of me was one yelling 'RUN FOR IT!'.

'Rory and I have been *talking* about you ALL DAY haven't we Rory?' Alexia continued.

I couldn't help feeling impressed. I mean, wow! I start running out of things to say about myself after half an hour. In fact sometimes I have to cut my sessions with my therapist short because I've run out of things to say. Other times I just make stuff up.

Rory nodded sheepishly which momentarily threw me off my guard, sheepish not being a part of Rory's facial repertoire with which I was familiar. Rory being one of life's wolves basically. His whiskey arrived and he downed it in one.

'He's told me *everything* about you, just EVERY-THING.'

'Everything?' I said. 'Ouch.'

I mean 'everything' is a lot of stuff. Let's deconstruct this statement for a minute. I've been paying a qualified therapist a living wage for over a year now to discover my inner depths with me and she's still just scratching hopelessly around the surface. Still scrounging for the most obvious of clues.

Frankly I think she's missing a lot of the best stuff, taking the Catholic guilt thing a bit too far but even so, *everything* is still a lot to know about any girl. Especially a deeply inscrutable, complex girl like myself.

Besides, I was thinking, Rory hadn't told *me* the first thing about Alexia. Not one measly thing!

'The thing is Evie, I AM completely FASCI-NATED by your life,' Alexia went on. 'Your career, your misadventures with men, your good deed with the turkey baster and the type of people you represent. And I have to be honest, all this wacky mix would make a GREAT comedy series. On the one hand you are a career girl and on the other you are, let's face it, a complete airhead.'

I wanted to grab her breasts and squeeze them till the silicone pads popped out. I reached out but Rory cut me down with a look of pure desperation.

'Rory told me that story about your first case, you know the guy with the steel plate in his head. I thought it was really funny. Didn't I Rory?'

This was all getting too much. 'Keith? My Keith? Head butting maniac Keith that I got off a charge of GBH years ago? You told her about Keith?' I asked, now feeling more than a little betrayed. This was intimate stuff – Keith was the first client I had shamed myself with.

I was still finding my training wheels as a barrister when Keith whipped out his dick during a pre-trial pep talk and unravelled his foreskin which concealed a photo of his pitbull terrier. It's not really something I like to be associated with. A case of letting sleeping dicks lie basically. Even my therapist hadn't been privy to the Keith Files.

'What is this?' I demanded, looking from one to the other. 'Expose Evelyn and humiliate her all evening?'

'Don't get excited,' Rory said, placing one of his large hands on my arm. Hands that had once been responsible for uniting all the orgasmic forces of my inner woman into a crescendo of spine-rattling ecstasy.

I looked at the hand now as if it was waiting outstretched for thirty pieces of silver. This was betrayal.

As Rory well knew, telling a girl of my emotional make-up not to 'get excited' is tantamount to pushing my emergency panic button. I glared at him – so as to pre-warn him that I was about to go into emotional rupture mode – but I don't think he took my glare on board. He began to move his beer around in small concentric circles.

'I'm sorry if I'm coming on too strong,' Alexia miaowed. 'It's just that the idea of your adventures as a lawyer appeals to me. I feel PASSIONATELY about your life.'

Gulp.

'Well hang on a minute here,' I said. 'Passionately? Are we talking about the same life here? I don't know what Rory has told you but I think you have been misled. Passion and I are barely on nodding acquaintance. Not even *I* feel passionately about my life – and I'm the one who wakes up in it every day. Sometimes, I'd go so far as to say that my life is a passion-free zone. In fact there has even been talk with my therapist lately that my life could use a cat – which as you probably know is an animal with an innate fear of passion or any other overwhelming emotion for that matter.'

'SEE! This is what I'm talking about here,' she squealed excitedly. 'It's your wacky playfulness that I love. You've got a total OFF THE WALL quality. You are so completely 'NOT' how legal women are viewed. You have feature film potential – not that film is really my line but I could recommend people if you're interested. Can't you imagine it Rory, can't you just see Julia Roberts or Meg Ryan or even Michelle Pfeiffer playing Evie? This girl-power thing could be really BIG.' She paused then and called for the bill.

I tried to rotate my head on its axis the way my osteopath does to relieve trapped nerves in my neck. Rory poked me under the table and mouthed the words, 'Behave yourself!'

'Well you see where I'm at Evie, don't you?' Alexia continued, using her finger to parenthesise words. Her nails were blood red and I felt like she'd been poking around in my stomach with them. 'I'm talking YOUR LIFE as star vehicle. This could be SERIOUS. Seriously. I mean what I say.'

OK, so here we were in harmony. Serious is what I do best. I mean, so when has my life not been serious? When have I not walked into Maddy's office and said, 'This is serious now, Mads,' and then gone on to sketch her a scenario serious enough for the big man Freud himself to want to check out.

I explained all this to Alexia and waited while she finished laughing.

'I'm SERIOUS too,' I told her. 'Let me assure you,

my life is no laughing matter. I even need professional guidance on how to live it.'

'Isn't she GREAT, Rory?'

Rory pretended to have fallen asleep. This was incredible – the woman wasn't just after my man, now she was after my life as well. It may not be the life of my dreams, I admit at times I would have sold it for a Mars bar. But it was the only life I had and there was no way I was going to let this blonde bitch with the silicone breasts get her talons into it.

'You need to be GREAT to handle a life like mine,' I told her plainly. 'My life makes *GI Jane* look like a Girl Guides' picnic. I doubt that a Hollywood star would be equipped for an hour down the cells of the Bailey with Keith of Shepherds Bush and his buddies.'

Rory started to squirm in his chair.

'Hey, think about it before you say no, Evv. A lot of girls would jump at the chance,' he advised.

I looked at him like he'd just pissed on my foot.

'You said it, Rory,' Alexia agreed. 'I was just thinking how great Liz Hurley would be in her life. Liz Hurley practically is her!'

I balked for a moment at the veiled implication that Liz Hurley might do a better job at being me than I had. 'I'm not an egotist or anything but give me some credit. I've been playing me for years. All my life basically, and while it hasn't been to any great critical acclaim, there has been the odd favourable review. Why, only last week my clerk Lee told me

I was brilliant! "Well done Evv, you're a star," he applauded after I'd just won a rather contentious appeal.'

I tried to get this idea across to Alexia without showing how furious I was. 'You've paid me a compliment Alexia but I really think you want to consider the health and safety of Liz *et al* before you start chucking my life at them. Check out their insurance for a start. I mean, my life is a dangerous one-woman disaster area.

'I've seen *90210* and *Melrose Place* and it seems to me that you LA babes have low thresholds for the kind of aggravation that I have to deal with on a daily basis back in London. Liz might not thank you for sticking her in a courtroom where Judge Morse is sitting. I mean, the man has serious gout problems and has to be handled with care and a great deal of port. It's not a lifestyle for an amateur.'

'Calm down Evelyn,' Rory whispered as my voice grew louder. 'You're sounding hysterical.'

'Bugger calm. My life is as far from calm as you can get. Even the shower pressure in London would drive you LA girls into six months in a Palm Springs spa. Have you ever had an English shower, Alexia? It's so masochistic it's positively kinky! You've got to be genetically bred for the British shower nozzle or they can destroy your self-image and make you completely ineffectual. Where do you think the grunge look came from? Huh? Straight from an English shower attachment, that's where!'

Alexia and Rory both had a supposedly calming grip on my arms now and were looking at me like I might have to be shoved under the table any minute. 'Don't worry about the details Evv, we'll get a good writer onto your life. It doesn't have to be set in London, what about San Francisco?' Alexia asked sweetly.

'Oh right, of course why didn't I think of that? I should have got a good writer onto my life and moved to San Francisco years ago. How stupid of me.'

Rory chucked me under the chin. 'Come on doll, don't lose your sense of humour.'

I know that what happened next was a big mistake 'HUGE!' as Julia would have put it but give me a break here, I was undergoing a rigorous and straining mix of emotions, many of them violent. The combination of getting writers onto my life, chin chucking and the reference to my lack of humour just made me snap.

'Rory, you are so right,' I agreed, smiling warmly as I rose from the table. 'A sense of humour is exactly what is needed here and rest assured, mine's just about to get into gear. In fact, here it comes now,' I told him, tossing his beer into his lap.

Needless to say my orgasm didn't get that test drive that night either. When Rory finally came to bed he told me off for giving Alexia a hard time. I turned on my side and played at being passive aggressive.

He was asleep before I was.

CHAPTER 6

'There's no sincerity like a woman telling a lie.'

Indiscreet, 1958, colour, Cary Grant and
Ingrid Bergman

I woke up the next morning in a Joan Crawford kind of mood. My frame of mind was off-centre, like a vertical hold crying out for someone to come and adjust it.

I started to think how it's often been said that it is not easy being a post-structural feminist gal at the *fin de millennium*.

But never by me.

I'm mostly pretty keen on the age we live in actually. More than happy to reap the rewards of the battles earlier feminists spent most of this century fighting for me. But now things are definitely on the up. Look at the evidence:

Girls are doing better at school than boys.

Female unemployment is dropping.

Girl bands are skyrocketing to the top of the charts.

Girls can even get overdrafts to buy their own tiaras.

Twenty-five per cent of my generation will remain childless by choice.

We have finally won the right to say no – to men, to sex, to housewifery, to throwing ourselves on funeral pyres, to circumcision, to cellulite and a whole host of other stuff our sex has been enslaved by for centuries.

More girls are breaking through the glass ceiling of upper management – slightly scratched and cut admittedly, but breaking through nonetheless.

Take my own profession even, once a great bastion of poo-bahs and satraps; changes are afoot. Positive discrimination has brought about a mass Silking of women barristers – and not before time. Any fool could see that garters, wigs and silk look so much nicer on girls. Sorry boys, lucked out again.

All things considered, even the most politically strident of my gender must agree that we live in an age of 'Way To Go, Girls!'

Apart from the great career strides, girls get all this fab physical stuff like multiple orgasms and G-spots and babies even – if the idea grabs you. Or not, if it doesn't – thanks to sponges, condoms and diaphragms.

And then there are the shoes, the make-up and the clothes. Think about it, while we've been discovering

Lycra and latex and spangles, blokes have to make do with cotton mix, micro-fibre and nylon baseball caps worn at a rakish angle to disguise baldness.

The really big prize though is female friendship, compared with the sad pseudo-friendships that men have – talking about ball teams and car parts. Or boys, asses and muscles if they're fortunate enough to be gay.

I'm sorry, post-structural feminists, but I just can't help feeling that girls have got the gold cup of gender comfort in the late twentieth century.

At least, that was what I had always thought up until this morning. As soon as I woke up and felt my head, the backlash began.

As I groaned awake, I wasn't focusing on any of the aforementioned privileges of my gender, see. In fact quite the opposite. Actually what I said (after putting on my Gucci sunglasses and checking last night's make-up in my compact mirror) as I turned to face Rory, still dribbling lackadaisically into his pillow beside me, was, 'God it's hard being a post-structural feminist in the *fin de millennium*.'

'What?' he inquired, without sounding very interested.

'I need sex,' I told him bluntly, in a coarse attempt to jump-start his interest in the conversation.

It worked. He opened one eye.

'I can't believe you talked about me to that, that, that' (I spluttered) 'surgically enhanced woman. I thought private eyes were meant to be, well, more or less private basically. And what about all that guff she talked – and the guff you nodded to? What happened to loyalty huh? What gives you the right etc.'

'You want a coffee, right?' he mumbled, closing his eye again. 'Is that what all this is about? You want me to order coffee?'

Then before I could start to rant again he smiled and pursed his lips so that I could kiss them, which I did. He really was extremely lovely.

'Oh what is the point?' I declared after a brief snog, agreeing that actually coffee was all I was ever after. Was all any girl was after actually and then I lay back sarcastically in my feather pillows until room service arrived on one of those lovely trolleys, pouring forth delicious aromas.

Rory was looking like a sex god by the time it arrived. His hair was slicked back, his six-pack of stomach muscles was making tantalising appearances through his robe and he flirted outrageously with the waiter as he poured the first cups of coffee.

I noticed a large parchment envelope on the trolley and when the waiter pointed this out and was about to hand it over, Rory snatched it up and created a diversion by offering the waiter a bread roll as he stuck it in his pocket. Sometimes I think he needs a few tips on being furtive, but this time I held my tongue.

Gazing upon the table layered in starched white fabric and the shiny silver pots with their precious cargo of caffeine and those baskets of delicious *brioches* my hard post-structuralist heart began to melt.

'What was the letter?' I asked in a more kittenish voice when I'd finished my first fortifying cup of coffee. I'd noticed him sneaking a look at it in the other room when he thought I wasn't looking. Whatever he'd read hadn't made him pleased it seemed. The corners of his mouth drooped so low I was worried he'd need surgery.

'Bad news?' I asked sweetly as he sat down beside me.

'Huh?'

'The letter? The one you just nipped into the other room to read.'

'Oh, nothing. Just a receipt.'

'Is there a problem with money? I mean, I know all this is your treat but I could have Lee send me some money out if there's a problem. I don't want you feeling that you have to pay for everything just because you've dragged me out here or anything.'

'Give it a rest doll. Nothing's wrong, it was just last night's receipt from dinner. I was just making sure it didn't go to the cleaners. Tax deduction, you know the thing.'

'Not well enough, actually,' I informed him.

He kissed me on my neck and I purred. I knew better than to probe. That was his job, not mine, and anyway my kittenish mood was getting the better of me. I moaned with pleasure as his kisses continued further down my body.

Maybe this luxury suite business wasn't too bad, I conceded as I snuggled into him – my Joan Crawford mood well and truly lifted. I was feeling all sensuous and blonde. Practically Carole Lombard-ish actually.

Perhaps I wouldn't just stop at going blonde, maybe I should go all the way I pondered. Peroxide my pubic hair even! I wondered if salons in Beverly Hills offered a pubic peroxide service and if they did, how much it cost and who administered the treatment. I mean, I wouldn't want to entrust Stefan with such a delicate task.

I asked Rory what he'd make of blonde pubic hair and he disappeared under the sheet to show me, while I snuggled into the pillows and purred.

Thinking that we were about to engage in a little light orgasmic sex, I was pretty shocked therefore when Rory came up for air and announced that he needed to rush out on business. After a perfunctory neck nuzzle, he left me sitting in the bed in my Marmont-issue robe, my libido on ten, surrounded by a pile of used napkins, *brioche* crumbs, empty butter wrappers and coffee stains, feeling well and truly orgasmically deprived. Bloody hell.

As the door slammed, I felt the walls of our enormous suite shrink. Luxury or not I was not cut out for hotel life. Besides, this was now day three in LA and still no sign of my paramour's once voracious sexual performance. How long does it take to get a shag in this town? I started to wonder and briefly toyed with the idea of ringing reception to find out.

This was the sort of hotel that would probably take that sort of enquiry seriously. They probably have some sort of historical reference library, a filing cabinet brimming with helpful information about their guests' behaviour. 'Well mam, notice here that Grace Kelly was here for well over a week before she got a shag. On the other hand, it says here that Gable was shagging before he even got out of the elevator. It was the first hotel elevator in LA too mam, says here . . .'

Daniel had said that if you're going to get into trouble, do it at the Marmont. I suppose it depends on what you define as trouble. At this point my troubles revolved around an inadequate supply of sex, and it's hard to make a scandal out of that. Maybe this was what happened to Hugh Grant?

Maybe he'd simply got tired of luxury suites, dinners at the Marmont with his agent and having his ears nuzzled by Liz. Maybe Hugh had said, 'Damn it, I'm going to get shagged tonight if it's the last thing I do.'

Maybe I too would end up with a hooker on Sunset?

Maybe my parents would wake up to morning papers emblazoned with headlines proclaiming my wrongdoings with street walkers: *London Legal Highflyer Falls With A Thud In LA Gutter*.

There would be a mugshot of me in runny mascara

and reading further down the page my poor shamed parents would discover that the rent boy in question had made ten times what I earn in a year as a barrister, selling the story of my indiscretion to *Hardcopy*. Rory would refuse to comment but concede (as Liz did), that 'marriage was the last thing on his mind'.

'She was very polite,' the male hooker would admit in an exclusive interview. 'We were listening to "Lonely Days and Lonely Nights" on the radio when the police discovered us. I didn't recognise her at first although I knew she must be someone important because she had a chauffeur and was wearing a Château Marmont bathrobe with a *brioche* in the top pocket. She said that I was the best thing to ever happen to her.'

Face it. I was joining the ranks of the great unshagged. And it wasn't as if celibacy was even hip now – god, how early nineties in fact. This was terrible, not only was I going to be desperate for sex but I was going to be unfashionably desperate for sex. It was probably going to be years before celibacy came back in. Decades even. My finger flirted with the phone pad. I was thinking that maybe it was time to call Mads for advice. Yeah right, I could see her on the other end of the phone, flicking through backcopies of *Psychology Today* for answers.

'Why can't you feel whole without sex Evelyn?' she'd ask, her features sharp with earnest interest.

Better still, maybe I should call Daniel's analyst. Maybe she could sell me one of those personalised self-affirmation mantra thingies? Maybe I was just lacking the right word or a simple numerological equation.

Normally Rory couldn't keep his hands off me. Before we had come to this town, I was fighting off his groping octopus arms with every weapon at my disposal. This celibacy binge was beginning to erode my self-esteem, which was only ever just a thin veneer anyway and not the solid sterling stuff of which Rory and his gender are possessed.

Like most women with a menstrual cycle, my self-esteem comes off with a bit of washing-up liquid and a J-cloth.

In an effort to restore my joy in life, I had just climbed into the powerful pleasure realm of the full-force shower when the phone rang. A predicament that normally causes some degree of consternation but in a luxury suite, all one has to do is reach out and a phone line is there for the grabbing.

'Yes?' I said, trying to sound like a busy woman with a full diary of important meetings and fab social events to attend.

'I have Alexia Dean on the line. Will you take the call?' a saccharine voice purred.

I thought about saying no, I really did, but given that she was my only rival in LA I graciously agreed to the transfer. I regretted my impulsiveness almost immediately.

Alexia was as bubbly and forthright as the night before. 'By the way,' she confided, 'I thought it was just GREAT the way you tossed his beer into his lap. It's something I've wanted to do for years.'

Years? She'd known Rory for years? This was not good and I implied as much by the way I replied.

'Well surely Rory's mentioned that he and I go back a long way?' she breezed. 'Anyway after you left, I told him he deserved a good soaking.'

Funny that, because I had turned to take a last look back, after the beer-tossing drama, and Alexia was on bended knee, crossly mopping up Rory's lap with her napkin. Not looking like she thought it was a bit 'GREAT'.

I reminded her of this but she just laughed. Not a full-bellied laugh, like a woman with a normal cellulite problem would laugh. No. More of a simpery tinkle, like those little bells they used to torture us with in exams. 'Time's up' bells.

She asked if LA was to my satisfaction. I told her that like Mick Jagger, satisfaction and I had conflicting schedules these days. 'I haven't had a window of opportunity for satisfaction for weeks really,' I explained.

Once again Alexia sent one of her tinkly little 'time's-up' bell laughs running up my spine. 'I was wondering if you were free for lunch?' she asked.

Which put me in the pathetic position of having to confess that my lunchtime programme was nowhere near as full as it might have been.

So like the two best friends that we weren't, we

agreed to meet at Four Seasons and hung up. I had no sooner set to, getting the conditioner into my hair, than the phone rang again.

This time it was Charles calling from London. Charles is my best friend in the world. We go way back and then some. In fact it was due to me that Charles and her lesbian lover, Sam, were able to have a baby – but that's another story altogether.

Suffice to say that Charles is the sort of friend who not only lends me her best red leather mini, but also takes emotionally draining calls in the middle of the night and always assures me that I behaved impeccably when we both know that my battle for impeccable had been badly and embarrassingly lost at a cocktail party the night before.

The best thing of all about Charles though is her refusal to utter that skin-crawling, hideous phrase, 'I told you so'. Even though she'd been at one with the multitude of men and women of my London acquaintance who had warned me that I was making a big mistake, committing myself emotionally to a man who called me doll and made a living spying on people's philanderous spouses, she was above saying 'I told you so'.

My analyst Maddy and my clerk Lee and almost everyone else I knew wouldn't have been able to resist a triumphant declaration of their farsighted wisdom. Not for a minute. Charles might think 'it' but she was far too well-bred to say 'it'. She was a Roedean girl through and through.

Feeling safe from condemnation therefore, I breathlessly outlined the entire misery of my predicament. Still under the shower, I told her about the narky 'girls who have trapped a man wanting the window seat' remark.

I told her about the 'I drive therefore I am' fracas at the Hertz desk.

I told her about the abandoned first day affront.

The bare-rump slapping antics.

The dinner with Alexia and subsequent beer in the lap lark.

I even revealed the distinct lack of reliably honest orgasms I'd had in LA so far. Total tally to date: none. And then, just to cap it all off, I admitted that, pathetic as it was, I was still in love with the man who had perpetrated all of the above. A man no post-structural feminist should go near without a hard hat and a castration tool. A man who called me doll.

I was a fool. A business class sadd-o. A brunette trapped in a blonde's role. My love was as doomed as nuclear power and I knew it as well as any ninety quid an hour analyst.

'Well, that's all well and good,' she said. 'But you've got to come back right now. I mean this is serious. Your problems are about to multiply and I am not talking orgasmically, Evv!'

She then went on to outline the disasters unfolding back in London.

Apparently, all hell had broken loose with my

analyst Maddy. Not as you might think because she had lost my patronage and was bereft with grief, but because Giles the super-bastard had left her – following an alarming confession that he was still in love with me!

ME?

Now for those of you who haven't followed my life from start to finish, Giles was not only my biggest mistake in attempted Coupledom but he was also a guy I hadn't passed the time of day with for the best part of a year.

The last two times I had seen him in fact, I had hit him. Once accidentally because I thought he was an intruder and once just because he was Giles – a man who voluntarily wears insteps for foot comfort.

Call me a pedi-culture snob, but a man in foamy rubber insoles has got to be the most unholy turn-off around – not counting toupée wearers, or worse, short bald men who drive convertibles in the hope that they will be mistaken for tall men, free of follicular challenges.

'He's on his way over,' Charles shrieked down the phone line. 'I mean it,' she insisted. 'Stick on your flat shoes and run. Back here, to the safety of London, your friends and your career. We'll hide you on the underground in one of those disused lavatories in Shepherds Bush where intravenous drug-users used to congregate.' Charles has always been one for ingenious ideas, that's why she's a divorce lawyer.

'I can't,' I told her. 'I've got to see this love thing through to its final conclusion.'

'You make it sound like a wisdom tooth that needs extraction,' she said.

'Well, it is more or less. I've just got to make sure, once and for all, that I am not made for Coupledom.'

'Not in Hollywood though, Evv,' she pleaded. 'It's not safe. I've been reading about El Niño and the earthquake probability and that's just the start of it. Hollywood will change you Evv,' she warned and then in typical legal fashion, went on to back up her case with irrelevant statistics, citing a million instances of how Tinsel Town had ruined lives. Sometimes even ended lives – one in this very hotel actually, where John Belushi died after injecting a heroin/cocaine speedball.

There was Natalie Wood (another Marmont guest) whose young life ended when she fell off a yacht.

Mama Cass (one-time Marmont guest) and her untimely end, courtesy of a ham sandwich.

Fassbinder and drugs. Or was it the four packets of fags he smoked a day? Charles wasn't sure.

River Phoenix – drugs or was it his name? Again, Charles wasn't sure.

And then of course there was the Scientology and the fringed jacket and cowboy boots issue, all equally dangerous in Charles' view.

The list just went on and on and on.

I put down the phone while she continued to

make her submissions and set to rinsing my hair. I know from my own jurisprudence experience that putting a solid case together can take time. Even on a long-distance phone line with the shower running and hair thick with set conditioner, I was moved by the powerful delivery of her case.

I had to give it to her, Charles had done her research well and she had a heartfelt presentation that would break the most hardened jury. Never a girl to trust something as unreliable as a gut instinct, Charles is a barrister through and through and knows the importance of research, detail and sheer drama.

'It's a fact, Evv, if the drugs and the Scientologists don't get you, *Hardcopy*'s always there to snap you when you're down. And whatever you do, don't get mixed up with underage boys. They stick you in prison over there for that.'

I promised her faithfully that I would steer clear of ham sandwiches, drugs, yachts, Scientologists and underage boys, and told her not to worry about my thighs because they were probably going to explode anyway.

Nonetheless she was adamant that it was time to abandon my heels and make a dash for safety.

'You don't seem to understand how serious this is Evv. Giles took a flight to LA last night, so he'll be there any minute. You've got to get out of there,' Charles' girlfriend Sam squealed, having snatched the phone.

'Sure Sam, what's Giles going to do to me? Flog me to death with a foam inner-sole?'

Charles' lover has never been a girl to steer clear of 'I told you sos', or to steer clear of very much at all actually. Sam is more a 'throw everything you've got at everything' sort of girl. A bit like those Spanish bulls that keep on jabbing at the matador even when they are speared to within an inch of their life. When any sane bull would be hot-footing it out of the ring, throwing in the glory of the fight as a bad lark and getting on the first boat to India or some other country where bulls get a bit of respect. Or is that cows? Whatever.

Love her as I do, now was not the time for raging bulls. I told her to put me back on to Charles who finally admitted that while she thought I should return, she had taken the precaution of deceiving the enemy.

She'd told Giles I was staying at the Clarion Hollywood Roosevelt Hotel, the best hotel in the world in which to go ghost-spotting. A lot of stars have passed through its grand lobby, from Montgomery Clift to Marilyn Monroe – and some haven't bothered to leave the place *post mortem*. Marilyn lived there for eight years and her room is still as she left it, which sounds a bit sick really. I dread to imagine what this room would've looked like in forty years' time without a maid service – and I'd only been there a few days.

Giles is a huge fan of the ultimate blonde babe

and I assured Charles that he would be too busy with Marilyn to get round to discovering my true whereabouts. And even if he did manage to unearth me, I would soon diminish his love for me with a few well chosen blows to the groin and send him back safely to Maddy.

Charles wished me luck.

My body was prune like by the time I got off the phone and set about the rigorous art of dressing to impress in Hollywood. Erring on the side of caution, I followed my standard four-point plan.

One: Aim to seduce.

Two: Aim to wear something that disguises the size of your thighs and emphasises the thinness of your waspish waist. Twenty-six inches on a good day in the menstrual cycle.

Three: Aim to try on every item you possess before eventually deciding on the first outfit you tried.

Four: Once you get into said outfit, realise it is badly in need of a dry clean and go back to point one.

After much hair-tweaking and make-up applying, I opted for the red leather mini I'd nicked from Charles before I left. Even with my insecurities about my body, I had to admit it didn't look bad. I stuck on my sunglasses and struck a few vamp poses for the Marlboro Man outside my window. He didn't look that impressed.

I started to have doubts. Maybe I was on an upstage of my cycle when I could kid myself that anything looked good, I told my ego. On the other hand, when nature saw fit to give me legs that go on for ever, it would seem churlish not to use them to torture the opposite sex, my ego argued back.

'Your legs are your best asset, girls' – my personal defence instructor had told us. She would always insist that a girl's legs were the most powerful part of her body and as such should be used against men at every opportunity, or as she put it: 'Use them to bring down the enemy.'

Kicking and kneeing came highly recommended but today I was going for straight exposure. Lethal in its own way.

I matched the skirt with a strip of Chanel *les rouges* across the lips and similar on the nails.

'The Tart is Back' the magazines were promising this year.

PS. So when was she ever out? I matched my tart-is-back look with lashings of Calvin Klein perfume, fishnet stockings, a plunging neckline and my new Patrick Cox satins.

Basically, it was an outfit I would live to regret.

CHAPTER 7

'She's a phoney all right, but a real phoney.'

Breakfast At Tiffany's, 1961, colour, Audrey
Hepburn and George Peppard

Why did the Japanese Kamikaze pilots wear helmets? Think about that for a minute. It is a question that has bothered me all my life. I mean, surely they knew that flying planes packed with explosives into American warships was going to end in tears? Yet on every mission those brave lads fastened on their safety helmets and hoped for the best.

Pretty much as I did on my suicidal mission to lunch at the Four Seasons that day. Knowing I was about to be driven to my death, I still fastened my seat-belt and hoped for the best.

I realised that it was the vain action of a fool who deserves to die as soon as we pulled out onto Sunset but nonetheless I clung to my safety belt and prayed.

My driver was no chicken shit though. I can state

this with some authority because I heard him yelling it out to fellow drivers every time we mounted the pavement or cut through several lanes of fast-moving traffic.

'What do you think I am, chicken shit?' he would bellow, shaking his fist out the window.

This was also the point at which I realised that I wasn't dressed for adventure. With every bump and swerve my breasts practically flew out of my bra and my skirt crept ever higher up my behind. This was an outfit designed for vamping the night away – not death.

My discomfiture was not aided by the fetid atmosphere within the cab itself in which there was a vague smell of a nuclear-based cleaning fluid having been brought in to clean up something of a nasty bacterial nature. Only it hadn't quite worked.

I informed my driver of my sensitive stomach and implored him to stop trying to impress me with his road rage skills. I warned him that I suffered from travel sickness and, *ipso facto*, required a steadyish ride. And when that didn't work I alluded to a propensity for projectile vomiting.

He laughed. He told me that I was talking non-sense and boasted that he could tell I was a woman who liked the wilder side of life and that what's more he was just the guy to give it to me. For one paranoid instant, I panicked that Maddy had been blabbing about me again.

My driver's name was Deano. I decided it was best

to get his personal details *before* the court case. Deano told me that he was normally a lover of blondes. His wife was blonde. I was letting out a sigh of relief when he told me that he was prepared to make an exception for me. Gee, thanks.

He promised me that keeping his eyes glued on my breasts rather than the road did not impede his navigatory ability in the slightest. Looking in his rear view mirror, I observed beads of perspiration gathering on his brow as he murmured Italian mantras of devotion to my body and soul.

By the time we were pulling up outside the Four Seasons in Beverly Hills, I was unfashionably late and in a state of acute disarray. My skirt was lassooing my midriff and my legs were all akimbo.

My next indignity came when my door was opened by a hotel issue Aryan, exposing my tart-is-back look in full fleshy glory. It was a style explored by *Vogue* only last season when Junkie Chic was declared the IT look. But I don't think my Aryan-issue bellboys saw it in that light.

I just wanted to chuck some cash at Deano and leg it to the safety of the women's loo but my *horror*scope had other plans for me that day. After I had torn my fishnet stockings trying to escape from my safety harness, my driver started to complain about his tip. This was a fresh concept for me.

In London, cabbies are just relieved if you don't sick on the seat or run off into the night streets without paying, bellowing a football chant as you flee. Rounding the fare off to the nearest pound is generally considered the done thing but I could tell by the way my driver reacted when I rounded off thirty-three dollars to thirty-five, that my British largesse wasn't going to cut the grass here.

It was all so hellishly stress-making that I broke a nail in the scuffle to hand over the acceptable toll and realised only then that I hadn't hitched my skirt down. In the end Deano drove off with fifty bucks – still looking none too happy, I might add. The battalion of valets and bellboys who had amassed to watch my baptism of humiliation, on the other hand, were delighted, although they had the good grace to disguise their sniggers behind obsequious grins.

'Head high, chest out (as a D-cup it wasn't a hard feat to master), straight back, walk tall,' my deportment teacher had coached us at the convent. 'Show the world the strength of your faith by the way you walk. Let the Holy Spirit put a spring in your step, girls.'

I followed Sister Conchilio's prescription to the letter, gripping my skirt around my buttocks like a condom but I doubt that I convinced anyone. Let's face it, I stuck out like a streetwalker in the sophisticated sea of beige, black and navy *en route* to the sumptuous marbledom of the ladies' rest-room.

I closed the door on my cubicle and, as I breathed in the intoxicating mix of Chanel No 5, Miss Dior and Versace, I moaned softly in relief. I love a good loo. For me the bathroom is the inner sanctum of a woman's world. The bog as they charmingly refer to it in England. Here at least I could feel safe from the derision of sophisticated LA.

I hid for a while in my cubicle and briefly contemplated slipping out the window and taking the nearest stolen vehicle back to my hotel room. But in all honesty, this wasn't the outfit to 'slip' anywhere without notice. The only place this outfit was slipping was off my body.

Pulling myself together as best I could, I strode out to the basins attempting to look like a grand, eccentric English rose. Tossing a five-dollar tip into the saucer of the Portuguese woman who passed me my towel, I pulled my cheeks into a haughty hollow.

She looked at my five dollars like it was a sachet of vaginal lubricant, not at all the sort of thing she was used to seeing in the intimate marble *sanctum sanctori* of the Four Seasons of Beverly Hills. Twenty pence usually satisfies them in London, and sometimes you even see the odd button left by some cheapskate duchess.

My confidence was still shrinking as I strode into the chi-chi ambience of the patio restaurant on the fourth floor, where I got the feeling that word was already out that I wasn't actually a madly wealthy and eccentric English rose at all. Simply mad.

My outfit, just the thing for the lunch venues and louche bars and clubs of London, clearly had no place in LA off Sunset Strip. 'Right, I will bloody well sue every British fashion magazine that promised me "the tart is back",' I muttered into my cleavage.

'Watch out, we've got a live one here,' I heard someone hiss into a Virgin Mary. It was almost embarrassing.

Alexia was already through her second spritzer by the time I arrived at the table. In a champagne-coloured two-piece, she was everything I was not. Physically bloody successful basically.

Cool and poised where I was perspiring and rattled. She had accessorised discreetly and taken care to apply her make-up in that painstakingly naturally gorgeous way that no Englishwoman I know has ever achieved or perhaps tried for. 'Not trying' is what the English like to think they do best.

Translate: making an effort = needy. If you are really cool in Britain you can't be bothered, or rather can't be shagged. Not being shagged basically sums up the British class system. Being naturally beautiful, intelligent, gifted, born rich and successful is no crime but looking as if you *tried* is a cardinal sin. Too uncool for words.

I know that Americans have a problem with the class thing but basically it is best defined as your level of determination *not* to bother. It is a person's absolute lack of aspiration that makes him or her cool.

Where Americans applaud a man or woman who busted a gut to achieve, the British see making an effort as somewhat gauche and needy. Somewhat middle-class, which is of course what the British are really best at – *petit bourgeois*.

It is written in stone in the Tower of London somewhere that the more you don't bother, the more kudos you have. The upper classes are defined by their ability *not* to care, and most importantly not to *show* they care even if they do care very deeply. Unless it is for a black Labrador or a horse, natch.

The employee who blows his or her pay cheque in an effort to look smart or who does overtime in order to get a promotion or who takes an evening job to pay for their kid's education is the real failure in Britain. The try-hard. It's this 'not caring', this 'not giving a toss', that constitutes the heart and soul of the stiff upper lip and *ipso facto* the British shabby appearance.

Since my short time in the States I had learnt to pick out the ex-pat Brits by their ability to impersonate tea-bags on their second time round the pot. It was the crushed suit and bad teeth kind of look.

That's why when British *do* bother, they do so with an eccentric flourish just so they are perceived as not giving a toss about convention. Better to shock than to be seen to care. Americans are coming from the opposite angle – 'reward for effort'. The kid from Queens who makes it as a movie mogul, gets res, bro.

In a nutshell the term 'class' refers to the subject in question's ability to look as though they have just rolled out of bed.

Alexia did not look as if she had rolled out of anything. Ever.

Alexia was a prime example of striving to succeed and proud of it. She was a woman who, not fancying her nose, went straight out to her plastic surgeon and demanded a new one. This was not a woman to let the grass grow while she haw-hawed at the Groucho or the Cobden Club. Not a bit. Alexia was a woman with people to see, things to do. In short, a woman with a schedule.

It wasn't until I had collapsed in a chair that I noticed that Alexia's schedule that lunchtime included another guest besides *moi*. A petite, rather gorgeous guest with the same blonde babeness and sharp eyes as Alexia herself.

'This is Katy,' Alexia said, air-kissing me to within an inch of my life. 'She couldn't WAIT to meet you either. She's been SO excited all morning. Haven't you darling? Why, you must have tried on your ENTIRE wardrobe, mustn't you Katy?' she gushed, patting Katy's rosy, fresh-faced cheek.

I gripped my skirt around my thighs even tighter and smiled my sweetest, warmest smile at Katy. I was in a bonding mood, reasonably presuming that *hauteur* wouldn't be taken seriously in this get up. 'I sympathise,' I told her. 'I tried on absolutely everything before choosing this skirt. Only I was feeling slightly more optimistic about the length of my legs then,' I confided.

Katy laughed. 'My daddy says you've got legs up

to your armpits but I think that would look funny.'
She crinkled up her nose and grinned.

'Your daddy?' My brain was still deconstructing
this sentence when Alexia put her hand on my arm,
the way nurses do after I've given blood. Right
before they ask, 'Are you going to be all right dear?'
After which I usually say, 'Oh yes, just fine,' and
then faint.

But Alexia didn't ask me if I was going to be all
right. Alexia was many things but she was neither
nurse nor fool. She held my wrist firmly, clearly
aware that the fainting thing was imminent. 'I didn't
want to tell you on the phone in case you got scared,'
she said kindly. 'I sort of assumed last night that Rory
hasn't told you about me, let alone about Katy. And I
sort of thought someone should.'

'And you thought that someone was you?' I said
bitchily, knowing it came out sounding like a bit of
bad dialogue from a day-time soap but not caring.

'It's all right,' she assured me, 'We've been divorced for a year now and I can assure you that there is
next to no chance of a reconciliation. It's really not
a problem, you see.'

'Well, it might be a problem for me actually,' I
said, trying to take in what she was saying, trying
not to burst into tears and trying to keep my skirt
from slipping up and revealing my panties.

'I know it's hard to take in, but it's better you know
where you stand. Our relationship shouldn't cause a
problem for you. Although I have to tell you that I

still love him and probably always will. Rory was never very good at monogamy you see. There were always *other* women. That was always the problem. Rory and his need for other women.'

She put so much force on the word 'other' I thought it was going to take on a physical form of its own and punch me in the face. She made Other Women sound like an illicit drug or a disease that Rory was powerless to control. There was a heat within my face, a sort of pumping hot rush banking up behind my eyes. I looked at Katy. She grinned at me.

'In a way we've been much closer since the divorce,' Alexia sighed, rearranging the ice in her drink with the straw. 'Rory's a great father and he stays with us as much as he can. When he's not involved with someone. He's absolutely devoted to Katy. She means more to us than any of our *affairs*. You're the first significant other he's ever wanted to bring here actually.'

Who am I kidding? This *was* a bad soap opera and Rory was the bastard director who had cast me in this shitty role. Bastard. 'I see,' I said, not seeing or feeling very much at all. I certainly didn't feel very significant. Far more 'otherish' actually. I couldn't stop staring at Katy. She was loudly sucking the last bit of her smoothy up through the straw and I wished more than anything that I could become part of that smoothy and disappear from this scene forever.

I was trying to imagine what Jean Harlow or

Carole Lombard or almost anyone clever and witty and wise would do if placed in my situation but I think the script was too lousy for even them to help.

'Don't do that pumpkin. You know it sets Mommy's teeth on edge.'

'On edge?' I muttered. 'On edge?' *I* was on bloody edge. I'd just travelled across the world to be with the man I love. I'd left friends and career and the London underground to be with the man I loved and wanted to make love to on a regular basis. I certainly didn't come here to end up playing the 'other woman' in a C-grade American day-time soap whose only audience was a three-year-old kid. I'd be better off locked up in a disused lavatory in Shepherds Bush.

Katy stopped sucking up the dregs of her smoothy and looked around the restaurant for inspiration. 'Can we order now Mommy? I'm hungry.'

And then it struck me with force that this little girl, this blonde angel was Rory's daughter. 'Let me get this clear. Katy is . . . ? Katy is . . . ? Rory is . . . ?' I stuttered, longing for someone to fill in the blanks. What was going on? I looked around – maybe I was at the wrong table, in the wrong scene? Where was the scriptwriter?

'My daddy thinks you're funny.'

'Your daddy,' I repeated. The word 'daddy' when applied to my man with a six-pack stomach didn't fit, a bit like my skirt in this restaurant, and yet I knew it was true.

'My daddy says you've got a terrible temper,' Katy giggled. She had a beautiful laugh, not a bit like Alexia's. It sort of tumbled out of her like breakfast cereal into a bowl and it was just too cute to be true the way she put her little chubby hands to her mouth as if to stop it. She was nothing if not adorable.

'Daddy doesn't know the half of it,' I assured her while trying to smile, only my face was numb and it came off more as a mean smirk. Katy hid under the table.

Great, so now I was terrifying her. All part and parcel of being the significant Other Woman. The bitch who steals fathers, and scares small children with tumbling laughter.

I've been in a relationship in which there was an 'Other' Woman and believe me, I know the depth of their evil. There is nothing these Other Woman will stop at. It wasn't a role I had even pencilled into my schedule. I am always the *only* woman. A one-true-love sort of girl. A believer in sisterhood and monogamy. I wanted the whole fairytale, not this post-modern-new-age-fancy-pants so called civilised relationship.

What was civilised about second best? I wasn't equipped to play the other woman. Give me a break! I hadn't even had time to learn my lines for the role of the one-and-only love of Rory's life yet.

'I knew he hadn't told you,' Alexia said crossly as if she was talking about a stained shirt collar. 'I told him he should tell you before you came out here.

He is terrible like that, isn't he? Even when we were married, he usually neglected to tell the Other Woman.'

'Terrible,' I repeated numbly.

'She's got a terrible temper,' Katy said, pointing at me. 'And legs up to her armpits.'

I wanted to cry but my vital functions had seized. Besides, I had to think of the children now. The child rather. Rory's child. I couldn't just start blubbering all over the restaurant. I mean, apart from not wearing waterproof mascara (a bugger to remove), I had to think of Katy. And besides, my script didn't call for vulnerability.

The Other Woman must be a hard and brittle monster, a dangerous threat to the morals of all decent women. A chain-smoker. I would have to take up smoking now. I couldn't possibly be a homewrecker and not smoke! And nails, the Other Woman sports long red nails, expensive perfume, saucy underwear and a sneer. I ticked these accessories off in my mind. So there were plusses, but not many. Judging from all the movies I'd watched as a kid, playing the Other Woman was a pretty nasty role to land.

The Other Woman turns devoted loving fathers into sex slaves.

The Other Woman makes other women cry.

'We discussed your relationship with Rory before we agreed to have you come out here to meet Katy,' Alexia said, summoning a waiter to our table.

'You discussed me?' Perhaps mine wasn't a speaking part after all, I thought hopefully. Perhaps if I stayed still enough and quiet enough someone with a clapperboard would walk up to the camera and say 'Cut! We've run over budget, this scene will have to go.' And my nightmare would be over.

'Oh obviously. We talked about you at length. For us it was a decision as to how much you should be allowed to *impact* on Katy.'

'Impact?' I asked. I was impacting here?

I scanned Katy for evidence of my impact. She was tipping out the few last drops of fluid from her smoothy glass onto the tablecloth. She didn't look like I'd impacted on her, well there was no obvious bruising at least. Which meant she must have sustained internal injuries. The sort of injuries that would eventually result in an expensive court case when she grew up and decided to sue me for gross nastiness or something.

God this was awful.

She pulled a face at me with her tongue protruding through a hole in her hands.

I remained monosyllabic after that, trying to limit my impact on Katy while Alexia rattled on candidly about her relationship with Rory and their projections for the future until it finally and inexorably dawned on me that this was not a practical joke thought up by the staff of Four Seasons to punish me for turning up in the guise of a street-walker.

Alexia really was Rory's ex-wife and Katy really

was their offspring. I really was the 'Other' Woman, the bit on the side – one of many by the sounds of it.

It was all true.

I had been shagging a *dad*.

CHAPTER 8

'Hollywood is a strange place when you're in trouble. Everyone's afraid it's contagious.'

Judy Garland (1922–69)

Mads is always telling me not to run from dilemma. In a perfect world she would have me running *at* it. No doubt without the aid of appropriate head protection.

When I ask who's going to pay for a new manicure once I've finished headbutting my million and one dilemmas, she falls back on her eternal argument that confrontation and volatility are the cornerstones of relationships.

I don't know where she gets this stuff but she's raking in the fast bucks with it. According to Maddy's theory, my happiness was right on course. I was feeling extremely volatile and confronted. Alexia on the other hand looked all serene and untroubled, more or less as Hitler did as he marched on Poland, I expect.

I managed to get a few leaves of something green down without betraying my humiliation and misery to my fellow diners. My pride may be as confident as a dish-cloth on a mop-up job at a homicide scene but it did the best it could in the circumstances.

I could feel my mouth moving to masticate and I probably made some semblance of conversation, but the reality was my brain was anaesthetised by an emotional cocktail of betrayal, anger and a *soupçon* of shame (one of my favourite mixers).

Being the Other Woman was a lot harder than I had hitherto imagined. Watching all those gorgeous Technicolor films as a moody adolescent with post-feminist aspirations, I'd always had this impression that playing the mistress was all about glossy lipstick and high heels – both of which I had in stacks.

Women such as Marla Trump, Yoko Ono and Soon Yi Previn seemed to make such light work of their Other Woman-ness that I was deceived into thinking I might slip into it with consummate ease.

These women had taken effortlessly to their role as usurper, even bringing a certain dignity to the part. Alas, like many women with busy careers and unrealistic romantic aspirations, I could never seem to find the time for dignity.

Throughout the lunch, I noticed that Alexia had a dependency problem with the word 'civilised'. She was a compulsive abuser of the term basically. As in – 'Rory and I believe in having a civilised post-marital relationship. We have tried to keep things civilised, for Katy's sake. Rory is very determined to keep things civilised.'

'Well drop my womb and scatter my eggs!' I exclaimed. 'Are we talking about the same Rory here?' I leaned forward intrigued. 'I mean, I have trouble getting him to be civilised with a sock. What's your secret?' I inquired confidentially.

She smiled in a saint-like manner and sighed. 'I suppose you don't have children so you can never really understand.'

'Try me.'

'Well, there is no great struggle of wills or anything. Rory and I have simply come to a civilised arrangement,' she explained enigmatically. 'If you can't behave in a civilised manner to the parent of your child, well, what's left?'

I know what Charles would have said, 'a bloody decent divorce settlement, that's what,' but I kept Charles' opinion to myself. Just the same, this civilised arrangement sounded a bit suspect from where I was sitting.

Civilised is a word I've never been big on but coming from Alexia's collagen-enhanced lips it sounded so hygienic it made me feel like a dirty no-good savage. I guess as a lawyer and a girl with a ruthless determination when it comes to sale-time, civilised is a word that I've never had a lot of call for.

As far as I could see, civilisation had led to a lot of ill-feeling in the last few hundred years. I mean the Industrial Revolution was meant to be a civilising breakthrough but it left us with a lot of ugly slag heaps. Anyway you deconstruct history, civilisation has been single-handedly responsible for the displacement of indigenous peoples.

Many a sin against humanity has been committed under the cloak of civilisation. On weighing up the pros and cons in fact, girls throughout history would have been better off without the yoke of civilisation. I worked this out as a teenager, basing my conclusion on my mother's list of 'uncivilised' behaviour which included:

Coming home late at night

Snogging Protestants

Overindulging in alcohol

Eating food in bed

Doing anything with too much gusto

Dancing and enjoying oneself in an unbridled fashion.

Basically anything worth doing came under the banner of uncivilised behaviour in my mother's book. Whatever, the image of entering into a civilised relationship with Rory and his ex appealed to me about as much as coming home early to do my accounts. Let's face it, love is uncivilised. Love is about doing all the things that heathens and teenagers have been warned about for millennia.

When it came down to it, maybe I would rather go for the role of the evil other woman than play second-hand rose in a *ménâge à trois* with Rory *en famille*.

'I should make it clear that my love for Rory is no longer sexual,' Alexia revealed as I carved up my artichoke-heart salad. Call me unreasonable, unrealistic and uncool but I didn't really want to discuss her sexuality with Katy there.

Besides, I don't really want my lovers to have sexual pasts which are immediately obvious, any more than I like the idea of 'staying friends' with an ex.

Bugger 'friends', I either want to fuck a man's brains out or blow them out. As Giles had learnt to his peril. Once I have entertained a man in my bed there is no turning back for me, no half-measures and certainly no option of a civilised relationship. There is nothing civilised about sex. The double-backed beast makes savages of us all.

No matter how hard Alexia wanted to sell the concept of Rory as father and ex-hubby it didn't wash. 'I'm a Generation X-er,' I told her. 'Not a free-love, beansprout, joys of futon extolling hippie. You've got more chance of getting me to wear a pair of Mexican slippers than of persuading me to move in with you and Rory.

'Get this down on tape, Alexia, you, me, Katy and Rory playing house is a non-starter,' I told her.

Katy seemed to concur with this theory, falling back again and again on her Daddy's claim that I had a terrible temper.

I pulled a face at her.

She fell about laughing. Basically Katy found

everything I said and did the height of hilarity. So who didn't? But I liked this kid. I really did.

When decency failed her, Alexia turned to insults, as in, 'if you really loved Rory you would love his past as well'. Something my analyst might have dreamed up on a bad day.

I responded with a look that I often use on judges who dare to question my wisdom. A look that either loses me the case or earns me a glass of claret and a pinched butt at the end of it. Needless to say Alexia didn't look like a big claret drinker.

She kept holding my wrist, no doubt trying to stop the blood supply. 'I know I was overwrought last night but I was terrified of meeting you,' she explained, with a pained expression on her face that my head clerk Warren gets when his haemorrhoids are playing up. 'This isn't easy for me,' she insisted. 'Rory has told me so much about you, he seems totally in love. I've never known him to be so into a person. It all just makes me feel uncomfortable.'

'Well that's something we've got in common,' I told her. I was so bloody uncomfortable with her still gripping my wrist, my hand was about to fall off.

'I actually meant what I said about using your life as the basis for a slapstick comedy though,' she told me later as she produced her platinum card.

'Thanks but no thanks,' I said firmly, slapping down my own less shiny gold American Express. 'If there is going to be any slapsticking going on where my life is concerned, I'll be the one holding the stick.'

'Promise me you'll think about it,' she persevered, taking hold of my wrist again. I looked at her manicured little hand like it was a shackle.

'I don't think we're close enough to exchange promises,' I told her grandly in my bitch-is-back voice. I was feeling very Joan Crawford-esque again, until I stood up and revealed my torn fishnets to the restaurant at large that is.

Alexia nodded sympathetically and looked away, like I'd just had a noisy public orgasm.

As we exchanged air kisses, I told Katy that we should empty a wardrobe together sometime and half meant it. Watched by the entire restaurant I made loud *mwa-mwa* sounds to my kisses to add to my ruse that I was an eccentric English heiress out for an afternoon on my trust fund.

I was contemplating suicide by chocolate as I climbed into my cab but opted instead for a debauched afternoon of shopping on Rodeo Drive where a sober little pant-suit by Donna Karan helped me find the will to carry on.

Let's face it, I needed a shot of consumerism that day like a judge needs his claret after a brisk day on the Bench. Rodeo Drive is just around the corner from the Four Seasons and mixes the very best of Hampstead in the summer with the best of Harvey Nichols when all the escalators are working.

Plus in Beverly Hills, all the staff are really desperate, being dependent on commission, so you don't have to put up with the 'shit on the sole of my shoe' attitude of the English shop assistant. They probably worked that much out from *Pretty Woman*.

I had my driver wait chauffeur-like while I traded in my tart-is-back look for a black crepe veneer of respectability. Candida, a QC back in Chambers, had been urging me to get such an outfit for years. Shopping always makes my heart swell with love for my fellow man so I bought my driver a perky little cap at Ralph Lauren but he refused to wear it, citing a Beverly Hills ordinance by-law or something.

Fortified by my DK purchase, I drifted on down to Philip Danes Cigar Lounge and reaffirmed my hip happeningness with a few cognacs (couldn't drink in front of Katy) and a hand-rolled stoogie.

I know it is a shocking revelation from a seriously vocal and on occasions violent anti-smoker like myself, but my historic distaste for smokers and their habit was never based so much on issues of health as style, cigarettes being the instant coffee of the nicotine world.

Plus it's an ancestral hatred. In her heyday, my gran used to deliver desperately mad philippics in the Hall of Lincoln's Inn on the slow-witted characteristics of the cigarette smoker. Her arguments were very profound and oft quoted in the pages of *Punch* and *The Times* in an age where women barristers didn't get their name in print often – unless they were a 'bolter' that is.

Declaring a fellow barrister a smoker was equivalent in Gran's books to announcing his or her penchant for incest or country dancing.

No one saw any hypocrisy in her manifesto in those days, even though she used to lip-ride Cohibas all over the Inns of Court. She was perhaps best loved for terrorising legal bigwigs into handing over their packets of Dunhill, which she would then ceremoniously crush under the sharp point of her stiletto while her victims choked on the clouds of smoke spilling from her own Cuban.

Given that Rory smoked roll-ups, I had recently modified my anti-smoking views although I have been known to secretly lace his tobacco with Chanel No 5. It is the stench of tobacco in my hair that I loathe the most.

He refuses to smoke cigars, deeming them too pretentious. This from a man who wouldn't know a cow if he fell over one coming out of Spago's but religiously wears cowboy boots nonetheless. Hel-lo?

Besides, cigars are beyond pretension, a virtual parody of a parody of pretentiousness if you like. A cigar is a work of craftsmanship, according to my supplier on Bond Street. A phallus like no other, with style, attitude and presence. Three virtues woefully lacking in the common and foul-smelling 'fag'.

Let's just say that cigars slink where cigarettes slump. Where cigarettes exude at best a down-and-out, trailer-park cool, cigars make you feel and look replete. A good Cohiba is like a Rolls Royce, capable of bestowing class on anyone who can afford to own one. A great leveller.

As my gran was always pointing out, people who smoke cigars are usually very powerful because you have to be quite strong to hold them let alone smoke them. Cigarette smokers in contrast are usually very nervy types, always worrying about bronchitis and wrinkles, who cough up stuff in the mornings – or worse, during important intimate moments.

I have dated cigarette smokers and there is nothing more disconcerting than having your partner call a halt in sexual proceedings because he has something down the back of his throat.

It is this essentially phlegmy nature of cigarette smokers that prohibits the sexual potency which a woman of erratic orgasmic ability such as myself so requires. One imagines cigarette smokers as having weedy, white torsos with patchy body hair and greedy, tar-stained tongues.

PS, scratch Rory from this comparison – his tongue and the way he uses it is sublime.

As I puffed away on my stoogie that afternoon, a largesse came over me. I actually thought about calling Maddy and chewing the cud on my newfound Other Womanness. I had a quiet driver this time, a man who knew his way around and didn't take his eyes off the road – apart from accepting his payment, when he was all rapt attention. No complaints about the tip from him – a polite fifteen per cent (and the

RL cap). I'm proud to say that we never even made it onto first-name terms.

Anyway, so I thought about calling Mads. I mean the thing was, I'd been seeing her all this time, sobbing about how life had impacted on *me* and now all of a sudden it would appear that I was the *impactor*.

Let's not forget that I was the sort of woman from whom men felt compelled to conceal their three-year-old daughters. I was a virtual totem of evil Other Woman characteristics. This little drama was going to make Maddy's brain follicles twitch.

Don't get me wrong, I'm not saying that Mads is a cold-hearted bitch more interested in my emotional damage than me; let's just say she loves nothing more than a psychosis that she can really get her teeth into. I sympathise with her. Really.

As a junior barrister I had dreamed of representing underdogs and fighting idealistic legal battles for maternity leave and equality. Instead, I found myself defending fraudsters and white-collar villains.

'Do you think pathetic cases like yours are what I went to Bar school for?' I have been known to scream at hapless clients when they whinge about the unfavourable judgement handed down in their case. Mads was facing those same career dilemmas within the court of the mind.

Let's face it, the Catholic Guilt Thing is OK as far as it goes but that's not nearly far enough for an intelligent woman like Mads. Despite the nuns' determination to see me walk tall and speak like a lady, they never actually managed to ruin my orgasm ability or my career drive, which is what really matters.

The nuns were all a bit of a letdown from Maddy's point of view. She likes something really complex and preferably sad and sick to wrap her analytical mind around – and who can blame her?

As perverse as it seems, I was somehow proud to finally be in a position to offer her something more substantial by way of emotional damage. My newfound role as the Other Woman was bound to stimulate Maddy's overdeveloped psychodrama gland no end. Hey, I was impacting on three-year-olds! My self-esteem was a mess. I needed major psychotherapy here. I couldn't help but be proud.

There was a party going on in the garden at the Marmont when I returned in my spectacularly sophisticated Donna Karan. Tall men in smart casuals and thin women in black suits such as my own were sipping champagne under the palms and laughing at one another's witticisms.

In my new pant-suit, I could have passed as an invited guest. I could have slipped in unnoticed and exposed my tonsils for the sake of bad jokes with the best of them. Which was slightly unnerving really for a fanatical outsider such as myself.

I eyed the women suspiciously, wondering how many 'Other' Women were out there. How many cold, evil-hearted dad-shaggers lurked amongst the fronds, looking for three-year-olds to impact on? Or maybe they were all enjoying civilised arrangements with one another's exes? This was California, after all.

'Oh, you've changed,' the girl behind the front desk announced as I swept into the lobby, trailing my plumes of thick smoke. 'Hang on a minute, you've hardly known me for a heartbeat,' I reminded her. 'Actually though you are right. My emotions have taken a slight U-turn and I am considering my role in life but that's a bit bloody incisive of you to notice. And hardly your place. I've got a hairdresser and an analyst for that.'

She blushed. 'I actually meant your outfit. You've changed outfits. I loved the one you were wearing earlier. We all loved it. We talked about it after you left,' she cooed. 'Normally people in LA look really casual. Boring really.'

She was wearing a high-buttoned white shirt over a sombre black shapeless skirt so she could easily have been being facetious but I was stupidly flattered. A shallow compliment was all it took to put a bit of a spring back in my step. Well not a spring so much as a slightly reduced hunchbacked knuckle-dragging gait, perhaps.

Our suite had been cleaned and all evidence of this morning's breakfast excesses swept away. The hotel-issue robes replaced with crisp new ones and not so much as a *brioche* crumb for miles. The message light was flashing cheerfully but I left it while I rushed to the bathroom.

I soon forgot the message actually, worrying instead about what I should do about Rory and our relationship and more importantly, perhaps, a rather nasty kink that had developed in my hair. Not that I was even sure if what we had constituted a relationship. Rory was not an easy man to pin down.

Unlike most of the men I go for who react enthusiastically to feminist concepts such as splitting the bill, Rory was the strong silent type with huge pecs and a washboard stomach, who pined for the days when he could open doors for women – or dolls.

Rory was up for Spencer Tracy levels of control. He used silence like a weapon and thought of the withholding of information as the most sacred of all human rights. I was forever on the edge of my seat where our relationship was concerned and I guess I kind of liked that. Rory had played his 'international man of mystery' advantage for all it was worth until now the veil had been lifted by his ex.

The proverbial game was up.

His hand had been exposed and there was an ex-wife and a three-year-old daughter amongst the aces and kings.

I guess I was kind of shocked. Quite apart from any personal hurt, I was feeling suddenly strong instead of weak, certain where I had been unsure, in charge where I had been under the thumb.

The power basis in our relationship had shifted and I wasn't sure I liked it.

Looking at the Rory and Evelyn thing dispassionately, I realised that he had insinuated himself into my life and my affections by making me uneasy. By making me unsure of where I stood with him, he had now given me an edge.

He had controlled my feelings by disorientating me.

Normally a control-freak, Rory had made me feel virtually childlike, although only in a symbolic emotional sense as Maddy reminded me before I left.

'You are responding to the symbolism of vulnerability,' she had reassured me. 'The promise that he will look after you gives you the power to relax and enjoy his love rather than attempt to control it.'

As the Other Woman – the woman who was impacting on his three-year-old child, it would seem that I was very much in control. His attempt to conceal Katy from me exposed his vulnerability. Revealing his doubts in my ability to love a man encumbered by the baggage of a family.

It was almost a compliment. After all, had he felt secure with me he would have told me about Katy. He would have wanted me to meet her. By leaving it to Alexia to fill me in on his daughter, Rory had shown himself to doubt my unconditional love for him.

The question I was now asking myself was, was he right to doubt my love? I mean was I made for a *Sleepless in Seattle* kind of love affair? One where the old wife wasn't dead? Yet. Was I up for a readymade family? Was I anywhere near civilised enough to cope with stuff like school runs and tooth fairies? God, only yesterday I was wondering if I was mature enough to embark on a cocktail without an umbrella on the side and now I had a readymade family waiting, with arms outstretched, for me to join them.

One thing was for sure. Rory and I needed to talk.

CHAPTER 9

'I looked for you in my closet tonight.'

Blue Velvet, 1986, colour, Isabella Rossellini and Kyle MacLachlan

When I next noticed the telephone message light flashing I was distracted by a knock at the door. It was one of the guys from the front desk known to Rory and me as the 'guy with the stud in his tongue' (as opposed to the guy with the stud in his eyebrow, the guy with the studded upper lips and the girl with the ruby in her nose. The same guy who'd helped me back to my room that first night as it happens. We were as bonded as two people who mean absolutely nothing to one another can be).

Today he was concealing his studded tongue behind a massive bouquet of flowers, but I knew it was him because the stud was so close to the tip of his tongue that it gave him a lisp.

The flowers were death lilies, my favourite. 'Explore

the symbolism of an act,' Mads is always nagging me. Whoever chose these flowers had a very clear message by her standard. This was symbolism with a neon sign attached. A sign that flashed SOMETHING IS ABOUT TO DIE. Or maybe I was just being paranoid.

'Put them over there,' I told him, trying to sound all alluring, irresistible and overpoweringly sexy. 'And if you could open the blinds for me?' I instructed, getting well into my Other Woman stride now. I wanted to play it like Marilyn Monroe only it came out more Jane Russell really. Maybe it was a blonde thing; maybe as a brunette I couldn't do a sexy, cute, disarming Marilyn.

Or maybe years of stereotyping at the hands of a suspicious mother had schooled me to believe in Other Women as bossy, hard-nosed sirens, well versed in the art of destroying decent women's marriages. Maybe there were perks to be had as the Other Woman, maybe I would become irresistible to all men – even gay ones and studded ones, etc.

I looked at the guy with the stud in his tongue as he arranged the flowers but he seemed to be having no trouble resisting me at all.

As far as I know my father had never had an other woman but my mother was always on her guard, ever vigilant in her role of Mistress Of All She Purveys. She never received so much as a single stem rose from my father which rather added to her suspicions, I don't wonder.

The flowers which the guy with the stud in his tongue arranged beautifully on the antique sideboard were heart-meltingly glorious. Maybe life as the Other Woman would be an improvement. If I could just be shot of the civilised arrangement and make more of my 'otherness', perhaps I would finally be empowered as a siren and my sex life would improve.

Maybe flower deliveries and compliments are all part of the Other Woman lifestyle? Maybe in time I would even manage to grow my nails long and stop my nail polish from chipping? I had little doubt that women playing second-fiddle in civilised relationships didn't get to have long nails.

'Anything else mam?' the guy with the stud in his tongue asked as I scanned my nails for signs of growth.

'Do you think my nails are growing?' I asked him as he hovered eagerly (perhaps beginning to be struck by my Other Woman-ness?).

'Yes mam, they do appear to be extending a little,' (or just wanting a tip possibly?).

I allowed him to toss me a few more well-guided compliments before letting him go. I told him that I might have him run me a bath or polish my heels a little later as I saw him to the door. Not certain of my tipping obligations a a *femme fatale*, I slipped him another five bucks. He didn't resist my cash for a moment.

The card attached to the flowers had most of the

words scribbled out, as if the sender couldn't make up his mind about what to say. In the end they had settled on 'Back (scribble, scribble) Home at eight.' There was no signature – that had been scribbled out too.

It was the word *home* that I found most unsettling. I may be deluding myself on many counts but not that. This suite was definitely *not* home. Don't get me wrong, I loved the place. Loved the stereo, the white chenille bedspread, the Frigidaire refrigerator, the view over the palm trees, the ever-replenished mini-bar and the little soaps, shampoos, moisturisers and complimentary gold condoms stacking up in an alarming pile in the bathroom cabinet each day. Love, love, love, love, love.

But despite what the Durex marketing men might tell you, a pile of condoms does not a home make. Men presume too much. The truth was, I was already pining for my loft apartment and my favourite restaurant where I was familiar with their sneering attitude and they were used to mine.

I was missing Chambers, missing my clerks, the only people in the world to refer to me as 'Miss Hornton'.

I was missing my friends and the freedom London offered to drink vast quantities of alcohol without everyone else in the bar panicking that I was an alcoholic about to admit to myself, my higher power and the bar at large, the exact nature of my wrongs.

Most of all though, I was missing my cheques.

Those comforting little reminders that I am a professional woman as opposed to an unqualified, amateur, dependent, Other Woman. The sort of woman men feel compelled to conceal their children from. The sort of woman that a man lies to.

The message light was still flashing troublingly so I picked up the phone and dialled the hotel message service. I had three messages. I can see now that I should have listened to them all but after hearing the first one I wasn't up for the future.

The message was from my analyst, Maddy. Diatribe might be a better word. From memory it went something like this: 'You bitch, you bloody two-faced bitch. If you think I'm going to let you get away with this, you're wrong. If you think I'm just going to wait while you run off and steal my man, you've got another think coming. I'll deal with you, you, you sick Catholic Bitch. He's mine now, not yours. So you keep your big hands off him.'

I looked at my hands as the recorded voice gave me the option of pressing one and deleting the message, pressing two to hear it again or three to save it. Ever a glutton for punishment (it's a Catholic Bitch thing) I elected to push two and listened to Maddy outline her detailed plans to deal with me for a second and then a third sickly masochistic time.

I needed a therapist now like never before, but by the tone of her voice I gathered that I was now *persona non grata* at her clinic. Even though her message didn't specifically mention striking me off her patient register, I considered myself struck off just the same and it smarted.

I know that I am always talking about giving her the axe and whining about her inability to analyse her way out of a paper bag but I don't mean any of it. Patients say cruel things about their therapists; it's all part of the patient–therapist thing. That's what I pay a therapist for. Otherwise I'd just use my hairdresser.

Truth was, I loved Maddy like a sister. After all, who urged her to have her nose job? I mean, she would never have stood a chance with Giles if I hadn't pushed the two of them together. Thinking of which, Giles would be in LA by now. No doubt wandering down the haunted corridors of the Roosevelt in his insteps calling out my name. Oh God.

Was the man mad?

Speaking to Charles that morning, the idea of Giles leaving Maddy for me had seemed like a ridiculous albeit flattering joke. I hadn't for a minute reflected on the reality of the situation or how Maddy might be reacting. Actually, I didn't expect that Maddy would react. After all, she was a trained professional. She was always telling me stuff like, 'Stop reacting and start acting, Evv.'

Like what was that supposed to mean?

Talk about calling the pot black, now look at who was reacting.

All the same I felt responsible, I felt ashamed. I felt guilty.

I relit my cigar and reflected on a course of action. I was determined to turn things around.

Looking back I should have listened to all the messages in one go but I was tapping into my guilt. I had decided to take control of my life and act. Bugger my manicure, I was going to run at my dilemmas like a quarterback with big shoulders. Only thing was I was more your pom-pom girl than gridiron champ. My shoulders were scrawny and my head was devoid of all protection and I was desperately afraid of personal injury.

My hairdresser would say that it was time to do something I should have done years ago, fly back to London and plant lawnseed in Giles' carpet. I have had it on good authority that seeding expensive carpet is the ultimate empowering gesture. If only Simone de Beauvoir had thought of seeding Sartre's carpet, the *Iron in the Soul* might have been avoided (v.dull). What fools we girls have been.

The Marlboro Man loomed outside my window with a knowing look, as if egging me on to leave. As if saying, 'I knew you wouldn't last in this town, kid.' Determined not to give him the satisfaction I blew cigar smoke at him and sneered right back.

I wasn't up for another transatlantic flight just yet anyway so I opted for a more immediate form of action. After all Giles was here – in the City of Lost Souls, creeping around in his insteps. Take that testosterone host into your hands girl, Gran would have said. And give it all you've got! That was it,

I decided, I would strike a blow for sisterhood and hunt him down – send him crawling back to Maddy on bended inner soles.

Armed with my resolve, I grabbed my bag, emptied my tart-is-back outfit over the bed and swept out of the hotel.

In the dark recesses of my subconscious a message light was flashing but I stuck on my dark glasses and ignored it.

CHAPTER 10

'Bill's thirty-two. He looks thirty-two. He looked it five years ago. He'll look it twenty years from now. I hate men.'

All About Eve, 1950, b/w, Bette Davis and
Marilyn Monroe

When the sun sets against the smog in LA and colours the sky a deep brooding crimson, it is almost divine enough to convince an environmentally aware girl like me that pollution is worthy of a heritage listing as one of the great wonders of the modern age.

As I made the journey across LA toward the Roosevelt, waiting for the traffic congestion on Sunset to clear, I thought about my actions very carefully indeed and what I might have done to have caused things to go so suddenly and so grandly wrong.

I had started off as a successfully single girl in

London. A small role but it had a certain kudos; I thought it one to which I was eminently suited. Hell knows, at least I had a script for that role. Now, suddenly, without even auditioning for the part, I'd been cast as the lead bitch in a family drama. Now I was shagging dads, impacting on three-year-olds and breaking up my therapist's relationship.

It occurred to me that maybe I needed method coaching or something.

I watched the pink pollution spread out against the sky like a red wine stain on a tablecloth and felt a great sadness descend upon my heart. A great big sorrowful sadness. A Mama Cass kind of sadness for all those Californian dreams that had ended up on the rocks, chased by a splash of whisky or a line of coke.

Another one-time guest of the Château, Cass Elliot, would understand how I was feeling now as I tried to dream up a plan to sort out my therapist's love life, she would have had a song for my mood. I offered up a little prayer to the fat angel and asked her to look down on her sister in need, and if she had the muse maybe she might throw a few pertinent song lines my way. Although I felt I should warn her before she got writing that it was going to take more than a tambourine rhythm and a muumuu to sort this mess out.

Humming the words to *California Dreaming*, I felt a slight urge to pop into a church. Maybe it was a lapsed-Catholic kind of thing but I couldn't help feeling that I had not been as blameless in my dealings with Giles as I might and I wondered if it wasn't too late to turn over a new leaf. If it wasn't too late to take up the final option, the final solution. Become a nun basically.

Giles and I go back a long way. I'm not going to lie; for a while I even fancied myself in love with him. He was my first English lover and without doubt one of the most attractive blokes at the Bar in London that year.

Back in Australia, I'd been schooled to believe in the British lover as the last word in small-penis sexlessness. It's a public school thing we were told. Poms are twisted, sexually warped and impotent. To discover that the converse was true made me fall all the harder.

Not only was Giles well-endowed but he was physically fluent in the language of love, call it cunnilingual. Stiff upper lips come in very useful when speaking that particular dialect. Unfortunately he was also a class-A pompous bore and should have come with an EU health warning.

Warning, this man has a high tedium reading. Spending long periods of time in his company could result in a coma.

If I had to spell it out I would say that Giles is the sort of bloke who makes itemised lists of his underwear. He is the sort of bloke who wears button-up collars and sock garters. On the week-ends.

Giles was not the man for me. I soon found (surprise, surprise) that other Englishmen have stiff upper lips and know what to do in the clitoral department, if pointed in the right direction and given clear instructions.

I was en route to the Roosevelt therefore to reason with Giles, to plead with him to give up his mad dream of a future with me. It was time to wipe the slate clean, give Giles back to Maddy and maybe even in time give Rory back to Katy. This last one made my pulse race a bit.

But it was possible that Charles had been right, she usually was. Maybe it was time to get back on that plane and go back to London so that my clerk might call me Miss Hornton and my friends might call me 'silly bitch'? It was time to put things right. Do the noble thing and step aside.

It wasn't as if I was equipped for Coupleland anyway. I didn't even have a visa for the place. Let's face it, I didn't have what it takes to make a double act. I was an illegal immigrant in the world of couples, an alien in the land of shared interests and Saturday nights at home. I may not have sighted the dreaded IKEA catalogue but I had seen the writing on the wall and Coupleland wasn't a neighbourhood I wanted to live in.

The majestic Roosevelt loomed out of the grittiest bit of Hollywood Boulevard. At one time the very hub of Hollywood and the once-famed venue for the Academy Awards, the scene had moved on long ago and left the Roosevelt behind. Now it stood in its 1920s splendour like a hungover guest collapsed in the post-party detritus after all the other guests have gone elsewhere.

There were rumours that the place is haunted, beset by the ghosts of Marilyn Monroe, Montgomery Clift and Mr Bojangles, and it somehow seemed appropriate that a ghost from my own past should have ended up here, giving new meaning to the term 'my favourite haunt'.

The Spanish Colonial lobby was thronged with an evening crowd drinking up the faded Hollywood grandeur. Tourists with their camera equipment and glamour junkies searching for a vanished era mingled around the desk wasting those last precious moments of the twentieth century, hankering for an age past.

Get on your keyboards, I wanted to yell.

Log into the future you fools.

Set your time/date consoles for the millennium.

But my calls would have fallen on deaf ears. No one in this place was looking for the now.

The Roosevelt was like a Tardis transporting people away from California today and into a California when people being gay had nothing to do with sexual orientation. When glamour meant chiffon and sequins, and talking in a baby voice was still considered v. sexy.

The Roosevelt reminded me of rural English tearooms, it was missing the point and proud of it.

'I'm looking for Giles Billington-Frith,' I told the guy at the desk who was remarkably unstudded.

'He's gone to a bar,' he snapped, not even looking

at me. 'The place on Sunset. The bar . . . what's it called?'

'"The bar – what's it called?"' I said, slightly lost and remembering a bar that I used to meet Giles in back in London. Years ago, before I realised how unsuited we were. Just by the Inns of Court not far from the tube, Benjamin Stillingfleet as it was then known was our favourite after-work haunt. Then it changed its name not once but twice until, thoroughly confused, everyone took to referring to it as 'the bar, what's it called now?'

Giles used to be there waiting for me after court. Sometimes he would have bought flowers, sometimes if he'd had a favourable verdict he would have ordered champagne. Sometimes he'd just be sipping on a Guinness, brooding over a lost case or dreaming of returning an especially ugly brief.

Barristers spend a lot of time both at the Bar and in the bar. We go there after court to wash away our cares or to gossip about one another or find people to sleep with. A world within a world, the bars around the Inns of Court reverberate with the chatter of men and women who might turn their learned selves to a murder or a fraud during the day and want to bore the ears off everyone else in the evening.

Of all the times I'd ever spent with Giles, the times at 'the bar what's it called?' were the best. He was never a great raconteur and sometimes we didn't have much to say to one another but his languid wit was at its laziest best of an evening over a Guinness and his hair flopped at its sexiest when the gel applied in the morning had given up its brave attempt to keep his hair lacquered and in place.

Giles was regular, responsible and noble in an anal sort of way. He was everything that the English do best, or rather used to do best before they started indulging in humiliating displays of cable TV-style emotion. Giles was English in the old-fashioned way. He was like an April drizzle, miserable but brilliant when the sun broke through.

'Bar Marmont,' the guy at the desk announced. 'That's it. Here it is, he left a message. Is your name E-V-E-L-Y-N?'

I told him it was but he didn't actually hand me the message, choosing instead to read it out.

'He said that he'll be at the Bar Marmont. If you want to see him, that is.'

This information made me pause. I mean, just thinking about Giles in Bar Marmont made my tongue loll. My gran had always warned us as children to never let our friends go unchaperoned. People change, she assured me, and not always in the way you might want them to. Surely Giles was the exception to this rule. Giles was what England did best before Cool Britannia. He was steadiness at its steadiest. Giles would never ever change, of this I was sure.

Giles didn't give a damn that other people might find him uninspiring or that being stuck with him in a dark corner of a cocktail party might be considered by some as the last word in tedium. Giles was arrogant in the way that only English public school men can be. It's something to do with the frock coat they wore up at Eton or a starch they used in the collars that renders them helplessly insensitive to the needs of others. As an Australian I actually admired Giles in a sick kind of way, only not in any lasting sense obviously.

But times are changing. Nothing is permanent, as Buddhists have pointed out with that smug knowingness that has always put me off Eastern religions.

'The Bar Marmont,' the guy at the desk repeated, looking at me with concern, clearly worried that he might have to call security. I guess I was staring madly into space.

'On Sunset. You know, the hotel where that John Belushi guy ODed.'

I nodded knowingly. I was used to receiving morbid directions in LA. It seems that most places are linked to a Hollywood death or a Tinsel Town crime at some time.

There's the Viper Room – you know that place where River Phoenix ODed?

The Ambassador Hotel – you know the place where Robert Kennedy was assassinated?

Corner of Sunset Boulevard and Courtney Avenue – you know, the place where Divine Brown gave Hugh Grant his best blow job ever?

As I climbed into another taxi I tried to think what the officios of that *sanctum sanctori* of cool would do with a bloke so consummately uncool as to wear insteps to support his falling arches. Even in my brief association with the Bar Marmont, I could say with some certainty that it wasn't the sort of place where my ex-boyfriend belonged.

No doubt he was about to be spat out like a processed cheese by a Frenchman.

Maybe it was just my exhausting day impacting on a three-year-old but I felt kind of maternally protective of Giles all of a sudden.

An inexplicable knot began to gather in my stomach.

CHAPTER 11

'You have no idea what a long-legged girl can do without doing anything.'

The Palm Beach Story, 1942, b/w,
Claudette Colbert and Rudy Vallee

Bar Marmont is about twenty-five yards from the hotel of the same name. The guide book describes it as a short walk but let's be serious, they are talking to people who wear trainers.

If you plan to go there in heels, drive, take a cab or climb on someone's back. Do not, whatever you do, try and walk. The pavements are deadly and men in fast cars might mistake you for a streetwalker. And no girl wants to be remembered for a mug shot – apart from the essential one they make you put in your passport. As great Hollywood agents have warned starlets everywhere, a mug shot is the only screen test a girl wants to avoid taking.

Stylishly dark and seedy in atmosphere, Bar

Marmont struck me as the sort of place where a girl could die in her cocktail and never be found.

PS. It is not the sort of place to hang if you don't have an agent. Even the agents have agents in this bar.

In decor at least it reminded me of the seedy club hangouts in London's Soho where the barstaff can give you a lot of information about a lot of things even if they can't work out how to get the espresso machine to work or how to pull a beer. But I suspect there was nothing that the staff at Bar Marmont didn't know.

The staff in this place were going places. There was a sense that any minute now they were going to be discovered. These guys had savvy implanted in their lips where most of the poor old English just had a droop these days. They had *cool* injected into their cheekbones, basically they were a super race of wannabes.

The staff here brought a new dignity to the word 'aspirational'.

These past few days in LA had more or less convinced me that my problem lay in my lack of aspiration. Anyway you looked at it I was aspirationally challenged. My problem was that I was aiming my aspirations too low. Way too low in some people's opinion. I had below-the-belt aspirations. People had gone down in search of my aspirations and never seen the light of day again. I had only ever aimed as high as the casting couch which some people might even call rock bottom.

In Blighty the verb *to aspire* is a derivative of the verb *to better oneself*, which is another way of saying, 'so you think you can raise yourself up from the slime of your sorry little excuse for a background? Just forget it!'

Along with feelings and caring, aspirations are another thing you have to conceal in the UK if you want any respect at all.

LA was the opposite.

To put you in the mood picture there was a humid bake-in-your-own-aspirational-juices atmosphere prevailing at Bar Marmont that evening. The place was packed with industry people and moviestar wannabes, and so thick with aspirations that people were practically choking on the stuff. I was beginning to worry about the effects of inhaling passive aspirations.

There was no getting away from it, an aspirationally challenged girl like me stuck out like a sore thumb in Bar Marmont.

Listening into the patrons' conversations, it seemed like everyone was trying to get something 'off the ground'. Careers and projects mostly. In London the only thing anyone is trying to get off the ground are the drunks who sleep and piss on your doorstep at night.

On top of the aspirations, the noise of flesh pressing against flesh, hormone rubbing against hormone and ego massaging ego was deafening. The air was tense with development ideas being swished around like non-alcoholic cocktails. Even the most cynical LA babe (i.e. me) couldn't help but believe that success might be just around the corner that night.

'Don't sweat it, doll. Life can turn on a dime,' Rory would always tell me whenever I complained about the hopeless aspects of a case. Here in LA there was a palpable sense that anything could happen. The future was a slot machine and you couldn't help but think that if you pulled the lever long enough, the jackpot eventually had to yield or explode.

'Nice boob job,' a full-faced man in glasses announced in my ear as I flashed my eyes about the darkest corners of the bar.

I looked at him as if he had just burped. He smiled knowingly and said, 'Don't tell me. They're your own.' Then he fell about with laughter as if he had single-handedly broken the humour barrier.

'No, they're my Aunt Kit's actually,' I explained, hoping to castrate him with my sarcasm. I kept forgetting that this was LA – the sarcasm black spot of America, but I refused to be deterred. 'See all my life my mother told me that I had Aunt Kit's breasts, and that's why I'm here in LA, scouting for the lucky bitch that got mine. You haven't seen them, have you? They're a neat little A-cup with pert nipples.'

'Hey, that's a beautiful thing,' he said, moving in his bar stool to get his groin in a more comfortable position. 'Ancestral breast exchange. A bit cosmic but I like it.'

Then I swear this is no lie, he reached out and

squeezed my left tit. I mean it. As God is my witness he took it tightly in his fist – as much of it as he could manage at least, and twisted.

We are talking about a large chunk of my anatomy here. I looked around for support or an automatic weapon or the PC police. A few people looked toward us self-consciously but presuming I was auditioning for something they went back to launching their projects.

'It's so soft. How do you get it like that?' he asked. Reaching into his pocket he pulled out a book with a pencil attached by a string and wrote something in it. I was beginning to feel very uncomfortable. 'Can I buy you a drink?' he asked.

'No thanks,' I said, deciding to play it straight. 'I'm looking for someone.'

'Well, you take care now.' He smiled disinterestedly and went back to writing stuff in his book. It sort of felt like I'd been dropped, and it seemed incredible that someone could be so engroped in me and my left breast one minute and dismiss me so easily the next.

Before my ego had time to become completely demoralised though I spotted Giles in a corner, stretched out full length on a club lounger. His feet, having overshot the available space, were resting on a small round glass table.

He was staring up at the ceiling as if considering a weighty philosophical discourse. Probably the latest breakthrough in in-step technology or the savage rise in last years' Legal Aid budget boding badly for *bona fide* criminal barristers such as he. Just looking at him made me want to yawn.

'Were you in here last night in a red sequinned floor-length dress doing Shirley Bassey numbers with a guy on a tuba?' a man in a Prince of Wales checked suit and a black T-shirt asked me. 'Because I thought you were great. Really talented.'

I looked down on him with abject disdain but my admirer didn't appear to notice. He offered me his card and patted me on the back. 'You've got a kind of corny talent. I might be able to get you a gig. Stick with it, kid.'

I took the card and shoved it down my bra as I continued to make my way through the obstacle course of chairs, tables and expressive limbs. Admittedly Giles was looking good. His blond hair had flopped engagingly over one eye and with his arm flung over the back of his chair, he really did look quite debonair. I have never denounced his looks although at times I have felt that his appearance exposed the inner depth of his dreariness.

Giles turned his head, clocked my approach and jumped up. 'Evelyn!' he exclaimed. 'I didn't believe you'd come.'

There were a lot of really amusing things I could have said to that but I wisely held my tongue. Now wasn't the time or the place.

Besides, everyone was staring. I could see their mental *Who's Who*'s clicking over as they tried to work out who I was or indeed if I was anybody. There are two types of people in LA: Somebodies and Wannabe Somebodies.

'You got my message then?'

'What message?'

'I've left Madeline,' he announced loudly to the bar at large. It was as though he was under a spotlight and judging by the way the bar crowd were staring at him, I guessed they were hoping he was about to strip down to a floor-length red sequinned dress and start bashing out the Shirley Bassey favourites of the night before.

Instead he adjusted his belt. 'I know it's sudden, but look here. I think we might have made a big mistake. I'm still in love with you and I can't believe you don't feel the same,' he blurted out. At this, everyone yawned and went back to their project launches, realising that I wasn't even a wannabe. Like I said, my aspirations were still focused on the casting coach.

I'd been reading a book by a tortured French sod of a writer in which the protagonist is constantly being engulfed by emotions from which he feels disconnected. Not normally one for the existentialists, I felt at one with that Frenchman now.

'Engulfed' pretty much summed up how I was feeling. Engulfed by men and their feelings for me. I was fairly sure that there was a Shirley Bassey number out there that could sum up the overwhelming sense of desperation I was feeling and I looked at Giles, hopeful that he knew the opening bars.

Instead he threw his arms around me and lifted me in the air. No mean feat for any man. 'Why did you leave me like that?' he demanded. It was one of the devices he used in court. Ask to have the evidence and facts laid out again and again until people's brains keel over with the misery of it all.

That way, sleeping judges can keep up with the dreariness of your defence and with a bit of luck the jurors will fall asleep and accept the judge's guidance in finding a verdict. Giles was the consummate master of slow and tedious repetition wins the race.

'Giles, I left you years ago. We've been over it a million times. You're engaged to Maddy now and I'm involved with someone else too.'

'You mean that obnoxious little Irish-American with the stupid name – what is it, Roly?'

'Rory,' I corrected. 'And he's not obnoxious,' I said defensively. 'He's very Irish-American, that's all. And he only threw you out of that party because he was protecting me.'

'Yes, well you've never been a woman in need of protection have you?' he sneered, which was pretty unpleasant from a man claiming to adore me.

I pointed this out to him.

'I'm sorry. Look, I've been doing a lot of drinking I mean thinking. I need to talk to you, Evelyn. I don't know if you've spoken to Charles yet,' he said, running his hands through his hair in a way I once found totally adorable. 'Look, can I buy you a drink?'

he asked. 'I simply have to talk to you. This might take some time.'

I asked for a bottle of champagne and sat down in the sofa waiting for drunkenness to save me.

CHAPTER 12

'Will you take your hands off me? What are you playing – osteopath?'

His Girl Friday, 1940, b/w, Cary Grant and
Rosalind Russell

We got through two bottles of champagne that evening. Probably not the best way to carry out a post mortem on a dead relationship but the only way I was prepared to undertake the task with Giles that night.

Giles had what Mads would call 'unresolved issues'. He also seemed to have 'false reclaimed memory syndrome' in regard to what our time together was really like. Whereas I remembered a stifling, largely boring winter of discontent, he recalled a golden age of boundless love and sexual perfection.

In Hollywood terms he was Spencer Tracy to my Katharine Hepburn in that film *Woman of the Year*. Only thing was, this was the late 1990s and I didn't care to marry someone who equated my ability to cook for him with my worthiness as a person. Besides, I relate more to Marilyn Monroe in *Gentlemen Prefer Blondes*, only I don't need to pay for my own diamonds. I have an overdraft for that.

Like most *fin de siècle* girls, I was looking for someone who could offer me more than I could offer myself, only maybe not a kid and an ex-wife.

'You've got unresolved issues,' I told him when he started to get maudlin and soppy.

'Oh save me,' he groaned, throwing his hands in the air in mock drama. 'You're starting to sound like *her* now. Speaking in that infuriating psycho-babble she specialises in. Can't you see? That's what drove me to the extremes of insanity with her. And yes, you're damn right I've got issues! I'm sick of having my brain taken apart like a Chinese puzzle. Why does everything have to come down to the way the fags beat me at Eton?'

Good question, I thought to myself. Let's face it, the images this revelation conjured were riveting. 'Well that's a question for Maddy,' I told him, trying not to smirk. I poured myself another glass from the bottle of Dom. 'I'm hardly qualified to decipher the underlying patterns of your behaviour.'

He nodded enthusiastically at this. 'Exactly! And that's why I love you so much,' he cheered, grabbing both my elbows and shaking them so that the champagne ended up all over my new trouser suit.

'Steady up,' I told him. 'This is Donna Karan.'

He ignored me. Giles had never had a lot of

respect for fashion designers. If you couldn't study it at Oxford it didn't really count as far as he was concerned. The tailoring genius of the sons of East End cab drivers eluded Giles the way that the mystery of Coupledom eluded me.

'It's true Evv, you can't deny that what we had was good. The sex alone was sublime. You can't tell me you've ever had better sex.'

Even though I could, I managed to muster enough sensitivity to let him down gently while using a cushion from the sofa to mop up my wet crotch. I watched sadly as the crepe crinkled up like feet that have spent too long in the bath. The cushion must have been Scotchgarded or something because it was totally ineffectual as a sponge.

The suit was ruined.

Donna can perform magic with a pair of slacks but even she's no match for French champagne. I could already feel the alcohol going to my head. If anyone was going to be the cause of crotch damage in this relationship, I was thinking it should be me. Giles was still harping on in my ear about good sex.

'"Good" is a subjective concept,' I reminded him sternly.

But Giles wasn't giving up without an argument. It's a career choice with him. 'OK, I'll admit I probably expected too much. But I'm a traditionalist, is that such a crime? Not to want the woman you adore to be stressed out about a career. I wanted you to be happy, is that a crime? So I wanted children, is that a crime? I don't want to spend every weekend partying with your bloody friends. Is that a crime?'

'Well, you're the criminal barrister,' I reminded him. 'The laws surrounding intent are a matter for you and your *Archbold*, I would have said.'

He laughed heartily and slapped me on the back, knocking still more champagne from my glass and causing more damage to my suit. I could see I was going to have to drink the stuff more quickly. I told him that neither my suit nor I appreciated his physical expressions of good humour, which made him laugh harder and slap me some more.

A bottle later and the evening was wearing to its open-ended conclusion. Periodically we were interrupted by industry people trying to muscle in on our 'project', asking us if we'd thought of so and so for the lead or whether we'd thought of approaching Disney with our idea. In my opinion that was where our relationship belonged – in Disneyland. Giles could be played by Mickey Mouse and I could be Minnie. I've always dreamed of being short.

Giles got very stroppy with our interlocutors but I was very encouraging. Face it, I was ready to lunge at any lifeboat out of our conversation, especially when he started getting the boot into Maddy.

Call me a mad loyalist but I had feelings for my therapist. She had guided me through thick and thin, rough seas and smooth waters. OK, so we'd had our differences and I felt she was a bit mad at times but apart from my hairdresser and my gran, no one knew me as well as she did, and in my experience it doesn't pay to dish the dirt on the people who know you well.

'And isn't she infuriating the way she says "breathe through it", every time you justifiably lose your temper over something?'

'Well I'm not as mad about justice as you Giles,' I pointed out. 'Like my gran used to say – "Justice is rarely served in the better-class establishment".'

He rolled his eyes. Giles was never big on Gran's pithy aphorisms. 'Well, you know what I mean,' he pressed.

'I don't actually, Giles. I mean apart from this irrational idea you have about you and me being an ideal couple, don't you think that you're being a bit hard on her? After all, you two were gazing into one another's eyes last time I saw you. Are you sure you're not just making a mountain out of a mole hill? Maybe you are afraid of commitment?' I suggested gamely.

He laughed and shook his head. 'You don't need to play devil's advocate with me. I've told her that I am still in love with you and I meant it. If she can't handle that I'm sorry but I can't help the way I feel. What you and I had surpasses anything I've ever felt for Madeline.'

'Giles, I'm going to say it again. We were never suited. You and I are polar opposites. We were terrible together! Most of the time we were at one another's throats and the rest of the time we were inhabiting another century, with you playing lord and master and me in the support role as chattel.'

'I like that,' said a woman sitting in the chair beside us. 'Do you have a director on this project yet, or is it still in the nascent stages?'

'Still in the Neolithic stages actually,' I told her.

'Oh forget it,' she groaned, rolling her eyes. 'Cave men? Been there done that. I think you want to go with the twelfth century. Twelfth century is really hip right now.'

I told her we'd think about it.

'I really think we should give it another go,' Giles continued.

'Give what another go exactly Giles? Huh? The endless rows, the nights in watching telly. The arguments about where I could and couldn't hang my stockings and knickers? Watch my lips,' I told him. 'You and I had nothing worth reliving. Nothing.'

'Why are you being so brutal, Evv? Did I hurt you so badly? What did I do to make you this harsh? I love you, Evv. What I'm really saying here is that I'm prepared to change for you.'

I laughed. Change was never one of Giles' strong points. Like most men even a change of socks knocked him for six.

I was still laughing when Giles threw himself on top of me and kissed me hard on the lips. Apart from the total unexpectedness of the action it all went badly wrong when his forced passion met with my teeth which sort of hurt a bit. Undeterred, Giles went on to give me one of his better kisses. Warm, soft and tasting of champagne.

It was strange kissing a man I now thought of as a fool but it was nice just the same. Maybe I was drunk. Actually I *was* drunk. Never drink with ex-boyfriends, my gay hairdresser has always warned. A by-law he introduced for the protection of his exes basically. Where Stefan is concerned his exes should never look back, lest they get stuck with alfalfa carpet or a shrimp in the mouthpiece of their phone.

The last time he bumped into one of his exes in a bar and had a drink for old times' sake the two of them ended up at the guy's flat in a night of reclaimed passion. Then the poor man woke up to discover the nipples and underarms had been snipped from all his Thomas Pink shirts.

'I just had second thoughts,' Stefan shrugged, although how he explained to the poor guy when he woke up and found his wardrobe destroyed, I dread to think.

Anyway there I was kissing Giles which turned out to be not at all as repulsive as I would have thought, only I couldn't stop thinking of what the kiss was doing to my lipstick so I pushed him off and reached for my compact.

It was while rubbing lippy off my teeth that I caught sight of Daniel. Over at the bar with a blonde. He had his arm lightly draped around her waist. She was laughing helplessly at something he had said. He was wearing the suit I'd seen him in that first night in LA, which made me reminisce. He was looking ruffled and tousled as if he'd had a hard day. Looking at him I felt like a vibrator had just been switched on in my stomach.

'I'm not afraid of committing to you,' Giles said quietly, as if giving me a cue. I shut my compact and faced him.

'Giles, you're on the wrong set. You're auditioning for the wrong role in the wrong movie. My life is a day-time soap just at the moment and frankly you're better off out of it. You deserve the role of the leading man in someone else's feature length film. Aim high, go for the box-office hit Giles, not the art-house flop that we had together.

'What we had was lousy. True, there was a certain chemistry but it was never going to last. We were always wrong. You and Mads suit one another. You're just having second thoughts now because it's getting more serious. That's natural. Go with it Giles,' I told him, knowing that I sounded like I'd swallowed a self-help book but pretty proud of myself anyway.

My attention though was across the room. I was watching Daniel turn his profile towards me. He was laughing at something the blonde said now. They were walking away from the bar, he was holding two drinks and coming towards us and that was when the vibrator fell through my stomach and into my groin.

Giles was bleating something but I wasn't listening. Daniel caught sight of me then. He smiled and waved. It was a wicked smile. A smile that said, follow me and I will lead you to a place of personal ecstasy before I make you miserable. Then I recognised the blonde he was with. It was Alexia. And I realised that he'd skipped the ecstasy bit and just taken me straight to the miserable part.

CHAPTER 13

'You know, the first man that can think up a good explanation how he can be in love with his wife and another woman is going to win that prize they're always giving out in Sweden.'

The Women, 1939, b/w, Joan Crawford and
Rosalind Russell

When I returned to the room later on that night, it was in darkness and despite the heat the air-conditioning was off. Even with the windows open, the suite was airless and sticky and there was a Tarantino-esque vibe in the place. I could hear the shower going though so I knew Rory must be back.

I stuck my head out the window in search of a sobering breeze but the fronds of the palm trees were as still as a stage set. The only movement outside was a fat girl in a black tyre, floating lifelessly in the centre of the pool. Looking down I started to get vertigo, which on top of the champagne made me feel slightly nauseous.

Taking in some deep breaths I gazed out at the overdose bungalows below and wondered if anyone down there was snorting coke or shooting up suicidal amounts of speed and heroin rollerballs and whether they might let me join them if I pleaded.

Someone's stereo below started pumping out a horrendous rock anthem about loving the wrong kind of woman, while from the bathroom I could hear Rory attempting to sing a bar or two of a Spice Girls song he professed to hate. 'If you want my future, forget my past,' he was wailing.

I closed the window, turned on the air-conditioner and peeled off my ruined trouser suit. That was when I noticed that the message light wasn't flashing any more, which meant Rory must have listened to all the messages

PS. Gulp!

That was the first signal to run.

The second was the beheaded lilies strewn over the floor that I tripped on as I stripped down to panties and bra. Fine, I thought to myself, we've been living together for under a week and already lilies are losing their heads?

Having noted the lilies, some might say that fore-warned is forearmed, to which I would say 'get a life'. Besides, I'd just consumed enough champagne to render me oblivious to all danger.

I was righteous and ready for catastrophe. I was like the fat girl floating in the tyre, daring the sky to fall, daring people in the suites above to throw up on her.

I rang the message service in case Rory hadn't wiped them.

He had. Including the vitriol from Mads. Oops.

The best form of defence being attack, I went forth into the bathroom and tackled Rory on his marital situation. I told him all about my lunchdate with his ex-wife and still very much current daughter. I don't know how I was expecting him to react but I suppose I probably hoped for a slight look of shame or sorrow or even perhaps a begging look of forgiveness and a plea to give him a second chance.

'Forget it, girlfriend,' Stefan always tells me when I ask whether my hair will grow back. 'This look suits you.'

By 'this look' I suppose he means my gormless sucker look which is the look I was wearing as Rory continued to lather his hair and sing. He was unrepentant. Rory was like Gregory Peck in *Designing Woman*. Marlon Brando in *The Wild One*. Cary Grant in about every film he had ever starred in and John Travolta in *Pulp Fiction*. A man who believes unreservedly in his own infallibility and more importantly in his right to lie and be forgiven – even if does get killed for his arrogance later on in the film.

When I confronted him about the whole Katy,

Alexia, ex-husband and civilised relationship thing, he simply shrugged his shoulders and told me to 'be reasonable'.

'Reason is a dish best served to the sober,' I told him, enunciating carefully and trying to keep my eyes focused.

He had just come out of the shower and was wearing nothing but a white towel around his waist which admittedly gave him the advantage. His whole body wore an expression that said, who wears the washboard stomach in this relationship, huh?

I spent the bad skin part of my adolescence watching Technicolor films in which women in gorgeous frocks swoon over Mr Wrong until Mr Right finally saves the day and the credits come up.

In the best films the men resort to desperate measures to get their true loves to even acknowledge their existence, usually resorting to some elaborate ill-thought-out ruse that will depict them as vulnerable or weak or in need of a woman's protection and love – the idea being that the woman in question will forget all about Mr Wrong and realise that Mr Right for all his flaws is just perfect. Rory only had to get out of the shower to render *me* helpless. When you've got a body like his you don't need elaborate ruses.

It was pointless to expect anything else. Like most of my arguments with Rory this one started with, 'Come on Evie,' and ended with sex. And the sex was worth sacrificing all the sorrowful looks in the world. Course it was.

Afterwards, lying on his chest musing on our tragic love, I started making mature, grown woman suggestions such as, 'Maybe we don't work together. Maybe I should go back to London and get a new analyst? Or a new hairdresser even?'

His riposte was to call me doll and bring me to orgasm again. It was that sort of relationship, where the physical perfection of it all justified a thousand sins and made me lose sight of all post-structural feminist issues. In his arms, all that mattered was the carnal. Sometimes reality doesn't compare to fantasy and this was one of those times.

Afterwards we watched television as if we'd been married for years and this really was our home and we really were the perfect couple and there wasn't a civilised relationship with another woman in the background ruining the idyll of our love. Who knows, I fantasised, maybe we'd pop down to IKEA tomorrow and check out their line in wall sconces.

After the Dave Letterman show ended, we sat in companionable silence. Rory was rolling a cigarette and I was smoking the butt end of my cigar from earlier in the day. I was thinking about calling my hairdresser, thinking about going blonde again and whether this would up my image or my aspirations, at least.

'Do you think I'd win more cases as a blonde?' I asked Rory as he kissed me on the top of my head and lit up.

'Nah.'

'Blondes have more fun they say,' I suggested.

'Maybe, but brunettes get more sex.'

It was so typical that a man would put more store by how much sex he'd get out of me as opposed to how much fun I'd get out of my hair colour.

'Is Alexia a natural blonde?' I asked, lying on his heart.

'Depends what you mean by natural,' he grunted.

It was about this time that the movie started. *Sleepless in Seattle*. Rory reached for the remote. I grabbed his hand.

'You don't want to watch that crap, do yar doll?' he groaned.

'Why not? Maybe I'll find answers to my dilemma.'

'Dilemma? What dilemma? One measly failed marriage does not a dilemma make, not for you at least. Jeeze doll, I'm not a widower and you're not a goofy blonde.'

I allowed my upper lip to curl into a sneer and gave it to him straight. 'Both scenarios which could be changed in an hour.'

'Don't make more of this than there is. My relationship with Alexia, failed or otherwise, is none of your damn business, doll. Period.'

'Period? Of course it's my business, You've got a daughter I've been accused of impacting on. As far as Alexia's concerned it makes me the Other Woman! And any way you look at it, your relationship with Katy makes me a dad-shagger.'

He met my sneer with one of his own. 'My daughter, my life, it's nothing to do with you. Have I asked you to be a surrogate mother?'

'A surrogate mother is when you farm out your sperm, smartass,' I explained, suddenly finding myself on the intellectual highground.

'Whatever. Point is, Katy's my business. Shit, I haven't even asked you to babysit. Save the dilemmas for another man, will you doll? Giles for instance. Now there's a man who probably wants you to have his baby. Maybe you should run to him?'

'What's that supposed to mean?' I asked, dumbfounded.

'Nothing. Only people in glass relationships shouldn't throw stones.'

'Glass whats? How did Giles enter this discussion?'

'He rang up earlier, left a message asking to meet you at Bar Marmont. When you didn't come home I went there but it looks like you two met up nicely. I also heard the message from what's her name, your mad analyst. What can I say? Sounds like you're not being very civilised in your own relationships, doll.'

'Oh that.'

'That.'

Basically we didn't watch the film. We had an argument instead. A stinker. A humdinger. And this time our verbal accusations weren't followed up with post-argument love-making. Quite the opposite really.

Put it this way, the headless lilies got off lightly. By the time we finished with the suite, it didn't recognise itself and nor did the poor guy with the studs in his tongue who came to see if everything was OK. When the Marmont starts asking questions you know you've taken your trouble a step too far.

Afterwards I took the plunge and did something I should have done while I was still a teen.

I peroxided my hair.

CHAPTER 14

'When you're in love with a married man you shouldn't wear mascara.'

The Apartment, 1960, b/w, Shirley Maclaine and
Jack Lemmon

'Throw the ball straight at my head, Daddy. Hard as
you can. Quickly Daddy, hard as you can.'

Rory threw the sponge ball with all his might and
sure enough it bounced off his daughter's head and
she giggled herself into a heap on the sand.

'He's *so* good with children,' Alexia said, staring
out to sea while I picked sand out of my cleavage.
'Don't you think he's a child himself in many ways?'

Turning around she looked at me enigmatically
over the top of dark Gucci sunglasses that hid most
of her face. 'But then *you'd* know that better than me,
wouldn't you Evie?'

I slumped back down in the sand, flattened by the

double entendre-ness of it all. Our dialogue together read like a B-grade thriller, only frankly it didn't thrill me at all. I think I preferred our scenes when they read like a day-time soap opera. At least I got to play the evil Other Woman then.

In this past week in which we'd rarely spent a moment apart, my role had been watered down into an inconsequential bit part. I was lucky if I got a line at all these days. Mostly I was just nodding my head agreeably or tearing up the leaves for a salad. We were doing a lot of salad eating, which frankly was ageing me.

I was still too young and reckless for salads; I was of an age for bingeing remorselessly on junk food and cocktails. For Alexia, sucking on a wheatgrass shake at an oxygen bar was her idea of letting her hair down. 'Are you sure all that H_2O is good for you? I mean don't you need some artificial colouring in these? I'd asked.

To which she'd replied, 'Gee Evie you are *soooooo* funny.'

Gee whiz, thanks.

My argument with Rory was now no doubt on file at the Marmont. I could envisage our antics going down in the mass database of Marmont legend. 'Château Marmont,' people would say, 'isn't that the place where Evelyn Hornton and her private eye had that big bust-up?'

Rory had decided to push my demand to know him better to the absolute limit. Either he was trying to break me or he took that saying 'know my ex-wife, know me' a little too literally.

Quite apart from the tricky interpersonal relationships involved in befriending my lover's ex-wife, I was finding the so-called pleasures of sun, sea and sand a bit of a challenge.

Joy in nature had always eluded me, perhaps it was the way the pony-fur heels of my Manolo Blahniks kept sinking in the wet sand, or the worry of salt damage to the red leather mini I was giving another chance to redeem itself, or maybe it was the way my tart-is-back cleavage kept filling up with sand. Whatever, let's just say I was not a successful beach babe.

I had the wrong attitude for the outdoors.

I had expectations that fresh air alone could never hope to fulfil.

Alexia on the other hand looked like a beach goddess incarnate. Her white bikini displaying her pert little boob enhancement job to perfection, her blonde hair windswept and positively natural looking in this environment, she was Marilyn Monroe (in her slim period) only altogether more sensible, intelligent, mature and Katharine Hepburn about it.

The woman had style. Not a style that would take her far at clubs such as Soho House in London or The Groucho at two in the morning. PS, I doubt she had ever stayed up beyond midnight in her life. But she had a certain undeniable cool, enough in fact to make me feel slightly chilly inside.

I was still very much in pain over Rory keeping such a monumental section of his past from me. I'd been resorting to melatonin to get to sleep. This morning I'd woken up at eleven in a dark glasses, selfish bitch sort of mood. I'd made so many threats before we set off that Rory was close to calling the excursion off.

PS, as if that would kill me!

'If she so much as mentions my impacting on Katy, I'll slap her so help me God!' I'd declared, digging out my most lethal heels in case I had to hit someone.

Manolo Blahnik should go down in history as one of the great weapon-makers of all time. I have this dream of US weapon inspectors uncovering a Blahnik shoe factory in Iraq and realising that Western hegemony as we know it is at an end.

'Calm down,' was Rory's advice. 'Alexia thinks you're great.'

So far though, neither Alexia nor Katy had ventured into any of the big no-no lands of my insecurity zones and as much as it was in my power, I was trying to be all dignified and Grace Kelly-ish in my forced casting as the Other Woman.

Alexia and I were behaving as model women basically. Both of us had something to lose, although she less than me. Both of us were jollying one another and the family at large along with our good humour and sunny outlooks. Complimentary, polite, respectful, not a talon or a tooth for miles. In the words of

Cliff Richard, we were walking, talking, breathing, faking, living dolls.

For all her clichéd, LA plastic babeness you had to hand it to Alexia though, she was surprisingly adept at these interpersonal relationship thingies. An expert at the safe detonation of emotional mines. Charles was on at me to ask her if she was a Scientologist or a user of mood-enhancing drugs.

'Get real Evv,' she said. 'No woman has a civilised relationship with their ex, let alone their ex's new lover unless they're a member of a cult or an intravenous mung bean user. Why, the best part of marriage is the settlement afterwards,' she assured me.

In her capacity of barrister to the rich and discreet, Charles has handled a lot of divorces. In fact, she was making quite a name for herself in the broken marriage field. *Vogue* had done a piece on her entitled, 'The Woman who has Legally Lynched a Thousand Feckless Husbands' Off-shore Accounts'.

After persuasive argument, I agreed to put the mung-bean use, Kabalah and Scientology issues to Alexia, but later on. Much later on – once we'd bonded – or superglued even.

It was a week now since Rory and I'd had our terrible argument, with me screaming about Alexia and Rory going ballistic about Giles and the poor bloke with the stud in his tongue lispingly trying to calm us both down. Although Rory hadn't admitted to witnessing Giles kissing me, I just knew he knew.

It paid to presume that Rory knew more than he was letting on because he usually did.

I guess it came down to jealousy. Maddy was always telling me that I must allow the people I love to have a past. 'Your love cannot erase a past love,' she would advise as I prattled on about my not-so-inner depths all those sessions.

In the light of Giles' rash dash to LA to declare his enduring love for me, perhaps Maddy was speaking from painful personal experience. I mean what if Giles had been going on about me? Boring Maddy with my masterful sexual wiles (very likely). Mysteriously I hadn't heard from him or Mads since the Bar Marmont kiss and I wasn't looking forward to that situation changing in the near future.

Katy, now wet and covered in sand, ran to Alexia, throwing her arms around her and kissing her all over her face. Alexia swept her into her lap seemingly content to have her white bikini muddied with wet sand and returned Katy's cuddles and kisses. In motherhood she was splendid, her plastic babeness humanised somehow by her love for Katy.

'Do you want a drink of water, pumpkin?' she asked, pressing Katy's little button nose.

'I want Coke, like Evvy gives me,' she said solemnly, referring to yesterday when Rory and I had taken her to the cinema.

'Coke dissolves your stomach lining,' Alexia explained primly, throwing me a dirty 'remember-whose kid-this-is' kind of look.

I blushed crimson. 'That's true Katy. I had to have mine replaced several times by the time I was ten.'

'Really?' she asked, staring at me the way she had on first meeting the new blonder me. 'My daddy says that blonde doesn't suit you,' she'd said solemnly. 'But I think he's wrong. You look nice.'

It was the greatest compliment I'd ever received and I loved her for it. Even if, as in this instance, her daddy was right. I looked frightful. Like a cornfed chicken, all yellow and dried out.

I'd rung Stefan in the middle of the night for a rescue remedy but he was so furious with me for daring to touch my own hair that he had insisted I put up with it. 'Let it be your sackcloth and ashes,' he'd insisted in his weird Russian-cum-North of England accent. 'Maybe then you'll learn to leave well enough alone.'

Rory came over and sat beside me, sensing nothing. As far as he was concerned he saw no reason why, as women who loved him, Alexia and I shouldn't get on famously.

He smelt of the sea and I wanted to lick it off him but dignity for once prevailed. If you want to be rendered frigid, just try kissing the man you love in front of his ex-wife and his child. Nothing like it for drying up the sexual juices.

Rory seemed to suffer no such qualms though. Licking my cheek, he declared me sweet. 'Why do you always taste like sweet coffee?' he teased, running his tongue over my mouth.

I blushed, feeling Alexia flinch beside me.

'Because I drink so much of the bloody stuff,' I laughed, deciding to play our intimacy in a jokey comedic sense as opposed to the smulchy. I looked over at Alexia to give her a smile but she was pretending to be absorbed in wrapping Katy up in a big fluffy towel. The irritation was steaming off her.

'You taste like that cappuccino ice cream, that's what it is,' he announced as he sat behind me and snuggled into my neck. I fought him off valiantly for the sake of Alexia's feelings and rolled my eyes at her in a sisterly 'men, who needs them' kind of way. But she ignored me and gazed out to sea where a group of supermen were waxing surfboards.

We chatted aimlessly about shark attacks for a while as the LA sun beat down on my chemically enhanced head and I thought longingly of air-conditioned hotels.

I was jolted back to reality when Alexia asked Rory to rub sunblock into her back.

There was nothing suggestive in the way she asked and nothing suspect in the way he took to the task but I could feel my brain moving away from its cranial moorings as a *Natural Born Killers* side of my character rose to the surface.

My upper lip must have curled because Rory made a face at me and set to applying the stuff with as little enthusiasm as he could muster without actually saying, 'This is a disgusting task that I wish I wasn't being forced to perform. At least not in front of my girlfriend.'

'Mmmmmm,' sighed Alexia, wriggling into the sand like an eel.

'Mmmmmm,' I replied, frisking myself for a weapon. Finding several – shoes, nail varnish remover, scissors and tweezers, I relaxed. We had *détente*.

'He's good at this sort of thing, isn't he?' Alexia joked when he spilt some on her bikini.

'A master,' I agreed. 'God knows why he bothers to do anything else. He should hire himself out on Palm Beach for fifty cents a back job.'

Rory scowled at me with a look that said I was going too far again.

I couldn't help it though. I was a savage in their civilised midst, unworthy to be in their please and thank you, let's-avoid-the-courts orbit.

I fell silent and seethed, laying out my weapons on my lap.

Rory asked Katy to race him down to the waves and Alexia said she'd join them. I agreed to mind the stuff, not being especially capable of running along the shoreline in high heels. The idea of taking them off didn't even occur to me – these days I wondered if I could even walk without a few inches' support in the heel department and frankly I wasn't prepared to risk the humiliation of trying. My gran was always saying that 'Heels maketh the woman!' and now wasn't the time to risk being unmade.

I watched them as they dashed along the shoreline,

this family unit I was struggling to see myself grafted to, laughing and joking and enjoying one another. They were clearly anything but dysfunctional, they were so functional in fact that it was hard not to feel like a spare screw left over after the making of a fine Swiss watch.

How could I ever be anything but a second-stratum citizen in their world? If Coupledom was complicated, this three-parent family option seemed three times as daunting. As to whether or not it was what I wanted, I couldn't hope to make a decision.

I could hardly chat to friends to ask what the three-parent family was really like. There were no support groups in place for erstwhile single girls wishing to graft themselves onto readymade families. Especially when that family has officially split. Was my love for Rory great enough to make the sacrifice?

The thing about being in love is that unlike cow manure it's really hard to know when you are definitely in it. You instinctively know you've stepped in something sticky but unlike shit, love doesn't have a distinctive aroma. Without Mads to guide me, I was lost. Drifting.

What's more I was due to go back to Chambers in another week and still nothing had been resolved. What had started out as an orgasm litmus test had turned into a family domestic pantomime. With me playing the back end of the donkey.

With Coupledom at least I roughly knew what I was getting – cosy nights in, compromise and the odd candle-lit dinner. When I'd asked Rory what my role would be he'd told me the only roll I'd have would be in the hay. But his smart alec remarks didn't comfort me.

Katy was skipping along the shoreline, her little feet splashing water. Rory was pretending to be terrified of the water and Alexia and Katy were enjoying trying to spray him with it. I was envious of their laughter and their easy way with one another and found myself wondering why they had ever split up. Rory was tightlipped on the issue.

When Alexia scored a goal, completely drenching Rory's face, it was hard not to compare myself with this woman who without doubt knew Rory far better than I. She had borne his child and taken those sickness and health vows. Both tasks to which I felt unequal. What had I ever done for him – put on his condom and lent him a T-shirt? Hardly a case for eternal love and devotion.

The mobile rang in Alexia's bag and without thinking I answered it.

'Lexy?' Hi, it's Daniel. How's it going?'

I froze. Cryogenics had its latest specimen.

I had tried not to think about Daniel since the night at Bar Marmont when I'd seen him put his arm around Alexia. Tried. There was nothing intrinsically sinister about the action, nor with Daniel and Alexia being friends – or lovers even, for that matter.

Alexia was a fully-fledged divorced woman after all, free to date and fuck whom she chose. But there was something very wrong with the vibrator in my stomach. Switched on full, it was drilling a shuddering route down through my body.

'Alexia? Are you there?' he asked.

I switched the mobile off and placed it back in Alexia's bag. They were running back now. Holding hands, the breakfast-cereal perfect family. Sitting there with the bloody vibrator still drilling away in my belly I had never felt more isolated, more confused, more lacking in breakfast-cereal qualities.

What braindead, sicko idiot said blondes have more fun?

CHAPTER 15

'It doesn't matter who gives them as long as you never wear anything second-rate. Wait for the first-class jewels, Gigi. Hold onto your ideals.'

Gigi, 1958, colour, Leslie Caron and
Maurice Chevalier

What became clear over the next few days was that Rory and I were treading water in this *ménage à trois* thingamy. Despite our attempts at bonding via beach picnics and shared salads, it was going to take more than a tan and a wheatgrass shake to get this three-parent concept off the ground.

Maybe it was my fault, maybe I just didn't have the will for it.

I was transferring, in denial and deeply regressed and repressed. For a girl just dumped by her therapist it was too much to ask me to compromise my needs as a deeply self-centred individual. For this relationship to work I had to make sacrifices that I wasn't sure I could make for any man, no matter how good his pecs. But I wasn't able to express this in a way that didn't sound hard-nosed.

I knew that it was shallow of me to allow Rory's past with Alexia and Katy to preclude a future for the two of us. Mads would have said I was running from dilemma again and she would have been spot on.

Rory and Alexia both had this idea that with a bit of effort on my part, I could annex myself onto their relationship as a sort of granny-flat on the main house. But I'm a girl who requires space, masses of it. I'm a natural born loft-dweller. Made for whooping it up solo in my spacious acres of cityscape loftspace, not living the life of an au pair in a basement flat.

Joining a couple required major sacrifices and maybe I'd been living too long alone to make those sacrifices.

Some girls might relish the opportunity of joining a readymade family but I couldn't help feeling that I was being asked to join a cult. A sort of Lovers of Rory Society.

'Just give it a try,' Rory would whine. 'For my sake?'

I told him that he sounded like a messiah when he said stuff like that.

Whenever a man asks you to do something for *their* sake you know it's time to hand in your chips. 'Girls stopped doing things for the sake of men years ago,' I told him. 'Sisters are doing it for themselves now Rory.'

'Well do it for Katy then,' he argued in a sort of 'this one's for the kipper' John Wayne voice.

The sticking point was never Katy of course. I loved Katy. Katy was a dream, about as problem-free as a girl could be. She could run courses for less dreamy girls.

The problem was her mother. When Alexia and I didn't mesh as ultimate Barbie sisters, I felt like I was failing in some grown-up skill, like I was an immature child caught up in a complex adult game. Rory kept reassuring me that Alexia really liked me but I found that hard to believe. Any way you looked at the situation between the three of us, it was obvious that she could live without me as easily as I could live without her.

I know this was California but despite Charles' suspicions, Alexia didn't look like an intravenous mung-bean user to me and she had vociferously denied any links with Scientology. She was a mother and a career woman who wanted the focus on her daughter. Now how could I blame her for that?

I suggested to her that as long I was here in LA making whoopee with her daughter's father, surely I was blocking that focus?

Alexia promised me that I had her all wrong. 'I want Rory to be fulfilled. Honestly, I hope that we can all be friends. I want to engage with you about your dilemmas and see if we can't work them out,

Evelyn. Rory and I have decided to honour our commitment as Katy's parents by staying together. That doesn't mean we can't explore fulfilling relationships with other people. It's called staying together for the sake of the children, nineties style,' she explained. 'We've taken the martyrdom out of the equation, that's all.'

Mads would have loved Alexia. These two could be psychological clones.

Just the same, my Catholic guilt couldn't help but kick me in the groin on this one. My conscience kept calling me names like 'home-wrecker', and watching Alexia and Rory together it was hard not to imagine them patching up their differences and getting back together. If only I wasn't involved.

They had an easy shorthand with one another that I remember finding so endearing in my own parents.

Even in argument they were a perfect match. They could push the elastic of their relationship out as much as they liked with the smug knowledge that it would bounce right back again. They had that kiss-and-make-up kind of way with each other as opposed to the fuck-and-make-up love which he and I enjoyed.

And then of course there was the Katy issue. How could I stand in the way of a father's love for his daughter?

Obviously I couldn't.

'Being the blonde seductress isn't as easy as it

looks,' I told Charles in a midnight phone call. 'The fun has still yet to begin.'

'You know it's not right Evv,' she said in her stern voice. 'Please come home to London.'

'I can't,' I told her. 'I'm in love with him. How can I walk out on a dad?'

'I think there's one of those *Hundred And One Ways To . . .* books on that actually, Ev. Do you want me to send it over?' she asked.

The most surprising thing about all this I guess was that Rory was such a brilliant father. He was so careful with Katy, so obliging and gentle and I loved him for it. I couldn't help feeling all Meg Ryan-ish whenever I saw him perform simple tasks like helping her on with her little sun hat so that her curls came out evenly around the sides.

But none of this Meg Ryan-ness could outweigh my own dilemma, which was tied up in a survivalist drive to drag Rory away from Alexia. I hated the thought of what she was to Rory – the ultimate role for any woman in a man's heart – the mother of his child. I was weak and greedy and selfish but I couldn't help it.

Even with method coaching, my script with Rory just didn't work with Alexia and Katy on the set. I was one of those primadonna actresses who have to play the diva in every play. Only hitch was I had one of those directors who wanted to stick me in a cinematic crowd scene.

Alexia and Rory could be as civilised as they

liked and Katy was without question the sweetest girl an other woman could hope for but the fact remained that Alexia and I were on the wrong side of the Rory divide. Me on the actively insecure and needing round-the-clock reassurance side, and Alexia on the secure, needing twenty-four-hour co-parent commitment side.

I was jealous. I was behaving selfishly and no matter how much I thought about it I had no intention of modifying my desires.

According to Rory they hadn't slept together for over a year but I wasn't so sure. There was a chemistry between them that suggested a more recent pairing. To add to my doubts, when I'd pressed this point, Rory had stormed out Clark Gable-like into the night. He'd come back in the early hours of the morning and made love to me.

But that only made me feel worse.

Without meaning to I had focused all my paranoias on Alexia and my attentions on Katy. Big mistake that. The way to any little girl's heart is through her mom but like I said, I was running from my dilemmas. I thought that this little girl and this mom were different.

I thought that if I could get a relationship up and running with Katy, then Alexia would go into fade out and a triumphant throbbing music would start playing as Rory embraced me and the credits came up.

I took Katy shopping for shoes at Barneys and

when Rory queried whether it was necessary to buy her fourteen pairs, I accused him of repressing her dreams.

'But fourteen?'

'Always start them young on their fetishes,' I told him. '"Choose a fetish and stick to it," my gran always said.'

Rory dropped it, knowing that when it came to one of Gran's theories on life he was beat.

'At least shoes are a relatively safe form of anti-depressant,' I reminded him. 'I'm not getting her hooked on prescription drugs.'

'Just don't let Alexia hear you say that,' he said, shaking his head.

The next day I took her to lunch at Spago's on Rory's expense account.

Spago's was where he wined, dined and met his clients in LA. Katy didn't just know her way around the menu, she knew her way around the kitchen and a good many of the guests' tables too. The kid had savvy.

Americans love a precocious child and she was a Shirley Temple rubber stamp, only without the puppy fat. Take a kid into a restaurant in London and you're made to feel like you're trying to smuggle in kitchen waste. It all came down to the hatred of aspirations thing again, I guess. As in, how revolting of you to aspire to the pleasures of adult dining before you can even walk!

She had started to sit on my knee. The night before

she had asked me to read her a bedtime story. Katy and I were so alike she could have been my daughter. Not that I have ever wanted a child, but if I had one I would want her to be just like Katy.

Together we took LA by storm, including all the corny tourist stuff like the Universal Studio tour where we posed as covergirls for *Barbie* magazine. We went to Grauman's Chinese Theatre where we tried out all the stars' handprints for size and squeezed into a photobooth together, and spent ten bucks pulling funny faces. But with every bond I forged with Katy, I was putting further strain on my already flimsy bonds with Alexia.

In his desire to see things work out between us, Rory had become a sort of carer, guiding me to enjoy family fun where he should have been guiding me into bed. As a consequence, our sex life suffered. Since our screaming row the week before, we had been talking into the night instead of writhing into it in a heap of passion.

Then, to top it all off, I had started having fantasies about Daniel.

It started off with a natural curiosity about the phone call I'd accidentally picked up on the beach. A normal enough desire to get to the bottom of who he was to Alexia. I've no doubt that if I was still seeing Mads in her professional capacity as my therapist, she would have had a lot to say about this.

I'd started fishing for clues. Asking Alexia about lawyers in LA as if I was thinking of setting up practice. But Alexia didn't bite. Despite taking to the idea with ill-concealed delight that I was considering my granny-flat option, she didn't mention Daniel's name once. Instead she gave me pamphlets on taking the Californian law exams.

I started asking her about her love life and progressed to bluntly asking her if there was anyone special? Anyone Rory was aware of?

'Not yet,' she'd answered demurely. I knew better than to believe her.

I started fingering Daniel's business card when I was alone. I told myself it was just a form of escapism. I tried to justify my erotic fantasies as harmless and irrelevant compared to my great and noble love for Rory. Yeah, right.

I flirted with the idea of calling his analyst for an appointment and probing her about Daniel but my traveller's cheques wouldn't have stretched that far.

'What about lawyers in a professional sense,' I asked Alexia one night at her house at Palm Beach. 'Is there anyone in particular you consult?'

It was my first invitation to dinner with Rory and Alexia's 'friends in common' as they referred to them. I started off on the wrong foot by saying that *Friends in Common* sounded like a bad sixties' rock band.

There was a couple from the beach-house next door, she was around fifty, an agent, and Bart was a model who looked fifteen although he made a big deal about being twenty-five.

'Yeah right and I'm Posh Spice,' I said.

Unfortunately he seemed to take this in all seriousness and proceeded to stare at me over dinner and cornered me before dessert to ask for my autograph.

There was an English ex-pat, Sarah, who was making loads of money as a sitcom writer. She was very quiet and became defensive when I asked about her work. Alexia explained that she found the creative process very painful and didn't like talking about it.

There was a guy with hennaed hair who used to play keyboard with a big eighties' heavy metal band and claimed to have attempted suicide in one of the Château bungalows. He wanted to talk about the conditions that led to his attempt on his own life for most of the night but I managed to cut him off at the pass by offering him our suite for another try.

There was a mute woman who turned out to be on a speech fast which I accidentally broke by admitting that the fur on my pony-fur Blahniks was the real thing. She became very vocal after that.

To save me from her guests or more probably her guests from me, Alexia linked arms with me and took me off on a tour of the house, in which Rory's room was pointed out with special fuss. Looking in I couldn't imagine Rory inhabiting the space for a minute. It was so clean and airy and minimalist, with a startlingly beautiful view of the sea.

We stood at the doorway together, two girls both

wishing we could look inside one another's heads this easily.

'Such a view,' I sighed. 'It's a wonder he can drag himself away.'

'Oh believe me he can,' she lamented. 'Duty calls the man from his pleasure, as you no doubt have realised Evie.'

I closed the door purposefully. 'Let's leave him *some* privacy,' I said leading her down the corridor of her own home.

'Now tell me about the lawyers you deal with in your work,' I pressured.

'Actually you should meet Daniel Silverberg,' she told me and that was when I knew I was in danger. The vibrator went off in my stomach again at the mention of his name.

'If you want to explore the selling of your antics as a woman barrister you should speak to Daniel,' she said later in the evening, tossing an oil-free dressing around the rocket leaves. 'Like I said, I don't really deal in film but Daniel would be able to advise you.'

Rory was over by the sink removing the cork from the wine and so he couldn't have seen the look on my face as I requested that she set up just such a meeting.

CHAPTER 16

'Whenever I'm caught between two evils, I take the one I've never tried.'

Mae West (1892–1980)

I woke up wrapped up in Rory's arms and legs. We had made *Fatal Attraction* love. I know I say that all the time but maybe it was true, maybe it did just get better and better, or was it just kinkier and kinkier? Maybe we were the perfect match after all. Maybe it was destiny?

Surely if the sex was the full Chinese fireworks sex that most people only dream of, our love must be destined? These are the sort of thoughts I was having that morning as my orgasms rushed through every fibre of my body. The guy with the stud in his tongue, to whom I'd started to turn for advice, said that if I had to question it all so much I had a problem. To which my riposte had been that if I don't question it, I've had far too much to drink.

After the *Fatal Attraction* sex, as the dawn light bathed us in pink, I'd held on to Rory like a duvet on a winter's night, as if trying to cover every inch of my body with his love and he had kissed me with small fluttering kisses that made me feel more feminine than I'd ever imagined possible without wearing heels from Agent Provocateur.

We had shared the same roll-up cigarette and while I was choking on a bit of stray tobacco that went down my throat, Rory told me he loved me more than he'd ever loved anyone in his life and asked me to stay in LA.

'I can't bear to think of life without you,' he'd mused while I choked to death in his arms.

But nothing was simple in our equation. For one I was meeting Daniel the next day. Alexia had set up the rendezvous. It was all so hellishly complicated and yet I had to meet Daniel again, I simply had to resolve this feeling in my belly every time I thought of him.

It was a madness that needed quelling, that was what I told myself as betrayal of my attraction to Daniel sizzled through my conscience like rain on a hot pavement.

One thing was beginning to dawn on me as the scheduled time for my departure drew closer, and that was that I wanted a man with a clean slate. Was that too much to ask? I mean, shouldn't that be a woman's inalienable right, like safe sex and clean sheets?

PS. Apparently not in the age of the post-nuclear family, according to my guy with the stud in his tongue.

With one in three marriages ending in divorce, there are a lot of relationships with baggage out there. Look at Giles! Without even marrying the man I had become his baggage. I mean it wasn't as if I had a say in the matter or anything. As far as he was concerned, he was going to carry me around for the rest of his life. I was weighing him down, making his life with another woman impossible. Bloody hell.

In my time-consuming attempts at happy family bonding, I guess I'd forgotten about Giles. I'd sort of hoped that he might have slunk back to Maddy – prehensile tail between legs sort of thing, and that all had been forgiven.

I'd been watching too many romantic videos at night, movies with love-conquers-all plots. Last count for *Sleepless in Seattle* – five times.

Anyway I was pretty damn shocked when Maddy turned up at Château Marmont that morning after Rory left to take Katy to her first day at playgroup. The first thing she made clear was that no such mushy scenarios were even close to being in the offing.

'You've ruined him for anyone else,' she told me as she flew into my suite like an Exocet missile.

I'd opened the door to her, hoping it was the guy with the stud in his tongue, bringing me my morning coffee and *brioche*.

'You'd better come in,' I told her, pulling the cord

of my robe tightly around me in case Mads had plans to rip it off and strangle me with it.

She looked unkempt and, well, mad really and I began to feel a little wary. Her hair was all frizzed up and sticking out and she looked like she might have even had a nose-job reversal. Only on closer inspection the problem turned out to be a huge pimple that seemed to throb when she yelled.

'What have you done to your hair?' she yelled. She looked as if she wanted to do a lot of yelling.

I stayed close to the door, ready to run, and hoped she'd exhaust herself with words before she got round to actual physical violence.

'Well I thought it might give me a bit of a lift,' I explained thinking that she was the proverbial pot calling the kettle black – or blonde, as was the case.

'You look like a corn-fed chicken,' she sneered, and then went on to detail all my physical imperfections and how my looks were fading. 'You'll be left with nothing but your legs if you're not careful.'

'I'll keep that in mind,' I told her.

'I suppose it means nothing to you that I've done nothing but gorge on chocolate since you stole him,' she sighed eventually, slumping on my unmade bed.

I didn't know what to say to her.

Here was the woman who had been guiding me down the dark forest tracks of my inner-self for months, like a French farmer with a prize truffle pig. Now here I was, positively sated with truffly goodies and she was looking as if she'd just been mauled. I wasn't in character for this role.

'Where is he?' she hissed, looking about the room as if I'd taken him hostage and hidden him.

I imagined Giles bound and gagged, tumbling forth from my cupboard. Nothing would have surprised me that morning.

'I haven't seen him for a week, I imagined he'd gone back to you,' I assured her.

That was when she started up again on the 'you've ruined him for any other woman' speech. Feeling a bit sorry for her, I went over and sat on the bed beside her, nodding sympathetically to her ranting, until she fell into a fit of uncontrollable sobbing and I had to hold her.

'There, there,' I said ineffectually, patting her on the back. For those of you who've never experienced the tears before breakfast of your therapist, let me tell you it's pretty disconcerting stuff. Not the sort of carry-on a girl's up for before she's been fortified with a few strong coffees and a bit of lipstick.

'He thinks that you are Elizabeth Taylor to his Richard Burton,' she blubbered. 'You can't live together but you can't live apart. He said he can't run from the dilemma any more,' she wailed, snotting into my hotel-issue robe.

'Brilliant, he can't run *from* dilemma so he runs *at* it,' I exploded. 'And guess who gets to play the role of Giles' dilemma? Me, that's who! Now

I've got him running at me like a berserker at a hallucinogenic mushroom and let's remember, I'm not the star in this production. I'm actually doing my own stunts here Mads, and I'm not even industry registered.'

She looked at me like I was unhinged but I carried on.

'I could get hurt and I didn't even audition for the role of Giles's dilemma. Have you thought of that Mads? I'm the passive party here.'

Mads laughed despite herself and I gave her a more comfortable hug.

'Have you got chocolate in your mini-bar?' she asked.

'Mads,' I told her, all proud of myself, 'I've got a maxi-bar with Toblerone for all. I've got enough chocolate for you to suppress even your strongest emotions.'

'I can't hate you despite my inner voice. But I do blame you,' she warned, snuffling up a Toblerone bar while it was practically still in the wrapper.

'And I don't blame you for blaming me,' I told her. 'Not that I did anything wrong Mads. Not a bit of it. It was all totally unexpected from my point of view. I love Rory now. Giles is a no-go area for me. You know how much I love Rory.'

'Actually, you weren't certain of your feelings for him last time we spoke,' she reminded me.

'Right, yes, that's right. Well anyway I'm definitely not still in love with Giles. I was always sure of that.

He did come here though and we did talk. I told him he was afraid of commitment and I haven't seen him since. I imagined he'd gone back to you on bended knee,' I explained.

Her face was brown with chocolate now but I could see she wasn't satisfied so I released the frozen Kit Kat from the freezer that I was saving for a special occasion. It was time to make sacrifices for the greater good of sisterhood, my inner voice told me.

Mads snatched it from me without a thank you, the way wolf children do in the wild. She was still chomping her way through the icy bits as she walked over to the window. I followed her, more or less panicking that she was thinking of jumping out.

'You're certainly comfortable here then,' she remarked with alacrity, leaning out of the window to take in the view.

'Rory's paying,' I explained hastily in case she thought I'd been putting off paying her bill under false pretences. 'Actually I'm having a lot of trouble in my own relationship,' I admitted, in an attempt at bonding. 'You wouldn't read about it, but it turns out that Rory was married to a blonde babe and even has a kid. Can you believe it – I've been having sex with a daddy? Not that the kid, Katy's her name, isn't adorable. I actually adore her, she's got a clothes fixation a bit like my own.'

'Huh!' was all she had to offer.

I continued. 'He's got a civilised relationship with his own room and he wants me to live a granny-flat sort of existence annexed to his relationship with his ex. Only as it turns out Alexia's not an ex in the strictest sense of the word. Not that they sleep together.'

'There he is, down there,' she yelled, interrupting my flow.

'Oh no, he's with Katy at her new school,' I explained calmly. The poor woman seemed a bit crazed. 'He's meeting the headmistress. Duty calls, or whatever that Latin quote is from Cicero. You know the thing.'

'It's fucking him I tell you!' Poor thing was beside herself.

'There are a lot of blokes with bodies like his down there. For London I know he looks like a freak but over here they breed them like that. It's the wheatgrass they feed them see.'

'He's bloody down there in a rubber ring,' she insisted, turning round and staring at me like she was about to take the strangulation by bathrobe belt option.

I began to feel a bit afraid, actually. I took a step back. Her hair was madder and wilder than before now, all over the place. And the pimple on her nose was throbbing, glowing yellow like a piece of active uranium.

The guy with the stud in his tongue arrived with the coffee just as Mads swooped out of the room, knocking his gorgeous little silver pot and white napkin arrangement for six.

'I'll order another breakfast for your, er, friend shall I?' he lisped.

CHAPTER 17

'Being a sex symbol is a heavy load to carry, especially when one is tired, hurt and bewildered.'

Marilyn Monroe (1926–62)

The poolside looked like the set of *Waterworld* by the time Rory turned up. Giles was in a semi-liquid heap. I was on the other side of the pool, standing by the suicide bungalows, while Giles was being sorted by a team of testosterone-enhanced medics. Mads was beside him.

There were about half a dozen sexy-as-hell cops milling about the scene, writing in notebooks and talking on walkie-talkies.

The cops wanted to know what, how, who and for how much this debacle was all about. I think they were still piecing together the basic clues as to why they had even been called in but I wasn't being much help. This wasn't the bunch of guys to get anything coherent from me. I wasn't up for anything more than ogling where they were concerned.

The sun beat down and the Marlboro Man looked on in scorn as if saying, 'With friends like these, and you think lung cancer's dangerous? Pah-lease!'

'I was having a bad lipstick moment,' I explained to the sexy cop with the pencil who had asked if I'd noticed anything. 'Strike that. I was having a *no*-lipstick moment. On top of that my legs needed shaving and my hair needed washing and no doubt there was the odd eyebrow hair that needed plucking. I wouldn't have noticed an earthquake in that state.'

The cops shook their heads ruefully and wandered away to get what they could out of the groups of gawpers who'd abandoned their morning ablutions, their sex, their personal exercise programme and their power breakfasts to come and watch the suicide chump by the pool.

Everyone there was asking stuff like, 'What's he been in?' and 'How was he trying to do it?' There was a nasty rumour circulating that it might have been an attempt at auto-erotic asphyxiation.

The little Australian guy who'd tried to sell me the snaps of the day-time soap star in the shower was out with his camera, looking all professional and happening. He had a tripod and expensive-looking lights. He was taking reams of shots of the distressed Giles, the equally if not more distressed Maddy and anyone else whom he mistakenly took for a Somebody.

Rory was gripping my wrists like I might join the

throng and become hysterical at any minute. It had more or less miffed me that his first question on arriving at the scene was not, 'Are you OK?' but, 'What are they arresting you for?'

'They're not arresting *me* for anything,' I snapped. 'I was innocently waiting for my breakfast to arrive.'

'So this whole mess here is nothing to do with you then?' he asked doubtfully, gesturing around the pool. 'Nothing to do with Evelyn Hornton and her well-known propensity for drama?'

'No, it's nothing to do with me,' I huffed. 'Well not directly at least. It was Giles, you see, you know my ex-super-bastard? He's had a bit of a disaster really with that black pool ring thing.'

Rory's initial relief that I wasn't being arrested for anything immediately turned to black fury when he heard the name, Giles. He looked at the scene on the other side of the pool again and clocked Giles, limp beneath a pile of Chippendale lifesavers.

Last time he'd seen Giles, I'd just recently slugged him, so Rory had only ever seen him in a pile of curls, curled up on the ground, nursing his manhood. Giles tends to have that effect on stilettos.

'What's the matter with him? Fall off his insteps?' he sneered.

I ignored his tone and delivered my explanation deadpan. 'He fell asleep in that tyre ring thing in the pool last night apparently. Anyway, when he woke up this morning he couldn't feel his backside because it had sunk into the middle of the rubber ring and all the circulation had stopped so he kind of panicked that it might have fallen off.'

'Let me stop you there.' Rory looked at me like I was a cabaret act about to shock. I was glad though that his jealousy was being overtaken by amusement. It was safer in the long run. 'His what got stuck?' he asked, controlling a smirk.

'His bum – you know, the lump at the top of the thighs, the glutus maximus? All right the ass.' I tried to keep all humour out of my voice as I explained the skeleton details of the case. It was one thing for me to laugh at Giles and his predicament but I didn't think either Giles or Mads would appreciate other people seeing the humour in this misery. It was a losing battle though.

Rory was already beginning to chuckle. 'Let me get this straight, this whole mess is all about Giles' ass. He got his ass stuck in a rubber ring?'

'Well more or less, you see it slipped in the ring thing while he was sleeping. It's not funny actually. A lot of people here are telling him that he should sue. I mean don't you think he should have been warned by the hotel management?'

'What for, sue them for not warning him about what? The dangers of sticking your ass in places it don't fit. Give me a break.'

'Whatever you might or might not think smart-ass, the fact remains that Giles fell asleep while he was lying in the ring, supplied by the management of this establishment.'

'Yeah? And?'

'Think of him there,' I said, feeling a bit of prose coming on. 'An Englishman in LA, looking up at the stars, thinking about his true love. Thinking about how he might have made a jolly big mistake running away from a commitment he now knows to be good and desirous. Perhaps frantic with worry that he might have lost his one true love for the sake of a long-dead infatuation. Some people might see it as a romantic accident.'

'Some people might think you need therapy.'

'Spare me.'

'Sorry. You've got to admit it all sounds a bit weird.'

'Whatever,' I said in my haughtiest legal mastermind voice. 'The fact remains that he was in that position for like hours, all night really. Think about it – his backside in cool water. Imagine waking up in that state.'

'I'd rather not if it's all the same to you doll.'

I could see that my efforts to get Rory's sympathy weren't working. He was still looking at me like I was about to introduce myself as the latest act at the Comedy Store. Only now the smirk was getting the better of him.

He was watching Giles on the other side of the pool.

Giles wasn't doing my case any good either. He was making a massive fuss with the medics who were trying to get some basic information out of him. Like what the fuck happened that led to the emergency services being called? They were really itching to arrest someone. Anyone. I could see their point. I mean, LA is the sort of place that gives the emergency services a pretty tough workout. You don't come here as a medic unless you are prepared for the worst. Skinny Limeys with their bums in rubber rings wasn't really what these guys were dreaming about when they signed up for basic life-saving skills.

Mads wasn't helping either. She kept making these noises that sounded like she was rehearsing for a role in an Alfred Hitchcock film. Eventually one of the Hollywood types (tanned, toned and fully oiled) threw a bucket of water over her which happened to drench one of the medics' nice white uniforms. He didn't look happy.

Rory chuckled.

I continued. 'It must be pretty terrifying waking up to find you can't feel your ass don't you think? I mean, he probably wasn't fully awake and he just kind of lost it.'

The muscles of Rory's face then gave up the fight to stay serious and he was openly smirking with a view to breaking into full belly laughter. 'What do you mean, lost it? His ass or his nerve?'

'Both I guess.'

'Let me do a reality check doll, just to make sure that we're both on the same page here. Giles here thought that his ass had fallen off into the pool. Are you kidding me. I mean you dated this guy! Not once but twice. Am I right?'

I ignored his slur on my romantic history and carried on with my explanation. 'Maddy saw him struggling from our room. She'd come to visit me and just happened to be looking out at the view.'

'Some view, a nerd with his ass stuck in a rubber ring. Christ, look at the guy.'

Admittedly Giles was looking like a bit of a Nancy boy – blubbing all over the medics. His behaviour was less than might be expected from an ambassador of the land of stiff upper lips. His lips, both upper and lower, were like jelly.

'They've both been under a lot of strain lately. I think you might show a bit more sympathy,' I chastised. 'You're becoming hard and brittle in your old age and anyway they've given him a shot of Valium now so he'll probably start to calm down.'

As I said this, Giles fell into a sort of limp slump and a very wet Maddy had to prop his head in her lap. I mean, they were my friends and all but I wasn't exactly feeling proud of them at this precise moment. Even though as far as the midget Australian went it was a sublime Kodak moment.

'So what about all the police? I'll buy the story as far as the medics go but surely it's not a crime to drop your ass in a pool in LA?'

'Oh yeah, the police. That's a bit complicated. Well when people heard all the noise they thought they had a rock star in one of the bungalows killing themselves or doing one of those auto-erotic asphyxiation things. Erring on the side of caution and all that, the hotel dialled the LA cops.'

'Will he be all right?' he spluttered, holding his hand up to his face to block his laughter. He reminded me of Katy when she laughed. The medics were looking at Rory – none too impressed by his sense of comedy, judging by the way their eyes glinted. The wet one was looking especially annoyed.

'Well maybe not *all* right,' I joked, failing in my efforts to be reasonable and appreciating how it must look to Rory – to anyone really. Even me.

In all honesty, Giles was never all right in the strictest sense of the word, well not in a late twentieth-century sense anyway. Giles was still having trouble getting himself hooked up to the century, let alone the world wide web.

Let's face it, this little incident was hardly going to improve his sense of contemporary worth. I mean in terms of reputation, this was not one of Giles' red letter days. Everyone around the pool was wound up in the excitement of the moment. In time though, they would see the inherent bathos in Giles and his butt. It was a good thing really that he lived on the other side of the world and would probably never have to face this crowd again.

But my sense of loyalty to him prevented me expressing this point. Instead I told Rory that in time Giles would recover. 'Anyway,' I said, dragging him over to Giles and his now incoherent, crumpled form. 'I want you to meet Madeline Bishop, my therapist.'

Madeline was leaning over Giles, sobbing her analytical little heart out so I just pointed down at her fizz and prayed she wouldn't look up and defame me as an ex-patient who had been sacked for stealing her man.

Unfortunately she did look up, only not to defame me. The pimple looked more hellish than before and her face was streaked with tears and grime. I can't deny it, love her as I do, she looked pretty damn horrifying at that moment – like she'd just been to a casting for *Things To Do In Denver When You're Dead*.

I made a mental note to pencil her in for a trip to the Aida Thibiant's European Day Spa down at Little Santa Monica Boulevard in Beverly Hills. It was the least I could do. Love her as I did, Mads was a woman who needed a serious going over with a loofah, a brush and a lot of expensive product.

Rory recoiled. 'What's the matter with her?' he hissed in my ear.

'What do you mean, what's the matter with her?' I hissed back in my no-nonsense barrister hiss. 'The woman's a therapist, a heart the size of a planet. OK, admittedly her personal dynamics are a bit strained at the minute but she had a nasty fright when she heard Giles screaming blue murder in the pool.'

'Yeah sure,' he said. 'I understand, loving a guy who just got his bum stuck in a rubber ring can't be easy but shit, will you look at the size of that pimple.' Rory, in all his perfection, wasn't big on tolerance.

'As a therapist she can empathise with his pain. A bit of empathy might suit you Rory,' I suggested, taking him aside. 'I mean it's a humiliating experience for a guy still dealing with the fact that he was bullied by his fag at Eton. She's grieving for his lost pride, that's all.'

'That'll take a while then. There's a lot of lost pride to grieve over in his case.'

I've got to be honest, there was no love lost between Rory and Giles. It's one of their guy rules. Guys don't like other guys that have dated their gal. I'd like to see a woman try to pull off what Rory was trying to pull off with Alexia and me.

I told Rory this after I'd organised a room for Mads and Giles and we'd finally got back to our room and ordered brunch.

'But it's completely different. Besides you and Giles never had a kid, so why on earth would you want to stay friends?' He laughed, a sort of fake insouciant chuckle, and I realised I'd hit a nerve.

'How about for old times' sake? How about because we want to stay friends?'

Rory uttered something incomprehensible and shoved a Danish pastry into his mouth. 'By the way, Alexia's invited us over for dinner,' he said, spraying crumbs everywhere.

'Oh? Well, I've already invited Giles and Mads over for dinner,' I lied, thinking that another dinner with Alexia might finish me off for ever. The woman was killing me with health food.

He laughed. 'You? cook? I don't think so doll.'

'Don't mock,' I said. 'So I'll have room service cook it in the kitchen but I'll do the placement thingamy. You know what I mean.'

'Alexia was actually going to cook. But hey listen, that's not a problem,' he said raising the palms of his hands, leaving me in no doubt that it was a very big problem indeed. 'I'll ring up Lexy and tell her you can't make it.'

I didn't like the way his tone was sinking into sarcasm but I held onto my cool and smiled coldly. 'No, you'll ring her up and tell her that *we* can't make it.'

'I *can* make it though. I've already accepted. Besides, you guys don't need me here cramping your style.'

He kissed me on the lips and pinched my cheek. I don't like to be patronised.

'No, we don't need you, you're right – but I want you here. Come on Rory, we've practically been living with Alexia since I got here. Mads and Giles aren't here for long. Come on, it'll be a laugh.'

'I've had all the laughter I can take with that guy. I'm sure as hell not going to miss seeing my daughter for the sake of a bloke who can't keep a grip on his own bum.'

'You mean you can't bear not spending the evening with Alexia,' I spat. 'Go then. I don't know why you got divorced in the first place as you don't seem to be able to be apart from one another for a single moment.'

'I go there for Katy and you know it. If you had any feelings for me at all you'd understand that. If you're so selfish that you can't see that, then maybe it's best that I keep my life with Katy separate from you. Like I did in the beginning only that seemed to be a problem for you as well. You can't have it both ways doll but one thing is for sure, if you've got a problem with me wanting to see my daughter then we've got a problem, because not even you are going to stand in the way of me seeing my kid.'

Put in those terms, I canned the idea of four for tea and warned him not to give me ultimatums.

He warned me not to say something that I'd regret.

I told him not to talk about regrets and then listed a few of my own off the top of my head:

Coming to LA under false pretences.

Falling for a bastard who didn't even have the decency to tell me he was a dad.

Shagging said dad.

Falling for said dad's kid when I really wasn't ready for the complications or commitment with a grown-up, let alone a dependent.

Everything got out of hand after that. We both said things we regretted and a lot of ultimatums were delivered on both sides. Mads would say that we'd engaged with our dilemmas but it felt more like a clash.

I did something I never do in arguments with men and started to cry, and Rory did something that men always do in arguments with me and cried along too.

I wished that my mother and Alexia could have witnessed us then – in all our uncivilised glory. Tear-streaked faces, screaming out abuse and hatefulness and threats. It was incredible that we didn't manage to make our heads revolve around on their axis really.

After we'd trashed most of the furniture in pure LA rock-and-roll-tantrum-style, we fell into a heap of tear-stained sex and promised that we would never ever again argue.

That was when Daniel rang to confirm our lunch the next day.

CHAPTER 18

'I'm a one-man woman. One man at a time.'

I'm No Angel, 1933, b/w, Mae West and
Cary Grant

Daniel was waiting for me in the lobby. Smart casual
– get the picture?

In Britain, smart casual suggests torn jeans and
marked trainers but not in LA. God no.

Daniel looked like the term had been invented for
him. He was a casual designer's dream come true.
While Rory's idea of style was to do a button up on
his shirt, Daniel knew his way around a menswear
store. Gucci to be precise.

He suggested that we eat in the garden of the hotel
and I nodded agreeably, not trusting my voice that
close to such machismo. When he laughed, and he
laughed a fair bit, my womb contracted. I was flirting
uncontrollably from the start.

Somebody stop me!

Outside in the garden, when he leaned toward

me to remove a purple flower that had fallen in my hair, I caught an exotic scent hovering around him. Something I couldn't place, and for a girl who spends most of her waking hours in the cosmetic department of Harvey Nichols that was saying something.

I was giving myself over to seduction, my G-spot cried out for me to surrender and a surge of oxitocin went shooting up from my ovaries to my nipples. It was one of those situations where attack was the only form of defence available.

I'd planned to play it cool, like Bogey in *Casablanca*, but it was useless. Try playing it cool when your G-spot is embarrassing you with its loud groaning.

Anyway, I was feeling slightly schizophrenic that day. There were two voices in my head, both of them nagging me and cajoling me like stereotypical fishwives.

Sorry feminists but it's true.

One of them was a cool, no-nonsense Susan Sarandon kind of voice – my therapist basically – telling me to 'engage my dilemmas'.

The other was an insane jealous voice that said Daniel was Alexia's lover and that I should keep my filthy glandular impulses off him.

This later voice was the most insistent and harrowing – more like my own really. It was hard not to listen to it because it was so deafeningly loud. That's libido for you. Loud and uncouth – not to mention downright embarrassing.

Throughout our lunch in the gardens of Château

Marmont, amongst the purple flowers, beautiful people, deal-makers, wannabes, palm fronds and *cosmopolitans*, which were becoming something of a habit with me, my clitoris kept nagging me to commit the ultimate sin against feminine solidarity – discounting not telling a fellow girl that she has lipstick on her teeth.

'Steal another girl's man,' it hissed.

A few people turned around to see where the uncouth hiss had come from.

There was a sense of trouble in the air.

It was palpable.

Dangerous even.

And yet?

Utterly compelling.

Cheating on Rory didn't bother me nearly half as much as ravishing Alexia's lover. It was the ultimate challenge for an Other Woman. I tried to justify it by telling my better self that Alexia had denied any involvement with the guy.

'See!' said my groin in a really loud, aggressive, wrong side of the tracks kind of voice.

'Sorry – doesn't wash and you know it,' said my RC conscience in a soft upper-class kind of voice.

'Fuck off!' said my Other Woman-ness in a Marlene Dietrich, heavily accented voice.

Daniel had gone off to the little boys' room. I was getting quite carried away with all my voices going at once when the large Afro-American waitress approached me. 'You've got a bit of lipstick on your, er, teeth actually,' she whispered helpfully. 'And there's a hunk of lettuce stuck on your chin too.'

'Oh! Fuck!' I exclaimed – almost livid with embarrassment. 'How good of you to tell me,' I said as I wiped it off. Then I smiled up at her, red teeth, lettuce and all as if I didn't care in the least, as if I was so cool that stuff like that didn't bother me.

She gave me one of those looks that said, 'Drop it sister, we've all been there. I know your pain.'

After she left I practically gave myself a hernia as I stressed out about how long it might have been there. I searched my bag for my trusty Gucci compact. I've got several but only the Gucci never lies.

Straight away, paranoia took hold.

Was it there when I regaled him with my famous case last year in the Royal Courts, when I'd made history with my shorter than short skirt? What a case that was. The judge had to be carried out. He was apoplectic with rage. There was talk that his tongue would have to be cut out.

He rallied later on in hospital after his clerk agreed to smuggle him in a bottle of claret, as a make up gift from me. My conscience again.

Daniel had laughed himself sick when I told him – but maybe he was more amused by my red teeth and green chin than the story?

Was it there when I struck a few *Vogue* poses and vamped it up while he decided what he thought about the new blonde me? And when he'd told me that he hadn't actually had time to get used to

the brunette me, was he implying a secret meaning?

'You want dessert or anything?' he asked when he
returned.

'No thanks. Coffee will be fine for me but don't
deny yourself,' I told him, fixing him with a dazzling
lipstick-free smile.

'Coffee for two,' he told the waiter.

All thoughts of my teeth and their lipstick status
were swept aside when he turned to me and said, 'Tell
me that we're not really here to discuss the virtues of
your legal adventures as feature film, are we?'

He'd sprung me there. 'Well Alexia was very
persuasive,' I told him.

'Alexia's a shrewd businesswoman. I've got more
time for her than most. She's smart, she's got looks,
brains and the rarest commodity in Hollywood – she's
one hundred per cent honourable.'

'I wish I could have a buck for every time someone
in this town tells me that someone else is honourable,'
I told him, fixing him in one of my smokiest looks.

'You two see a lot of one another?' he asked,
ignoring my cynicism.

'Sure we do, she's so much fun to be around,' I
lied.

'Oh miaow, hiss.'

'Shut up.'

'No sorry. I just wish I had a buck for every
girl who's told me that her arch rival is fun to be
around.'

'Touché! Do you know Rory at all?' I asked.

'You mean your, um, friend? No, I met Alexia after they split. She doesn't talk about him. I gather there's still a lot of love to be lost there, am I right? Or is it only on her part?'

'You think they'll get back together?'

'You're fishing in the wrong lake here. You're involved in another couple's relationship and if that's what you want, you're going to have to make sacrifices that even the martyrs only dreamed about.'

'That's OK, I come from a long line of martyrs.'

He laughed. 'That I doubt, but getting back to the selling of Evelyn's legal adventures, the professional woman in jeopardy scenario, seriously, where do you stand? I'll tell you now that Alexia's got a nose for a story. If she says something's got legs you know that you're talking Cyd Charisse. There aren't many noses like hers that I'd trust.'

I thought of a number of things that I could say about Alexia's nose or rather lack thereof – but I wasn't that drunk.

He was staring at me now with those Richard Gere eyes that made me feel I was being laughed at. I couldn't help wondering what he looked like when he cried – did people take his sadness seriously?

I asked him.

'Sorry,' he said, 'I wasn't listening. I was looking at the way your eyes change from brown to green in the light.'

PS, yes I was flattered.

I lost my train of thought, even ignoring the cliché element for a moment. We were both looking at each other like amnesia victims staring into a mirror.

'So you trust Alexia's judgement on this – is that what you're saying?' I asked, blinking to rally my brain. The way he looked at me with those smiling eyes felt like I was under a stage-light for my big audition and that big things were expected of me.

'I'm very attracted to you,' he whispered, taking my hand. His eyes laughing at me. 'I mean it, I haven't stopped thinking about you since I first laid eyes on you at the airport,' he admitted.

'Oh pah-lease,' I sighed, rolling my eyes. 'It's just your libido talking. Mine goes on and on at me all the time. Just ignore it.'

He laughed, his head thrown back, his Adam's apple jiggling about like he'd swallowed a bee. 'I'm serious,' he said. 'Let's make love before we both go out of our mind with small talk. I know I'm being out of order, so just tell me to stop if you don't feel the same. Otherwise I vote we take a room.'

A silence fell between us then as the coffee arrived.

'Don't,' I said when the waiter had left. 'I mean it, don't. This is like the last thing I need,' I told him, stirring my coffee. 'My life is a maze of complications right now. I'm in love with a man in love with another girl. His daughter to be precise.'

'So?'

'So, I'm a one-man woman, or at least one of those serial monogamists. I'm just not in the habit of inter-relational affairs,' I told him, not having any idea what I was talking about.

Maybe I'd had one too many *cosmopolitans* or something but his eyes seemed to be going from blue to green to black again. It was as though they were consuming me like some sort of alien thing off *The X-Files*, siphoning off my brain. What was left of it.

I was terrified of these feelings he was expressing, maybe because I felt the same. But I didn't let on that part. Instead I told him that I should go. 'I've got to take my friend to the salon, her um, her hair's a mess,' I explained.

'Let me repeat,' he said. 'I am so attracted to you I would gladly sign a prenuptial agreement here and now, vow everything to you and condemn myself to a life of fruitless lawsuits, just give me your body for the afternoon. That's all I ask.'

It was so typical I was thinking that as the lead man he should get to say all the best lines. As the lead girl, I bet all I got was to take my clothes off and let him adore me.

PS. Sounded OK to me.

'It's probably just the er, the um, the wine,' I suggested, pointing to his untouched glass.

'It's you,' he said, without a trace of cornyness in his voice. 'Take me to your room and make love to me Evelyn or consign me to a life of paralysis and misery.'

'The misery part I can handle,' I told him. 'Only I have to say, the paralysis part seems a bit extreme.'

Somewhere along the line we'd started holding hands across the table. He had such beautiful long-fingered hands and I wanted them on my body. I heard myself moan.

He called for the bill.

All the way up in the claustrophobic elevator, inhaling his amazing scent, my vagina throbbed with anticipation at the sin I was about to commit. Meanwhile that vibrator thingamy was whizzing up a smoothy with my lunch. What can I say? Huh? I was allowing my Other Woman voice to control me, that's what. I was allowing the Other Woman within me to lead the other girl, i.e. me, astray.

I was leaping from one uncivilised behaviour to another without sparing a thought or a feeling for others.

The outcome, once inside the suite was as predictable as a *Melrose Place* plot. We closed the door. I put on the chain. I felt a flash of guilt as I turned around to survey the room, the room I shared with Rory. Our 'home' as he'd referred to it on the card attached to the lilies he'd torn apart in a fit of jealousy. I'd kept the stalks in the vase on the sideboard and one look at those headless flowers left me in no doubt that I couldn't go through with the sexual infidelity thing.

I've been a classical bad girl in my time but I was drawing the line at committing a sin I couldn't even pronounce after a few *cosmopolitans*.

I burst into tears.

CHAPTER 19

'If you have a vagina and an attitude in this town, then that's a lethal combination.'

Sharon Stone

I just wasn't made for giving myself over to abandoned sex with a practical stranger. I know that because no matter how much I've had to drink, I can never relate to the lyrics of rock and roll anthems which nearly always extol the virtues of uncommitted sex.

Men always complain that girls don't enjoy throwaway sex, that we can't separate our emotions from our need to nest. Hetero men always say that gay men have got it easy because other men don't have a problem with casual sex. Gay couples on the other hand sometimes have a problem with this.

Men talk a lot of shite really, but as far as I'm concerned they are right on this. I don't like throwing anything away and sex is no exception. It's part of my middle-class background. I mean my wardrobe has got to practically explode before I'm willing to part with anything and then it's got to be a really good cause like AIDS charities or anti-tree chopping programmes. Sex is no exception to my rule.

But Daniel didn't need charity. Daniel was a physical insult to anyone in need actually, the man exuded so much ease in himself that he should apologise to those men less fortunate and offer them bits of his body and a few inches of his own superior virtues. From his shorter than short hair and his olive complexion the guy could launch a thousand flirtations with the mere raising of one perfectly sculpted eyebrow.

From his psychological soundbites to his throaty laugh the man was a sexual cert. Something about the way he expressed himself with his hands made me secure that he was not the sort to skimp on the vaginal orgasm. Moreover, I could tell by the length of his legs that he was an all-the-way type of guy – especially in the wrapping a girl up in his body sense.

He also had a seriously good sense of humour, which if you believe the personal columns is the be-all and end-all of personal attributes. If you've got the GSOH thing sussed you can be bald, fat and still get laid.

PS. What a load of shite.

The thing I've found is that most blokes have some degree of laughter-development delay with me and my sick sense of comedy. It goes something like this:

I say something funny, they wait for a bit – as if expecting the PC police to come charging in and arrest me, and only once they're sure that I haven't been caught will they snicker along with me.

I've found without exception that a girl can measure a guy's dick by the time it takes him to laugh at one of her jokes. I read that on a desk calendar once so it must be true.

The cutest thing about Daniel though was that he didn't seem to know how cute he was. Even Giles was aware of his vulnerable charm. In bars he always liked to bend over his Guinness a bit to expose the non-existent Irish poet in him. And as for Rory, he had an ego on him the size of a producer's.

I guess Daniel was so wound up in his inner-self or the 'inner world' as he called it, that he forgot about the perfection of his outer shell. I couldn't help thinking that Daniel was the sort of guy that Rory would actually like if he got to know him.

PS. It would be a whole different story though were Rory to catch me in bed with the guy.

Once inside our suite, Daniel didn't even make cursory enquiries about my mini-bar or my view. Now is that sophisticated or what? Even the Marlboro Man sneering at us with his habitual supercilious, accusatory look, didn't warrant a comment.

Actually he became very passionate which kind of took me by surprise. When you're in a relationship, the turn-on comes from the familiarity of your lover's touch, their smell, their taste. It's like you know what you're getting so there's no need for warm ups. You're already limbered up and you can surge straight into active eroticism.

Snogging someone else when you're in a relationship is a different kind of turn-on. It's like being turned on under the influence of sin. Every sensation is heightened by the risk. You can actually feel your eggs popping. My hormones were so wound up when Daniel touched me, so overexcited, they were tripping over one another in a clumsy chase around my lower torso.

My libido was on full-throb. It was like one of those souped-up cars with the exhaust pipe taken off. People in the pool below could hear my desire yelling out for mercy.

My womb was miaowing like an alley cat and my vagina was so wet I had to keep my legs crossed. Very undignified stuff, Sister Conchilio would have said. I tried to justify my cheating by telling myself that I was engaging my dilemmas by snogging Daniel. But when push came to shove, I had to kick my pheromones in the groin to get them to stop. I couldn't sleep with Daniel.

Could I?

For one, cheating on Rory wasn't that easy. Part of the fun of the cheating thing is not being found out. I learnt this from my gran who was a renowned and oft-copied cheat at her bridge club. But Rory would find out, there was no getting away from that fact. He found out everything – it was his job. It was uncanny in fact the way he always knew precisely what I'd been up to before I'd even got up to it.

Apart from that, there was Alexia. I mean, I'd already stolen her husband. Bit much to steal her lover as well, my better self reasoned. On the other hand the Sharon Stone within me told me not to sweat it. 'What kind of hard-as-nails bitch are you that you don't have the guts to steal your boyfriend's ex-wife's lover? Huh?'

I guess I just wasn't the Other Woman I made myself out to be and I asked Daniel to forgive me as I shoved him away.

'What for? There's nothing to forgive,' he said, placing a necklace of kisses around my throat as I pushed him toward the door and told him it was best that he left and that we never saw one another again.

'I'll agree to the first suggestion, not the second. Nevers, I don't believe in. Promise me that you'll give me a call or I won't leave,' he said, all Jack Lemmon-ish.

I nodded, fearing my voice would fail me and I'd cry out 'Stay! Stay and ravish me you American beast! Do a Kevin Kline on me and tear off my clothes and suck as hard as you can on my Gucci steel-heeled boots!'

'Hey,' he said, sweeping my hair up into an Audrey Hepburn bun. 'Don't sweat it. The sex I mean. I don't know what came over me. I shouldn't have pushed the point. You're involved with someone else. I totally respect your commitment.'

'That's kind,' I said, a bit annoyed that he wasn't putting up more of a fight.

'One thing before I go though?'

'What?'

'What's with the beheaded flowers on the sideboard? It's been bugging the hell out of me since I got in here. Didn't you fancy the lilies I sent? Or was it the sender whose head you wanted to rip off?' He was pointing to the flowers that Rory had decapitated in a jealous fit.

'Funny,' he continued. 'I had you pegged for lilies, something Gothic lurking within you I figured. Maybe it was just a height thing though.'

'The flowers *you* sent? No, you've made a mistake, *you* didn't send me those flowers. Rory did. He tore the heads off them because . . . Well, it's a long story.'

'He buys flowers to decapitate them? Now that really is Gothic. You want to watch him round Halloween. Funny really, I actually sent you a similar if not identical bunch from my favourite florist – heads intact and all. Wrote the card myself.'

'I didn't receive them,' I told him.

He looked troubled. 'And how I agonised over what to say,' he said shaking his head. 'Do you know, I practically resorted to my Dalai Lama desk calendar? I was terrified that you wouldn't even remember me. I wanted to tell you that I was under your spell, madly in love, counting the minutes till I saw you again but I lacked confidence in my poetic abilities.

'If my memory serves me, I opted for, 'Going to Italy tomorrow for a week. Back on the 8th. Hope to see you when I get back from Rome.' Something like that anyway.'

I retrieved the card that purported to be from Rory. In an attack of sentimentality I'd kept it with my make-up. Looking at it now it did look dubious. Rory must have scribbled out selective parts of Daniel's message and written his own, replacing *Rome* for *home*. My conscience glazed over.

What a cad, what a cheapskate bastard, I fumed inside. There was a breeze blowing in carbon dioxide fumes from Sunset and I wanted to faint. I noticed that the message light was flashing and a letter had been pushed under the door but nothing happening in the now mattered to me.

The bastard had deliberately changed the card so I would think the flowers were from him. Typical really but it was enough for me to weaken my resolve to throw Daniel out of my room.

Something just went click inside me. The little switch on my morals, maybe? I pulled Daniel towards me and snogged him furiously.

We were tearing one another's clothes off within seconds, crushing my conscience underneath us as we writhed around the floor. I was so given over to the passion of the moment I wasn't even worried about carpet burn. All I could think about was the velvety touch of his skin and how I'd never felt anything so soft in my life.

That was when the phone rang. Some idiot impulse forced me to pick it up and believe me I kicked that idiot impulse to death when I heard who was on the other end.

It was Alexia, sounding pretty distraught. She was down in the lobby. And she had to speak to me right away.

Daniel was going to work on my nipple as she spoke and I couldn't dislodge him. I had to take the whole call with my hormones surging full pelt round my body.

'It was Alexia,' I screamed when I put down the receiver but even that failed to move him.

'Will you stop it,' I asked. 'This is real life, she's down in the lobby now.'

'So?'

'Can't you see?' I was frantic.

'No, I'm blinded by your beauty. These things are real, aren't they?' he asked, running his hands over my breasts.

'Don't be outrageous.'

'I fully intend to be more outrageous than I've ever been in my life. Forget Alexia, she can wait. We on the other hand have urgent business to attend to.'

CHAPTER 20

'Don't fuck with me fellas. I've fought with bigger sharks than you.'

Mommie Dearest, 1981, colour, Faye Dunaway

A chauvinist I once kicked in the groin used to say that girls start off playing with Barbies and grow up to play with minds. Sitting in the lounge of the Château Marmont amongst the Addams Family fixtures and fittings with Alexia, I was beginning to understand the wisdom in his sexist aphorism and I had to concede that perhaps I'd been a bit hasty with my stilettos. Maybe he had a point after all.

Oh well. Time heals all wounds.

In the end my guilt got the better of me and I found that I just couldn't go through with the full penetrative sex thing with Daniel. Something about the whole deal felt wrong and let's face it, the shade of carpet hadn't helped.

I'd pushed him off in a last minute attack of the

'I still love Rory's. What was it with me? I was starting to concur with Mads, maybe the nuns made me do it.

'It's hopeless. I just can't do it,' I told him. 'I still love Rory. I can't have sex with you,' I explained, taking his poor shocked gorgeous face in my hands. 'I like you and everything and you're obviously the most fanciable man alive, but I can't help it. Shit that he is, I love Rory.'

'What?' Daniel had cried, this not being what a man with an erection wants to hear about another man.

Unfortunate as it was, I left him somewhat indisposed as they say and after throwing on some clothes I rushed downstairs asking myself what the hell I was thinking of, engaging in such a serious flirtation with another man when I was already involved. What kind of behaviour was that for a serial monogamist?

What had come over me? What had made me think I could sort out one complicated situation by developing another? I tried to tell myself that it was a case of too much sun and not enough walking around shopping malls that did it.

Daniel and I had things to sort out but they didn't seem as imperative as they once had. Actually when I thought about it, my life was a bundle of loose ends. A veritable bag of tangled relationships left to the devices of a bunch of wayward kittens.

Still, image is all as they say, and when my

emotional self is at its most dazed and confused, I like to put this saying to the test.

To put you in the frame as far as my image that evening went, I was wearing a short tight black Prada number that was so skimpy it might even be illegal for use on people under the age of twenty-one in some states of America.

My guilty eyes (and a good part of my face) were well-hidden behind large black Gucci sunglasses. The main defence tools in my battle with my conscience were a pair of six-inch nail-heel stilettos and a Rigby & Peller bra that would make Fellini weep.

Before our cocktails arrived, I puffed on an old cigar butt I'd found in my pocket. I was trying to focus on how drop-dead cool I looked rather than on Alexia, who was weeping quietly and explaining in detail what a bitch she had been and to a large extent still was.

I wonder what Mads would have made of us that evening. Two women in love with the same man. One the mother of one man's child, the other the thief of both.

Alexia was wearing LA-tourist white Chanel, small white sunglasses, white shoes, no jewellery and pale make-up. The good fairy to my bad, if you like.

Everything she was about to tell me was the truth, she assured me, sucking hard on a Marlboro Light like it was an oxygen mask. People who see fit to warn me that they are about to tell me the truth make me suspicious from the outset, I guess, so I can't claim to have given her speech my full attention.

Coming down the stairs I had thought I was going to get sprung for cavorting with Daniel, so to find that my indiscretion had been interrupted for a confession slightly irritated me.

I settled back in the velvet of my armchair under the Gothic window and basked in her testimony, counting my lucky stars that I wasn't in the frame. In a nutshell the theme of her submission was 'blame'. As in, she wanted to hog it all for herself. As a Catholic I thought of this as a bit greedy actually.

According to her interpretation of events, she had manipulated the situation with Rory to suit herself. It was time to face the truth she told me. Rory no longer loved her (pause for sob) – if he ever had (pause for vacant gaze into space).

Rory loved me (Evelyn) and she wanted to confess to me that she had, until now, been selfishly asking him to forsake that love for her (the mother of his child).

Pause to wipe stray tear making its lonely way down perfectly sculptured, pale, vulnerable cheek.

'Don't sweat it,' I told her, toking nonchalantly on my cigar as Michelle Pfeiffer walked in. 'A mother isn't just for breastfeeding,' I assured her. 'She's for ever.'

She told me not to be so damn understanding and explained how she had planted doubts in Rory's mind about my ability to deal with his domestic arrangement. 'Can't you see Evie? I actively tried to turn him against you. Do you understand?'

I shrugged my shoulders and went right on puffing away. What did she want from me, an Our Father and two Hail Marys?

'You see, I knew that by telling him you wouldn't want to be strangled by his domestic arrangement with me that he would distance himself from you. That's what he does if he wants to test your mettle. He pulls away and waits for you to fall. Can't you see, he's been waiting for you to fall!'

Hiding behind my plumes of smoke, I was thinking about Daniel waiting for me upstairs and how I'd felt when he'd kissed me and how Rory's wait hadn't been all that long actually.

Sitting there in the lobby watching the comings and goings of stars and producers and their minions, I couldn't help but feel detached from my troubles, and Alexia's for that matter. It all seemed so insignificant when measured against the lives of all these stars, this Hollywood firmament of men and women whose every mood and move is captured by the press and eagerly followed by people like me – the men and women that no one would ever want to read about in a million years unless we were unfortunate enough to become a victim of an atrocious crime or something.

Now if I was Sharon Stone sitting here in the lobby with the ex-wife of my lover, it would be a different matter, especially if it was known that there was another man upstairs waiting for me in his underwear. The press would be swarming.

I turned my attention back to Alexia who was still chatting away about her sins. Her lips were moving, sound was coming out but I sensed I'd missed a really important revelation by the way she paused as if giving me the chance to slap her across the face or something.

I looked at her and tried to weigh up what was going on. I mean, here she was, thinking she was graciously stepping aside for me to swipe her old man while I was harbouring her new man in my room upstairs. I was the Other Woman, for God's sake – what did I need to do here to make her realise that I was the ultimate baddy in this scenario? Have BITCH tattooed on my forehead?

But Other Women are cold heartless duplicitous bitches. Instead of making a full disclosure, I held her hand and soothed her. 'Alexia, it's not your fault,' I assured her. 'You're an important part of Rory's life, that's a fact. You'll be the mother of his daughter for the rest of your life. No divorce court in the world can change that fact. You are in Rory's life to stay, and any woman he gets involved with will have to recognise that.'

She took a white handkerchief from her white purse and dabbed at her eyes behind the sunglasses. 'Do you think so, Evie – really?'

'Really I do,' I promised, tilting my dark glasses on an honest angle. I did actually. My duplicitous speech made a lot of sense. Mads would be proud of me.

'I can't believe that you're being this understanding,' she said.

On an empathy roll, I carried on. 'I wouldn't want Rory to choose between Katy and myself, and if he did choose and that choice was me, I wouldn't be able to love him. You must see that.'

'Rory told me you would think that.'

Bastard, I thought to myself – how dare he presume my saintly willingness to put his daughter first? I mean a girl doesn't spend twice what she earns in a year to look hold-your-testicles gorgeous only to step aside for a three-year-old. Surely that was taking sisterhood too far?

'Rory would never choose me or any other woman over Katy. And in choosing Katy he chooses you by proxy, and all my selfish need to be the only woman can't change that fact.'

Alexia blew her nose loudly.

All around us the beautiful people milled. Men and women in designer casuals shook hands, airkissed and generally behaved in a civilised manner toward one another. In their midst I was beginning to feel like the anti-Christ – hellbent on evil. But maybe it was just that time of day.

My mother used to call this time of day 'arsenic hour' – the hour between sunset and dark when children whinge and husbands don't come home and meals burn in the oven. She used to give us laxatives to make herself feel better. I had an overwhelming urge for a strong purgative now. Something that would strip my colon and my conscience.

Alexia was tapping her fingers on her cigarette packet.

'I can't bear this,' she said, leaning towards me like she was about to plunge her cigarette into my eye. 'How can you be so noble?' [Dramatic pause.] 'Your decency only makes me feel worse!' she cried, loudly enough for a couple of passersby to stop and stare.

She blew her nose daintily into her white hanky. Everyone in the lobby turned their full focus on me as if recognising a sinister presence. This was the end of my secret life. I had been outed. I could see the headlines, *Evelyn the Bitch Exposed in the Lobby of Château Marmont.*

I wanted to scream like one of those Born Again Christians on television. 'I am an evil duplicitous bitch, hell bent on havoc and the ruination of your personal happiness.' Instead of making a confession though, I inhaled deeply on my Cohiba and choked up a larynx. A man in a Ralph Lauren cap – similar to the one I'd given my taxi driver in Rodeo Drive – tapped me on the shoulder and asked if I would mind not smoking.

My head really was on the block tonight. I complied with his request and stubbed it out. Actually my lungs weren't up to this smoking lark, whatever the benefits to my image. Besides he looked like the sort of bloke to sue a girl for inflicting passive-smoking syndrome. The sort of bloke to track a girl down fifty years from now and strip her of her assets as soon as help her cross the street on her Zimmer frame.

Alexia, the white witch of this coven, smoked on regardless.

'Rory has good taste in women,' she said ruefully, tossing back her non-alcoholic cocktail as soon as the waitress handed it to her.

I toasted her with my double alcoholic one. 'Alexia, I think you're giving me way too much credit here. Hate me,' I insisted. 'No I'm serious. Go right ahead and hate me. It's the least I deserve. In fact I'd feel a lot better if you hated me.'

'I do hate you,' she said, taking off her sunglasses and staring me in the eyes. 'I hate you because Rory loves you far more than he ever loved me. I didn't think any woman could ever hold his attention for more than a week. But Rory was right. Now I've met you I can see what he means. You two were made for each other.'

This graciousness was more than I could bear. I had to broach the Daniel issue. I took off my own sunglasses and asked why that would matter so much, given that she was in love with Daniel now.

'Daniel?' she asked. 'Who's Daniel?' She looked genuinely puzzled.

'Daniel, the lawyer, I saw you with him at Bar Marmont the other night.'

'Daniel Silverberg? He's a business acquaintance,

a lawyer that's all. How could you ever imagine I would date *a lawyer*?'

'Well, hang on a minute, I'm a lawyer.'

'Well, yes, but that's not the point. He's a media lawyer. A shark, a nice shark but a shark just the same. Who told you I was seeing Daniel anyway?' She sounded very irritated.

She leaned forward and looked me straight in the eye. 'I don't think we're on the same page here Evie. I've been sitting here the last ten minutes explaining to you that I'm still in love with Rory. Haven't you listened to a word I've said? *I've been screwing Rory since you arrived in LA!*'

CHAPTER 21

'Once in her life every woman should have that said to her. I thank you for being the one who said it to me.'

The Inn of the Sixth Happiness, 1958, colour,
Ingrid Bergman and Curt Jurgens

It was as if Alexia had stuck one of her long, perfectly manicured hands down my throat and pulled out my heart – plus a few other vital bits and pieces I needed to go on breathing. I fell forward, my head in a slump.

Alexia recoiled.

I gasped and considered whether or not it would be appropriate to sob.

'Come on Evie don't look so bloody shocked,' she sneered in a superior tone of voice that didn't quite match the mottled blush creeping into her cheeks. 'You must have realised that Rory was no saint. Let's face it, he's a James Dean not a James Stewart.'

She made a funny little coughing sound at the back of her throat which I gathered she meant to be a brittle laugh. I was thinking not for the first time how ridiculous she looked.

'He's not James bloody anything. He's my bloody boyfriend, you stupid bitch,' I told her, finding now that my breath wasn't quite as lost as I'd thought. It's amazing really what a bit of white-hot anger can do for a girl's eloquence.

'And he's the father of my child,' she snapped tartly. 'You think you can prance over here with your smart talk and your reactionary views and turn my life upside down.'

I raised one eyebrow quizzically. 'Excuse me for mentioning it but you haven't exactly put mine on a steady course.' I was about to go on into even greater oratorical brilliance but I saw Rory approaching so I decided to save my strength.

It didn't escape my notice that Alexia went a ghastly shade of purple when she spotted him, which all in all sort of clashed with her suit. This was the first time I'd ever seen her looking ruffled.

Stubbing out her cigarette she rose from her seat and in her fluster knocked my drink to the ground. It smashed onto the polished floor but nobody in the vast and busy lobby seemed to take the slightest notice. We were nobodies with no audience interested in watching our play. Alexia brushed the pieces aside with her daintily clad foot.

'What are you doing here? Where's Katy?' she

asked Rory as he looked from one of us to the other. I expect she was trying to gain some sort of ground as a responsible parent, the one who wasn't to be questioned.

Rory didn't look very happy with her; in fact he was staring at her with pure contempt. I stayed seated, shrinking into myself, lapping up her discomfiture like a cat with a saucer of sweetened cream.

'She's with the nanny. Now why don't you tell me what's happening here Alexia?'

She smiled stiffly and turned to me. I smiled back at her with a little more sweetness and raised one eyebrow again. This was where all my years playing the role of the ingénue in Chambers paid off.

We looked at each other as if daring the other to speak, like naughty schoolgirls caught out committing a prank, daring one another to blow the culprit's cover.

'We were just er having a chat, weren't we Evie?' Alexia breezed, still smiling stiffly as if demanding my complicity.

I was damned if I was going to give it to her.

'Don't call me Evie,' I told her in a voice I reserve for recalcitrant witnesses in court. 'My name's Evelyn. E-V-E-L-Y-N. I'm sure you can manage it if you try.' Then I stood up and faced Rory.

We were inches apart.

His hair smelt of the sea and pheromones and my anger began to melt. I almost swooned. I hated him for having this effect on me but swoon I did. The idea that I still loved him flashed like an e-mail message across my synapse. I heard a voice that sounded like mine rise out of me. 'Your charming ex-wife here was telling me about your sex life together and how it is still very much, how should I put it? On heat? Now if you'll excuse me, I have someone waiting for me.'

I tried to wriggle out of the space between the coffee table and Rory. He was looking me up and down as if his eyes were micro-computer cameras, storing images of me on a chip for future identification. Then he put his hands on my shoulders.

'Give me a chance,' he pleaded, looking into my eyes. 'One chance.' Then he held up a finger in case I hadn't done my maths. It didn't sound like a lot so I paused. I think I was paralysed with the misery of all the information about him and Alexia which I was still trying to digest. Besides which he was holding onto me firmly so that I couldn't move.

He turned his gaze onto Alexia and it was as if a wave of pure hatred flowed from him to her. I'd never seen him look at her like that before. I was gripped.

'Alexia?' he asked in a voice with a subtext that read – what the fuck are you up to, bitch?

Alexia was perspiring. A trickle of sweat was racing its way down her make-up like a snail trail. I almost felt sorry for her, she was clearly in a nasty corner and the girlfriend side of me wanted to give her some support, some sisterly solidarity.

'I don't know what she's talking about Rory. She's babbling. You know what she's like,' she started.

Scratch the 'almost felt sorry for her' bit, I was almost ready to scratch her eyes out.

'Go,' he told her quietly. Not a muscle of his face moved as he spoke. He reminded me of Roger Moore in his young Bond days, only he rather spoilt the effect with, 'And don't forget to bury the goldfish before Katy finds it. I left it in the oven.'

'What happened?' she asked, as a loyal wife and mother might ask a devoted father just in from work.

He shrugged. 'Don't know. I think she might have overfed it. The fish food was almost empty when I looked.'

She nodded, bit her lip and then looked up into his eyes. 'I simply won't allow you to let your affairs affect Katy, Rory.'

Rory stared into her eyes and dropped his voice still further. Whatever he said next sounded quite dangerous but I didn't catch it.

Alexia didn't answer, she was gone in an instant. She was sobbing quietly and I knew in that instant that what she'd told me that afternoon wasn't true. We watched as she disappeared down the stairwell and then waited in silence as her shoes clattered down the terracotta tiling of the steps to the garage like a drum roll.

He sat me down then and summoned a waiter. I felt vaguely unreal, like part of my consciousness had floated off.

'We have to talk, doll, but not here.' He pulled

out his tobacco and commenced rolling a cigarette. I watched his fingers, long and brown, spread out the paper. The faint smell of the tobacco wafted up to my nostrils, redolent of every post-coital cigarette he'd ever lit.

'First up, I don't know what Alexia's told you but you have to know it's shit. This whole thing has been a fuck-up from start to finish. I know now that I was asking too much, bringing you here.'

I nodded. My head was spinning, I wanted to cry but I felt if I did I mightn't be able to stop. It was as if someone had wrung me out and rolled me over with a rolling pin. Rory didn't look at me as he licked the paper. I stared at his tongue as a million reasons to cry stung at my memory.

'I guess I thought that once you saw Katy you'd understand,' he continued, putting the cigarette to his mouth.

'I love Katy,' I told him truthfully. A breeze came through the window carrying the scent of purple blossoms that had got caught in my hair that afternoon.

'I know that,' he said. 'But it's not enough, is it?'

I shook my head.

'I want you in my life Evelyn. I want you here with me all the time.'

I nodded again, gazing out onto the garden where industry people gushed and laughed and schmoozed one another. I felt too empty for speech. A pigeon flew in and flapped about the fan, panicked, and flew out again. I wanted to chase after it – it had all been a mistake, all of it. A dreadful, complicated, painful mistake and now I wanted to fly back to England and hide underneath the duvet of London and its comfortable, miserable drizzle, far away from the delirium of all this heat.

Rory looked at me as if he might be about to cry. 'Shit, I've fucked up,' he said. He was saying what I had longed for him to say since we arrived in LA. Only I wasn't quite sure it was enough anymore.

We lapsed into silence. The waiter came and cleared up the glass, Rory ordered coffee, the lobby began to empty as people left for bars and restaurants. Someone in one of the bungalows was playing a loud rap song. Even with the noise of the music there was a stillness in the dying light of the evening, a finality, a closure. Sitting there under the swishing fan sipping our caffeine fixes, both of us uncertain as to what was going to happen next, it was as if we were in fadeout, waiting for the titles to come up.

In all the drama of revelation and emotion I had forgotten about Daniel and even as I remembered him it didn't occur to me to act.

'I think you were right with your "engage your dilemmas" advice,' Rory announced as the darkness finally settled. 'Maybe I should have talked to you more? Told you stuff. Let you in on what my life involved.'

'Maybe,' I answered. 'I don't know.'

'I guess I'm not big on revelations.'

'No,' I agreed, smiling despite the fact that I could feel tears in my eyes.

'In London with you it was just that everything seemed so, I don't know, so simple, so straight-forward.'

'You didn't see my Harvey Nichols store account bill.'

He smiled. 'I did actually.'

I looked at him aghast. 'How dare you!'

'Only joking.'

We laughed then and it was as if everything suddenly made sense or at least seemed worth it, as if somehow all the complications and the demands of the nuclear fall-out family ties drifted into insignificance compared to what we felt for one another. Whatever that was.

Surrounded by the fabulousness of LA, this paradise of palm trees, smoggy sunsets, the stars and their scandals, the plots and the subplots, we had shoved aside fun in our rush to get the project of our relationship off the ground.

There was a small group of loud women in faded jersey and leather sandals sitting in the sofa ring beside us now, laughing raucously and talking excitedly about a party that they'd been at the night before. One of them turned to me and looked for a second as if checking us out. Then she clocked the mess that was my hair and gave me an understanding wink that said, 'Relationships hey, they take a toll don't they?'

Looking at Rory sitting opposite, his checked shirt half-unbuttoned, his brown belly peeking through a gap, I closed my eyes and smiled. Yes, they take their toll, I was thinking. When I opened them he was smiling back at me and it was as if his muscular Chesterfield arms stretched out over the top of the chair were inviting me to embrace him but I didn't move and nor did he.

I had a sense of something lost and a part of me wanted to throw my script aside and ask if we hadn't been too ambitious. Maybe we had wanted too much from one another? Maybe we should have gone for something more low budget? More arthouse, kind of?

'I think the problem was that I wanted the lead role – no strings, no supporting actresses taking out the Oscar on me,' I told him.

He pointed to himself. 'Am I the Oscar in this metaphor by any chance?'

'One of them,' I said, suddenly remembering Daniel – naked at the foot of our bed last time I'd seen him. I started to hyperventilate. Terrified that this amazing mutual exposure session with Rory was going to end in me exposing more than I wanted, I shook my head as if to shake off all this languid remorse. I needed to think straight.

'Fuck! Fuck! Fuck! Fuck!' I said, jumping up.

'My dear, you do say the sweetest things,' he laughed.

'No! I've got to go. I've got an important thingamy. Won't wait. I mean – back soon. Wait here. That's it, wait here. Don't move a muscle. Won't be long. Oh no!'

CHAPTER 22

'In Hollywood a girl's virtue is much less important than her hairdo.'

Marilyn Monroe (1926–62)

My journey to our suite took longer than I meant it to, thanks to an earthquake. It was as the lift rose between floors three and four that it stopped. I didn't think 'earthquake' at the time – you have to have lived in LA for a while to think 'earthquake' immediately. I thought it was just my emotions playing poltergeist.

There was a shudder as the lift stopped and then I was plunged into total darkness. I closed my eyes and said a prayer, expecting to go into free fall but after one more shudder all movement stopped. It was like one of those sensory deprivation tanks only without the dolphin dreaming music and the wet feeling.

On top of the burdens of my misery, my shame and my confusion I now had an earthquake to deal with. I suppose it had to happen then, my life-script – now rewritten as a disaster movie – demanded another crisis situation. The lift was just about large enough to sit down in but not large enough to have a fit in, so I sat down, wrapping my arms around my knees with absolutely no thought for my dress.

PS. Shows how utterly distressed I was – this little sweetheart being a Prada no less.

After shedding a few pathetic tears of self-pity I started yelling and pounding my fists on the walls until I became exhausted with the futility of it all and collapsed into another self-pitying slump (see above). After a bit I tried to search for inner resources as out-lined to me by Mads in one of her chattier sessions.

'Dip into your inner well,' she had advised one after-noon, dunking a camomile tea bag in her *Hug-Me* mug.

'Dip into that well of inner resourcefulness and you might be surprised.' So I had a bit of a dip but there was nothing more surprising than a few murky secrets and a nagging feeling that I shouldn't have tried to make it as a blonde. Who was I fooling with my yellow fluff anyway? Did I honestly think it was that easy being sultry?

After a bit I gave up on my inner resources and turned to my amazingly incisive brunette-style intel-ligence and pressed the alarm. The noise practically blew my head off.

It rang like a pulse for what seemed like for ever before the guy with the stud in his tongue armed with a torch and a calm voice rescued me. By then I was beyond hysterical – I was deranged.

I threw my arms around his freckled neck as if he was Superman rather than the weedy gay guy with the lisp who brought me my coffee in the morning. I sobbed with the damp sobs of the damned into his Versace-scented chest.

It was a pretty moist moment in his brief life and I could tell that my lifesaver wasn't entirely comfortable with my labile emotions. He patted my back awkwardly before feeling it was safe to prise me off and say, 'Actually this shirt has got to last me until the end of this shift, so how about I take you to your room and pour you a drink? I find alcohol is always more effective than tears. Tastes better too,' he assured me encouragingly.

He held the torch between our faces and smiled at me kindly and I nodded bravely until he convinced me to give in to the humour of the situation by a series of imitations of my wobbling lower lip. Then he held my hand and told me it was going to be all right and sucker that I am, I believed him.

'Earthquakes are great,' he promised me, chucking me under the chin and when I looked as if I didn't believe him he said, 'Hey, believe me! Earthquake time is party time!' And then he wiggled his hips, thrust his fist in the air and yelped.

Holding hands we climbed the stairs to the fourth floor, checking out everyone we passed with the torch. There were lots of people milling around the stairs and the corridors with torches and candles, laughing and singing and sometimes snogging. Some groups had champagne buckets set up for little impromptu parties.

The atmosphere reminded me of dawn raids at boarding school when we used to sneak along the corridor and pour jelly into the beds of younger girls. Those were the days. My inner resources imagined what fun it would be to tip jelly into Alexia's bed.

The guy with the stud in his tongue told me that his name was Barney and that he would prefer me to call him that from now on instead of 'the guy with the stud in his tongue'.

Barney was only working at the hotel while he paid his way through UCLA, where he was studying script-writing. We'd got to know one another pretty well in a sort of ambivalent way in the time I'd been staying at the Marmont but he had never told me his name – his was just a shoulder I'd cried on occasionally, only not in the literal sense before tonight.

He unlocked my door and went straight to my fridge for the champagne while I groped around in the semi-darkness and satisfied myself that Daniel wasn't still around. He must have got bored of waiting and left, I surmised. Somewhat relieved I began to rally.

'So is this your first earthquake then?' Barney called out from the kitchen and I called back that it was. 'Well let's celebrate,' he sang out over the clatter of ice being shovelled into the bucket.

I opened up the curtains where the Marlboro Man – still illuminated thanks to his very own generator – cast an artificial moonlight in the room. 'You still here?' seemed to say. Maybe I was just getting used to him, but his sneer didn't seem quite as derisive as before. Were we bonding possibly?

'I think the Marlboro Man may have started to warm to me,' I suggested to Barney as he walked in from the kitchen with the champagne.

'Yeah, he takes a while with women but you can win him round. He has to like your style. He's quite a cool dude actually. Like most men he's had to moderate his image over the years. He's become quite camp recently – that coat he wears for instance. Pah-leese! Even I could go for him – if he used a breath freshener, that is.'

He had shaken the bottle so that when he pulled the cork it sprayed all over us and it felt like we should be toasting something. Barney must have had the same idea because he held his glass up to the glow of the Marlboro Man and said, 'To good men and true!'

'And to Other Women!' I saluted.

'Other Women?' Barney asked, raising an eyebrow. 'Do I detect a miaow?'

So I explained how my 'Other' Woman status had come about and how I had sought to deal with it without so much as an inner well of resourcefulness or a therapist to back me up and he did what all good listeners do, nodded as if he was paying attention and said, 'Men are such assholes and believe me, I should know!'

We set up picnic with the chenille bedspread and pillows and guzzled champagne by the window under the watchful eye of the Marlboro Man.

We opened bottle number two, then Barney told me about how the Italian guy he lived with wrote scripts that were frequently optioned but never made into films. This made the Italian moody and he was always threatening to move back to Milan.

Barney said that he wouldn't really care if he did – the relationship having run its course. He was a great believer that relationships had set time-limits on them. Some were 'three-weekers', most were 'three-monthers' and rarely did any last more than three years. Three years being the ultimate watershed of true love. If you made it through the three-year barrier you were stuck with one another for better or worse.

We were both doubtful that we were made for a three-yearer.

Barny had been with the Italian twenty-seven months – he gave it another six months and he predicted that the last three of those were going to be hell. 'It's when it ceases to be dysfunctional and starts to work like clockwork that I want out but most of the guys I go out with want to stick with it till we kill one another with mediocrity,' he explained.

I thought of Giles.

When the champagne was finished, we moved onto

the whisky. I told him about my stint with Rory and my almost but not quite fling with Daniel.

'I think you're an idealist like me,' he said sagely. 'We don't want to sacrifice everything we are for the sake of love. We'd rather stay single. Let's face it, it's nice having the bed to yourself.'

'Tell me about it,' I groaned, thinking of the way every man I had ever been with had snored and hogged the blankets.

'Our parents expected to take the rough with the smooth and all that sickness and health shit, but our generation – especially the ones of us who aren't breeders. We don't want to compromise our happiness for the sake of love. When the going gets tough, I get clubbing,' he lisped.

We were very drunk now.

'I knew your love life was in trouble when I saw your hair,' he teased, drinking straight from the bottle now. 'God, one look at that colour and we all said, "That girl is in P-A-I-N!"'

'My hairdresser back in London says I have to put up with it,' I told him, feeling quite disloyal towards Stefan as I said it. 'But you know, I think it's just making everything worse. I haven't got the right lines to be a blonde.'

He passed me the bottle. 'I'm not surprised, you look hideous. You may be a blonde trapped in a brunette's body but that's better than being a chicken looking for an oven to hide in.'

The lights came back on then and I realised how

much I'd drunk. Things were whirling around the room and when I looked out the window, there was a whole boulevard of Marlboro Men. En masse they were even more intimidating, like a battalion of macho condescension.

Barney didn't seem to be in such rough shape as me – at least he could still do stuff like talk and stand up and move around without needing to grab on to things, and I guess that's how he got me to agree that I should let him fix my hair. Before I really grasped what it was I was agreeing to, he had left for the chemist across the street.

I took the time on my own to drink a gallon of water while the Marlboro Men looked on censoriously. 'What you need is a fag girl,' they advised and I thought they might be right. I thought about going down to find Rory for a roll-up but I didn't want to risk another earthquake.

On his return, Barney promised me that he knew exactly what he was doing and told me to wash my hair in the kitchen sink. This was easier said than done though and in the end Barney just tipped the slush from the bottom of the champagne bucket over my head, which brought me round pretty sharpish.

'I don't think you're meant to do stuff like that to paying guests,' I gasped.

'I'm off duty now anyway. I'm just your regular Good Samaritan.'

I began to feel afraid but given the way he was holding the scissors, I didn't want to run and risk tripping over. I'd seen *The Postman Always Rings Twice* the night before.

'Besides, my sister's a hairdresser in Beverly Hills,' he told me, as if that might be a sort of quasi-qualification. 'She's always going on and on about how the hair is the pathway to the soul.'

'Isn't that the eyes?' I asked.

'Eyes, hair, what's the diff?' he said, snipping around my ears.

After a bit he applied the colour, which he told me was going to change my life but actually when I saw it I realised I was probably going to have to change my name to live with it.

We were in the bathroom now and looking in the mirror, I realised that I no longer resembled myself in any way whatsoever and that wasn't just because I couldn't focus properly.

'Fuck!' I said.

'You like it, huh?'

'Well, I'm not quite sure.'

'I told you it would change your life, didn't I?'

I nodded zombie-like at the beautiful face before me.

The cut was very short, quite professionally done, it was feathered but shaped into my head so that all my features sort of jumped out where they had more or less hidden away. The colour was arctic white and even with the barest remnants of make-up remaining on my face, I looked glamorous and sexy and totally unlike myself.

I looked stunning, totally head-turning. But was it me? Did I have the right to look this good? From brown bob to corn-fed chicken to sex icon?

'Is that really me?' I asked.

'Well it's not the girl next door, that's for sure.'

CHAPTER 23

'Cigarette me, big boy.'

Ginger Rogers (1912–95)

I read the letter at 6.00 a.m. while the light was already demanding extremely dark sunglasses. I'd just said goodbye to Barney when I noticed the message light flashing. The desk clerk told me there was a message for me at the front desk, which I asked him to bring straight up.

I guess I just presumed it was from Rory. No doubt saying his goodbyes and wishing me the best – I imagined it would read something simple like, 'see you around – R.'

I was booked on the flight to London the next day and any thoughts I may have harboured of changing my departure date and extending my stay to bask further in this Californian sun had evaporated with events the evening before.

My mood, still energised and hopeful, thanks to my new hairdo and Barney's slap-on-the-back company, went into a speedy decline as I contemplated the state of play vis-à-vis my relationship with Rory and its clumsy ending.

The ending moreover that wasn't really an ending at all, just an inexorable realisation that Rory and Evelyn didn't work. Period.

We could never ever be a couple in the true sense of the word. No matter how we did the sums, one plus one would always equal three or four even if I counted Katy, which I did. I couldn't hack it as a triumvirate any better than Alexia could.

I had to face facts. It was time to trudge back to London, back to the knowing looks of my friends and colleagues. Time to dig up that map to my G-spot. Time for another minimalist purge. Time to go back to casual sex (when I could get it). I mean it was embarrassing. I·hadn't even made it as far as IKEA, my friends wouldn't be able to stand up for laughter. It was sad really.

When the envelope was actually put into my hands though, I knew at once that whoever it was from it wasn't from Rory. It was the same, distinctive sort of envelope as the one I'd noticed Rory pick up from the breakfast cart that first morning after he'd introduced me to Alexia. The envelope he had run into another room to read and then shoved into the pocket of his robe like a guilty secret.

My name was written in large energetic letters. I grabbed a bottle of Evian for support. Daniel's letterhead paper hit me like a snort of speed.

❋ ❋ ❋

Evie – (I was getting quite used to the name really)

Sorry not to have waited till you returned. I hope your meeting with Alexia wasn't too traumatic – she's all right really once you get used to her. I thought I should explain what happened to make me run out on you like that.

After you left to meet Alexia, Rory walked out of the bathroom. As you can imagine, he must have heard what passed between us or rather what didn't pass.

He was very civilised about it, asked me if I'd mind getting dressed and offered me a drink. He didn't seem interested in my apologies or my admittedly pointless justifications. Anyway, just thought I should warn you. Stay in touch.

Daniel S.

Sticking the heavy paper back in the envelope, I began to shake. The Evian was absolutely no help. I thought of going for something stronger but even I can't drink before I've put on my make-up. Mascara requires a steady hand – as I have learned from bitter experience.

Could it be true? Could Rory really have witnessed me tearing Daniel's clothes off, I asked myself. Did he actually see the bit where Daniel sucked my breasts? I ran over to the bathroom and peered out through the crack and realised that the answer was yes. He could very well have seen every gory detail. And just to make myself really abject with misery, I replayed those scenes in my mind.

Then my thoughts turned to how Rory had been so calm in the lobby last night, giving no clue away as to what he knew.

I put my face into my hands and wailed. What had I done? Daniel was nothing more than an aberration, after all. A mad flirtation that I'd allowed to go too far due to my total lack of inner resources and the fact that he laughed at all my jokes. I was so confused I didn't know what to feel.

Even so the vibrator had started off in my belly again, drilling its way through my vital organs which were already feeling a tad tender thanks to my alcohol consumption. I convinced myself it was just hunger – for all the champagne and whisky Barney and I had consumed, we hadn't got around to eating last night. That's all it was – hunger. Course it was.

What must Rory have been feeling, lying down on the bathroom floor peering under the crack? What can he have been thinking? What foul images must be haunting his dreams this very minute! He must have been utterly devastated.

Or a total pervert.

Not certain where Daniel might be now and even less certain about what I was going to say to him, I began to panic. Maybe he'd spent the night downstairs in the lobby. Maybe he was still down there. Unlikely but I decided to check. Engage my dilemmas so to speak. I took a last look in the mirror to make sure the new me was still looking utterly consumable and then I walked down the stairs to the lobby.

PS. This girlfriend wasn't doing lifts ever again!

The lobby was virtually empty when I tottered in on my new Jimmy Choos. Apart from a few people checking in – looking none too fresh after longhaul flights – there was a janitor-type person lazily vacuuming the floor – and Rory.

He was still where I had left him and my heart began to ache when I thought of him keeping vigil there all night. He was such a darling really. How could I have thought of tossing him aside for a careerist yuppie like Daniel? A man more at home in his Gucci than in an uncomfortable chair waiting for me. I didn't notice Daniel waiting around for long. A brief note and he was off.

This thought of Daniel got my libido going again. I needed something to take my mind off him, so I asked the girl at the desk to send over some kippers and a few eggs. Rory lifted his hand as I approached but he didn't look up. He was reading *Variety Daily*, his eyes hidden behind his Ray Bans.

There was a steaming cup of coffee on the table beside his feet. Basically he looked like someone who'd been waiting twelve minutes, not twelve hours. After I sat down he made a grunting sound as if I was asking him if it was all right for me to do a bit of dusting and then went back to his article.

'He saw everything!' my conscience screamed at me. 'E-V-E-R-Y-T-H-I-N-G. Get It!' it yelled.

'Coffee?' he asked, still not bothering to look up and face the scarlet woman.

'He must really hate you,' my alter ego taunted. 'You said it,' added my ego proper. Not even my ego was on my side, I thought miserably. 'Face it, your actions have been indefensible,' they jeered. 'Did you honestly think a new hairstyle would get you out of this?'

'I would have ordered you one but I wasn't sure when you'd be back,' he said dryly as I wriggled uncomfortably in my seat trying to block out the voices in my head.

'There was an earthquake,' I explained. I had pre-planned a little speech earlier – before reading Daniel's note – a speech all about natural disasters and confused head-states and altered reality principles and how I wasn't mature enough for a *Sleepless in Seattle* scenario – especially one where the ex-wife wasn't dead. But my speech was blurred by the spinning images of what Rory had seen me doing with Daniel.

I heard myself making an inane little enquiry about what he was reading and then I heard him make a grunting noise like he'd been shot, although I think he actually said something like, 'Oh nothing much.'

Barney had advised me to rely on my new haircut and a series of smouldering looks he'd taught me while cutting my hair but given what I now knew

Rory knew, I decided to shelve the smouldering looks part and as for my haircut – he hadn't even given me a cursory once over as yet.

'Face it, he can't face you any more,' my conscience yelled.

I made another remark about the earthquake.

'Yeah – I thought the chandelier was going to drop,' Rory responded.

'But it didn't?' I enquired chattily, smiling sweetly, willing him to look at the new me and be dazzled. I was thinking that maybe the new me might be enough to pave the way to a new start. Maybe we could sweep all the old stuff away and start fresh. That's what America was all about, wasn't it? New frontiers, new beginnings.

'Nah, just swayed a bit – wasn't much of a quake, probably six on the Richter scale tops.' He turned the page.

'I got stuck in the elevator.'

'Thought you might have,' he drawled as if we were discussing where I'd left my sunhat.

'Well, you could sound a bit more interested. I mean, you don't seem very concerned,' I huffed, suddenly feeling unloved and unwanted. OK so I might have behaved reprehensibly, but given the circumstances of my near brush with death – well with a very confined space anyway – I thought he might have been a bit more worried about me.

'No I wasn't – not too concerned anyway. Says here that—'

I cut him off. 'I don't give a shit what it says there. I could have died you realise. I could be dead now. Stuck in an elevator in the middle of an earthquake. I could have plummeted to my death. It's incredible that I'm still here! I mean, *I could have died.*'

'Probably not,' he replied staring intently at his page.

'What do you mean, probably not? Of course I could have died. People do it all the time. This hotel is a veritable blackspot for unexpected deaths. I mean, there I was all alone in a suspended lift. I could have run out of oxygen. How did you know I wasn't gasping for air, trapped in that pendulum of death. I don't think my friends and family would be too pleased to hear that I died alone in a metal coffin caught between two floors in a strange country,' I told him, getting progressively more agitated by his lack of concern. 'I defy you not to have been concerned.'

He wasn't smiling but there was a mirthfulness playing around his lips, I could just tell. But he kept on reading despite my oratory. He should have been a lawyer.

Notwithstanding his pretence of macho cool, I wasn't put off my case – not for a second. 'They probably would have found me by now, lying like a broken beggar woman, stiff with rigor mortis, my nails broken and bloody from having carved my last communiqué to the world. The words *Evelyn Hornton lost her battle for life in this lift, 1998, due to Rory's lack of concern.*'

I was feeling quite emotional and raw now and maybe it was lack of sleep, too much alcohol or something that happened to me as a child but I really was feeling very tired and upset.

'I don't think you could have carved all that in metal, with your fingernails. Not in that time anyway.'

'Well I might have just written it in lipstick then,' I lied, knowing full well that I would never be likely to waste such an expensive lipstick even in the face of death. 'And then what would you have told the police huh?' I asked him. 'When they enquired as to why you hadn't thought to search for me in the rubble after the earthquake.'

He looked up from his paper then and took a sip of coffee. 'There was no rubble. It was a very slight tremor. I doubt very much if it was even six.'

'What?'

'There was no rubble. The electricity was disconnected for about twenty minutes. The chandelier shook. The girls who were sitting on the chair beside us screamed and one of them knocked the table over as she dived on my lap. That was it really.'

'Well, I hardly think now's the time to be pedantic about time frames and the whereabouts of a chandelier. I was practically killed in an earthquake while you sat here calm as a cucumber with a strange girl in your lap, not sparing a thought for me up there in that death trap fighting for my life like that girl in *Towering Inferno*. And now all you can do is talk Richter scales!'

'I did go and look for you,' he interrupted. 'They said in reception that the guy with the stud in his tongue had rescued you. He came down later and when I asked about you, he said you were drinking champagne and whisky on the floor with him and that he was going to buy scissors and dye to fix your hair, which by the way looks great.'

After that his mouth gave up the battle to hide the grin that had been playing around his lips since my arrival. My anger (which was only a mask for my guilt really) dissipated.

At least it had by the time we went back up to the room and made love.

CHAPTER 24

'All they have to do is play "Melancholy Baby" and my spine turns to custard.'

Some Like It Hot, 1959, b/w, Marilyn Monroe,
Tony Curtis and Jack Lemmon

We saw Mads and Giles off that same afternoon. Rory and I held hands even though it was far too hot and sticky and we both knew it. It was all very *Midsummer Night's Dream*-ish, the way we had paired and unpaired and then paired again. Giles would have been just the man for a sonnet too but he had other things on his mind. He had – wait for it – thrown away his arch supports!

It was all very moving and even Rory managed not to smirk – too badly at least. Maddy had invented a little ceremony to signify his letting go-ness. On her insistence, Giles made a few awkward pronouncements about how he was ready for personal growth and ready to open himself up to a foam-free existence

and then bang, it was official. California had had its
way with him.

We waved them off in a taxi, Madeline looking
radiant and at peace, Giles looking uncomfortable
and crushed in his teabag suit – another of Maddy's
changes. When he turned back to wave at me, he
seemed to be pleading, begging for something – like
those plastic dogs that used to nod in the back of
Ford Cortinas.

Afterwards Rory and I drove down to pick up Katy
to take her for a last supper at Louis's Trattoria, on
Montana Avenue. It's one of those affluent areas
where they don't let you in unless you can name
all your chakras and demonstrate your ability to do
yoga exercises without artificial stimulants.

To Rory's annoyance, Katy and I were both on
hyper pilot, screaming with laughter and girltalk and
generally troubling calm spiritually at peace people
who just wanted to sip their wheatgrass shakes in
peace.

There were a few other precocious children there
as well but they were focusing their intelligence
in a very enlightened and wholesome way, giving
their parents dissertations on the virtues of creative
learning in a mixed gender environment. Etc.

Rory was very subdued although occasionally I
caught him staring at me in a concentrated way
which I found a bit heavy. He wanted an answer
to the 'us' question, even though he knew I wasn't
in a position to give him one. How could I possibly

think with all this health and yoga going on around me? I asked him. I needed to get back to London, back on my stress wheel, clear my head with a day or two of hard shopping in Harvey Nichols.

'Will you come back to take me shopping?' Katy asked me solemnly as she picked listlessly at her dessert.

PS. It was fruit salad, who can blame her?

Rory put his spoon down pointedly and looked expectantly at me – creating one of those pregnant pauses.

'Well I'm not sure really Katy, we'll have to wait and see won't we?' I replied, turning to my fellow diners, who, sensing the tension, were checking out our group with lingering sidelong non-judgemental glances.

I grinned inanely.

'That is so lame,' Rory said, pushing his plate away in disgust and glaring at me.

'I *feel* lame,' I told him, realising as I said it that from Katy's point of view this was one hell of a lame conversation that we were embarking on. She giggled at me from across the table and a small piece of cherry escaped from her mouth. She giggled louder as she caught it.

Rory reached for my hands. 'I want you here. We'll get a place. You can sit the law exams here. We can have a great time.'

I ignored him and pulled a funny face at Katy, hoping that Rory would take the hint and shut up.

I felt his hand close around mine tightly. I began to feel claustrophobic.

'Wouldn't that be great, doll? I could cook for you. We could jog around the beach front together.'

I looked at him like he'd just swallowed his tongue. 'I'd rather take up asthma than jog,' I snapped, wondering if I could really have enjoyed wild sex with a man who could suggest something like jogging to me.

It wasn't like Rory to be so expressive and, well, needy really.

'Mommy jogs,' Katy told me.

'Precisely,' I said, and then not wanting to sound bitchy, I added, 'Mommy's very fit.'

'I can jog,' she said. 'Do you want to see me? I can jog real fast.'

'Will you at least think about it?' Rory said, taking my face in his hands and rubbing my nose with his.

'I've already told you, I'll think about it. What do you want from me? I've allotted every brain cell to the thought. My medulla is exhausted with all the thinking I've been forcing it to do. I mean, my brain hardly has the cell room to deal with basic stuff like breathing. My bodily functions are suffering because my mind is so engaged with studying the big question of our relationship.'

'I don't believe you.' He kissed my nose and then made for my mouth.

I looked across at Katy then but she was gone. I

pulled away from Rory and looked under the table
– no cute little girls there either.

'Where's Katy?' I asked Rory who was now
nursing his face in his hands like students do in
exams when they don't know answers to any of the
questions.

'What?' he grunted, not moving.

'Katy – where's she gone? She's disappeared,' I
said, a little more urgently.

This brought him back to the real world. 'She
was just here!' he said, pointing at the empty space,
checking under the table and then when looking
around the restaurant failed to produce his daughter,
jumping up and running off.

His chair fell to the floor with a crash and everyone
looked at me.

I heard him yell her name as he opened the door
to the street.

I saw her skip past the window in the direction of
the sea. 'Look, there she is,' I shouted, throwing some
money on the table and running after him. I grabbed
his shirt and pushed him in her direction. She was
jogging away from us, pretty quickly actually and
about to disappear from view.

Rory raced after her and on reaching her, he
picked her up with one arm and kissed her. 'Don't
scare me like that, pumpkin.'

'I was showing you how I can jog, Daddy.'

When I caught up with them, I stroked her on her
silken head which smelt so sweet and dear to me now.

My heart was pounding with the relief that she was safe. 'You're miles better than me,' I told her. 'And hardly even puffed out.'

She was still moving her legs in mid-air like a little wind-up doll.

Rory carried her all the way to the car. He was wearing his ubiquitous unbuttoned shirt and blue jeans. His hair was due for a cut and his six o'clock shadow had gone into nine o'clock overtime and watching him there with his daughter tucked under one arm like a surfboard, I loved him more than I had ever loved anyone in my life.

I loved him and I adored Katy and her fierce determination to show her daddy her running style even as he held her. So what was my problem? Why couldn't I commit, why couldn't I make the necessary sacrifices and become part of this family?

I gave Rory a kiss on the cheek which he didn't acknowledge.

We took Katy home after that and Alexia gave me a hug at the door and invited us in. I had my hands in the pockets of my jacket. I felt awkward and out of place.

'No thanks,' I told her. 'I've got to get packed. Holiday time is over for me now.'

She gave me another hug and said that she was sorry about the way she'd behaved and told me that she hoped I could forgive her one day. I nodded and said that it was all fine and meant it.

She was trying to catch Rory's eye as she spoke but

he refused the contact and said nothing, hanging back in the shadows of the porch like fathers are meant to do on access visits.

He was pissing me off and I told him so when we got back to the car.

'What do you expect me to do after what she did? Fall all over her? She tried to break us up. Doesn't that piss you off?'

'What did she do? Huh? Tell me that? She loves you, she tried to keep you for herself. She was practising sound survival techniques if you ask me,' I told him. 'Defending her territory.'

'I'm no one's territory,' he sulked.

'You're not John Wayne either,' I told him. 'So drop the attitude.'

'Women,' he sighed. 'You've got a justification for everything. Why do you side with her after what she tried to do? What's in it for you? Can you at least tell me that?'

'I respect her, I don't blame her. It's suited you to keep the relationship open. You got your cake and you got to eat it. You got to see Katy as much as you wanted and on top of that you had Alexia running around after you as well. She's still in love with you. You must have realised that.'

'That's her problem.'

I mimicked him. 'That's her problem? Well, that's a nice attitude. You can't take advantage of the way someone feels. She needs closure and so do I.'

'You've been in California too long doll. You're ~~starting to sound like a native.~~'

'Whatever. I think you've got some issues that need sorting, that's all.'

He looked annoyed but he didn't say anything. When we got back to the suite he turned to me and asked the question I'd been willing him not to ask all day long. 'What about Daniel then? How's that for an "issue"?'

I looked to the Marlboro Man for help but all he did was look down Sunset Boulevard. It had cost Rory a lot to ask that question and it didn't feel right to toss him over with a throwaway justification. In the silence while he waited for my answer, the phone rang. And rang. And rang. And rang.

'I'm sorry,' I whispered as the ringing stopped. 'That was stupid. We had lunch and I don't know why it happened. It felt wrong Rory. I guess I don't know what to say.'

A nerve twitched in his cheek and I wanted to kiss it. I felt stunned at all the pain I seemed to be causing and yet incapable of even attempting to heal the wounds I had inflicted. Anything I said only rubbed more salt in both our wounds. I wished I could stop feeling and sounding so wooden but I was afraid to.

Rory sat down and rolled a cigarette and I sat down beside him. In both our minds it was already over, I think. Later we gazed out at the lights of Sunset

Boulevard and he told me that he knew I was in love with Daniel when I left with him that first night at the airport. He knew.

I didn't know if he was right or not, I just knew that I was unequal to the sacrifices that love was demanding of me. Coupledom never looked this complicated at parties. I'd always imagined that Coupleland was a dull place, occupied by facile people who got excited by words like 'cosy' and 'cute' and the prospect of a 'night in'.

I had no idea that Coupledom could be so emotionally charged and complicated and draining. Up close and personal, I was starting to feel like I might be the one who was too inane for Coupledom.

A voice within me told me that I wanted too much and was prepared to give too little. I hung my head and went about my packing while a Jim Morrison song wafted up from the pool.

Even as I gathered my shoes together to put them in the little bags emblazoned with their designer's name – a task that would normally put a song in my heart and a spring in my step, I felt tears prickling my eyes.

I saw the message light flashing and rang up the operator. Daniel's voice sounded syrupy and safe. 'Call me,' was all he said but it was enough to start my heart racing.

'It was Daniel wasn't it?' Rory said when I put the phone back in its cradle.

'It doesn't matter,' I said, hanging my head. 'Daniel's

got nothing to do with anything,' I added, knowing how worthless my excuses were. I was pathetic.

'He's defending his territory,' Rory called out as he walked into the other room. 'Fighting for what he wants. I don't blame him.'

'*Touché*,' said the Marlboro Man, and we both spun round to face him.

CHAPTER 25

'To err is human, but it feels divine.'

Mae West (1892–1980)

I was travelling coach.

I was giving up cigars.

I was never going to fall for a man on a purely physical basis again. PS. That could be dull!

I was going to have to face up to the grind of work again.

I was going to have to do my own cleaning and my own cooking.

I would be lucky to ever see a breakfast trolley again on my pay.

Worse than all of the above, though – I was going to have to face my hairdresser, the sadistic dominatrix, Stefan, with a hairstyle given me by someone else!

Life had never looked bleaker.

The worst moment came when the steward directed

me to turn right and my inner voice (the one that
had picked up a lot of high expectations in LA)
sulkily told me that I should be turning left. In my
arrogance I imagined that all the passengers behind
me were whispering, 'Ooh, and with that hairstyle
and those clothes, I thought she'd be travelling first
class, definitely.'

I tried to think positively and not hyperventilate.

Maybe the plane wouldn't be too full.

Maybe I would have a row of seats to myself and
be able to stretch out and sleep my way through time
zones and jet lag.

Maybe I would get one of those exit seats with the
leg room (the ones you have to take a vow to help
frail and hopeless passengers off the plane, to get).

Maybe I'd be sitting next to someone really neat,
a soul-mate, a masseuse, a best friend from years ago,
a hunky guy, a famous designer who chose to sit in
coach 'to get ideas'.

Wrong.

An oversized bag which someone was stuffing into
an overhead locker fell on my head.

I decided to go for the hyperventilation option after
all, deciding that the best thing that could happen to
me would be to suffer a total collapse and get whizzed
off on a gurney to Mount Sinai hospital, and flown
back home on a ventilator machine.

'Watch out,' the asshole said as he picked his bag
off my neck and went back to his task. I made my
way further down to the back of the plane where

my seat lay in wait for me, ready to envelope me in all the misery that modern-day travel inflicts on the aspirational. 'You think you deserve to travel, cheapskate? Well I'm here to teach you a lesson.'

My companions, who were already seated grimly on either side of my seat, were evil incarnate. In the aisle seat was every girl traveller's nightmare – a fat man who looked like he intended to leer and fart his way back to Basingstoke. He was picking something out of his teeth when I arrived and when I asked him to excuse me, he leered and wiped his hand on the front of his polyester jumper.

In the window seat was, well, there was probably nothing intrinsically wrong with this guy, let's just say that he was the person who had the window seat I wanted.

I had been assigned the black seat, the seat in the middle, the seat marked 'jerk'.

Maybe I had been too eager to flee the *Sleepless in Seattle* lifestyle after all. Actually, maybe not. Basically it hadn't been one of those 'parting is such sweet sorrow' goodbyes. Just plain sorrowful really.

Rory and I had left Château Marmont at the same time. Rory bought me a bathrobe as a parting gift, I bought him a shirt with all the buttons still attached. After a clumsy cuddle and a failed attempt at a snog, he left for the beach house with Alexia and Katy.

We promised to phone, which was an ironic sort of ending to it all really because the whole point of

me coming out to LA in the first place was to save
~~on phone bills. But I didn't say anything.~~

I hadn't confirmed my seat which is why I ended
up in coach rather than business. I was lucky to get
on the flight at all, they told me. 'Luck is relative,' I
told them.

I know my therapist would have advised me not
to but I'd rung Daniel the night before while Rory
was out setting up some counter-surveillance system
in a studio boss's house.

I don't know why I did it, just to say goodbye
really, just to hear his voice, just to make sure the
vibrator was still working. He had answered the
phone on the first ring as if he'd been waiting for my
call all night long. Men are so sure of themselves.

The guy in the window seat turned to me as we
were taking off. 'Isn't this just too grim for words?'
he groaned. He looked at me, rolled his eyes and
slumped forward with mock drama and I realised
that just when you're about to write off your fellow
man as a waste of space and an eyesore, someone
surprising crops up to make you change your mind.

He was immaculately dressed in a pair of black
Versace jeans, a velvet jacket and a chiffon shirt. He
was about my age, dark hair and legs that were at
least as long as mine. I looked into his eyes – green
– and down to his smiling mouth with their perfect
American teeth, and we bonded. OK, so he was gay.
All the best ones are.

'What I usually do is pinch myself until the drink

trolley arrives and then become insufferably drunk and boorish and annoy all my fellow passengers and then fall asleep. After that I usually spend the next two weeks trying to recover. How are you planning to cope?'

'Pretty much the same as that,' I told him.

His name was Mike, he worked in Versace in LA and between us I figured we could just about make it to London with our humour intact – which in a way practically justified coach travel. Practically.

Mike was true to his word. An hour into the flight, he was asleep, exhausted from his tussles with the drink distributors and his arguments with fellow passengers who had taken umbrage at the nicknames he had attributed to them. Some of them were a little cruel.

I was just about to reapply my lipstick and join him in the boon of sleep, when the stewardess tapped me on the shoulder and told me that there was a gentleman in First Class who wanted to see me.

I squeezed out of my seat and said good bye to Mr Fetid as Mike and I had nicknamed our companion. He leered and pinched my butt. I guess that's what they mean by an anti-feminist backlash.

I knew it was Daniel before I got there. I knew it was him because the vibrator went off in my stomach as I stood up and because he had been so careful to take my flight details when we'd talked the night before. Furthermore, I was as certain as I've ever been certain of anything in my life, as I walked through the fragrant curtains into the first-class lounge, that I was going to join the mile-high club.

Wanting to inspect the facilities and make sure there was room, check my appearance etc., I took a peek in the first-class loo and he was there waiting for me.

'I knew you'd check out the loo first,' he said, dragging me inside and snogging my lips off.

The rest as they say is history.

[THE END]

PS. I am still deeply afraid of commitment, especially with men who take their socks off with their toes and men who leave the loo seat up. On the other hand, I am no longer 'in' therapy and have joined another gym which I actually use, so that's progress. I also got rid of the futon and the minimalist look that was cluttering up my Visa bill. Maximalism is in, it's official.

My girlfriends and co-workers didn't say 'I told you so' once, and in fact said lots of really nice stuff about how well I looked and how much a tan suited me.

One look at what Barney had done to my hair and Stefan declared me *persona non grata* and refused to touch it again (promises, promises). I am, in consequence, living in fear of having the crotches cut out of my pantyhose. Men!

TYNE O'CONNELL

Latest Accessory

Every modern woman knows the importance of getting her accessories right. This year, like most of the gorgeous young things in London with an overdraft and a Harvey Nichols chargecard, Evelyn is investing in a Prada handbag, saving up for a jacket by Alexander McQueen and thinking about a pierced navel. Somehow, though – without even needing to queue – she ends up with a stalker!

Evelyn, the lawyer with attitude and a penchant for Mr Wrongs, has moved into a loft in Clerkenwell and her anxiety levels are way up. She's got problems with debt, problems with builders, problems with her girlfriends, her love life and the usual problems at work. Add a stalker to the equation and you've got disaster. Or have you? Evelyn's about to find out that sometimes the solution is so much worse than the problem . . .

'Brings to mind Kathy Lette and Jilly Cooper'
Mail on Sunday

0 7472 5614 4

review

ISLA DEWAR

Giving Up on Ordinary

When Megs became a cleaner, she didn't realise that if people looked at her a cleaner would be all they saw. Megs has as full a life as the people she does for, Mrs Terribly Clean Pearson or Mrs Oh-Just-Keep-It-Above-The Dysentery-Line McGhee. She's the mother of three children and still mourning the death of a son; she enjoys a constant sparring match with her mother; she drinks away her troubles with Lorraine, her friend since Primary One; and she sings the blues in a local club.

Megs has been getting by. But somehow that's not enough any more. It's time Megs gave up on being ordinary . . .

'Explosively funny and chokingly poignant . . . extraordinary' *Scotland on Sunday*

'Observant and needle sharp . . . entertainment with energy and attack' *The Times*

'A remarkably uplifting novel, sharp and funny' *Edinburgh Evening News*

0 7472 5550 4

review